DARK FAE

THE FAE SERIES

JANE ARMOR

Dark Fae Copyright © Jane Wallace February 25, 2020. Registration # 1166607

All rights reserved. No part of this publication may be reproduced, stored in a retrieval system, or transmitted, in any form or by any means, electronic, mechanical, photocopying, recording, or otherwise, without the prior permission of the copyright owner except in the case of brief quotations embodied in critical articles or reviews.

eBook ISBN: 978-1-9990089-0-1

Book ISBN: 978-1-9990089-2-5

CHAPTER 1

The kitchen door stood open a second longer than necessary, and that was all Rella needed to slip inside without anyone noticing. The human servants were tired and not very observant. Everyone at the long tables wore gloves and masks to chop, mix, and blend the drugged food.

Pulling the corner of her turban over her marked face, she scuttled into the shadow of an alcove, where the smells and humid heat surrounded her. Rella had to be careful not to get near any trace of the food. The last thing she and her brother needed was for her to become an addict too.

One long wall in the kitchen housed a bank of ovens, where the servants prepared the prisoners' food, every morsel laced with the highly addictive dragon's blood poison. Kitchens catering to the human servants and guards were located on the far side of this lower level—well away from here. The citadel was massive. She knew only enough of its layout to get her from the kitchen doorway to her brother's cell and, if necessary, out through the secret cave. It was all she needed to know.

At the sound of booted feet, Rella looked up. Damn, Percy was on duty. He was the only guard who'd ever caught her, and he'd threatened dire consequences if he ever found her inside again. Rella pushed back into the corner, lowered her eyes, and prayed he didn't notice her.

With her head dipped, all she could see from below the rim of her turban was her own dirty feet on the stone floor. Percy's boots scraped along the flagstones as he drew near her hiding place. Rella held her breath. He walked right past her.

It was another two hours before cleanup in the kitchen slowed, then the servants left to find their beds. By that time, Rella was stiff and cramped. She waited nervously until no one was watching then slid out into the corridor. It wouldn't be long now before everyone in the citadel went to sleep—except her.

For some reason, whenever the vizier slept, so did all his human servants. This was her time to find her brother and prepare him for escape. Unfortunately, however, the vizier slept in short bursts. That meant the whole citadel came to a stop twice a day, but not for long. How the human servants and guards dealt with it, she didn't know.

Rella reached the edge of the prison cells located within the thick curtain wall and stared down at the energy-sucking floor. It appeared almost liquid in nature, bright blue and silver with undulating shades of mercury running through it. She hated having to walk on it but dared not use her magic to avoid it. It was like walking on icicles: cold, sharp, and slippery.

Rella reached Calstir's cell and lifted her bare feet onto the horizontal metal bar of the gate so that she didn't have to stand on that floor longer than necessary. She almost sobbed when she saw him. He lay beyond the bars on a low cot. His famous, long, blonde hair, so typical of the light fae, fell to the floor, dirty and unkempt. His gaunt face, ravished by addiction, made him look like a stranger even to her.

She noticed he'd eaten a good part of his meal laced with dragon's blood and shuddered. "Calstir, wake up," she whispered.

"I'm not asleep," he said.

"Then come here," said Rella.

He rose slowly to a sitting position, then, turning, worked his way to the end of his cot, but that took almost all his energy. "Have you found someone?"

"I think so."

"Then make it soon, or I will be dead," he said, falling back against the wall behind him, which undulated with the same substance that made up the floors.

"Here, take this," said Rella, pulling a fresh loaf of herb bread from her cloth bag. The food she'd brought would allow him to eat less of the food laced with dragon's blood that the vizier fed his prisoners. She hoped it would make him strong enough to leave.

"Mmm, that smells good." He turned to look at her, and Rella saw him wince when he looked at the disfiguring brown mark that wound up her body from her calf to her face. Together with her dark brown eyes where once bright blue had shone, it declared her sacrilege and her sacrifice.

Calstir reached out and put his finger on her face. "Little Rella, my once beautiful sister, what has happened to you?"

"You know well enough. There is always a price to pay when you bargain with the dark fae. Now, take it," she said, pushing the fresh loaf through the bars.

"What happened to your magic? Did it die with the kiss of the Dark Emperor?"

Rella could see he was confused. He didn't mean the

cruel things he said. "If I use my magic inside the citadel, I will be discovered and put in a cell too. That's why I need a human to help me. I think I've found the right one," she hissed, unable to completely hide her irritation.

Calstir chewed a morsel of the healthy loaf. "Who?"

"Have you heard of the Halfenhaw brothers?"

"Aye, they're in here, one floor down."

"Not all of them." That got his attention. She saw him struggle through the fog of his addiction. "The fourth brother is here in Hedabar? The human one?"

"Aye, and he looks strong enough to carry you."

Calstir shook his head as if trying to break through his confusion. "Don't trust him. Tell him only what he needs to know, no more. It is too dangerous."

Now he sounded more like a prince of Casta. "I won't. Eat the herb bread. It will strengthen you. If all goes well, it will happen tonight."

Calstir's shoulders straightened, and he swept his knee-length hair to one side. "Don't worry, my sister, once I'm out of here, I will deal with the Dark Emperor. He won't want me for an enemy."

Rella smiled. "I know. Now, promise me you won't eat any more of that poison."

"I promise, but if you don't return tonight, I will break that promise come morning." A deep sadness clouded his eyes. "I won't be able to stop myself."

A shudder passed through her. "I know," she said. "I must leave. I've stayed too long as it is. If Percy catches me, he'll beat me, and I don't trust myself not to use magic on him if he does."

Calstir stood, and for a fleeting moment, he was once more a royal prince of Casta. "Take his beating if you must, Rella."

Dagstyrr circled the citadel again. His frustration grew daily. There had to be a way in, yet all he could see besides the perfectly smooth wall were the one hundred steps he'd been thrown down by the guards when he'd first arrived and his brothers were imprisoned. There was also a small postern gate for food deliveries. Both were clad in iron and heavily guarded.

He'd take on the guards if he thought it would result in his brothers being set free. But the guards were too numerous. Eventually, Dagstyrr would fall. Then who'd rescue his brothers? He was all that stood between them and eventual madness and death.

Dagstyrr raised a hand and rubbed his neck stiff from gazing up, always up. Rounding a corner, he saw a boy being thrown out of the postern gate as a miller's cart exited at the same time. Dagstyrr recognized the waif. He'd been following Dagstyrr for days, grateful for a coin or crust thrown his way. He saw the boy scuttle under the cart, but the guard called a halt to the carter and reached under, dragging the boy out by the rags he wore. "What'd I tell you last time? Eh? Well, you're going to get it now."

"Let 'im go, Percy, he's done no harm," said the carter.

"Oh, no. This time, he gets what I promised."

Dagstyrr's step quickened when he realized the boy was about to get a beating from a man three times his size. "Leave the lad be!"

"Oh, aye? Says who?" said the guard, spoiling for a fight.

"Dagstyrr of Halfenhaw, that's who," said Dagstyrr, gripping the hilt of his sword. The gesture worked. The guard dropped the squirming boy and turned to Dagstyrr.

"I'm captain of the vizier's guard, and no one on Hedabar tells me what to do, not even a fancy lord like you."

"If you want a fight, you've picked the right day," said Dagstyrr, drawing his blade. His irritation was egging him on to accept this oaf's challenge, even though he knew the man was an unworthy opponent.

"Don't fight him, mister. He fights dirty, and he ain't worth it. Not for my sake," said the boy, and Dagstyrr heard real fear in his voice. That was curious.

Dagstyrr and the guard squared off against each other. They were well matched in size and weapons, and Dagstyrr itched to expend some of his pent-up energy. He suspected this man's cursory training would not yield a good sparring partner.

Growing up with three fae brothers he'd learned to be fast—very fast. He leapt into the air and spun around, the sun bouncing off his blade as it scythed towards his opponent. At once, Percy was in retreat, desperately trying to hold off his opponent's blows by gripping his sword two-handed. Dagstyrr didn't give the man a chance to strike, just beat him back with every hit.

Suddenly, Percy turned and leapt onto the cart, giving himself an advantage. Dagstyrr smiled. This was going to be fun. The guard's blade lifted, inviting him to fight, but Dagstyrr would not be hurried. Suddenly, his opponent threw a handful of grit in his eyes. It stung and temporarily blinded him. A shout of protest went up from the onlookers who had stopped to watch the spectacle, but Dagstyrr parried his opponent's blade blindly until his sight cleared.

He saw the look of fear on the man's face when it became apparent Dagstyrr wasn't about to give in. With a yell, Dagstyrr leapt onto the cart beside him. It was slippery from the spillage of grain covering the boards underfoot.

That must have been the grit Percy had thrown in his face. No wonder it stung.

Dagstyrr's gaze caught the panic in Percy's eyes as his blade drove him backward until he tripped and landed on the ground with a thud. In a trice, Dagstyrr landed lightly on his feet beside him. Like all bullies, Percy was a coward. He threw away his weapon, begging for mercy.

Townspeople had gathered to watch the fight. "Let 'im 'ave it, sir. Show 'im 'ow a real knight fights." As they jeered at Percy, the coward's face turned deep red with anger. Dagstyrr's sword was at his throat, and Percy froze, recognizing the fury in the knight's stance. A hush fell about the gathering.

The tone of the small crowd quickly changed. "No, don't do it, sir. It'll only cause trouble for them inside!" called the carter. Others walked away, not wanting to witness whatever followed.

Rella watched from her hiding place as the tableau in front of her froze. Then the human knight slowly stepped away, turned his back in contempt, and marched toward her, leaving Percy to get up and retrieve his weapon from the dust.

She could see Dagstyrr's large frame quiver as he fought to control his anger and frustration, which he dared not take out on Percy lest he bring harm to his brothers inside. It was the same way her muscles used to cry out for fulfillment on the practice field.

As he passed by without noticing her crouched against the wall, Rella sensed the immense control coiled inside him, his fists still clenched at his sides, and his breathing slow and steady. He was ready for a real fight, and she had a use for that energy.

Terrified about revealing her secret way into the citadel to the wrong person, she observed him carefully. He might think she was selfish, rescuing Calstir without saving the other prisoners. But a full rescue of prisoners would require an army to back her up. Most of the captured fae were close to death and in no shape to put up a fight. Surely, he would see that.

He was Dagstyrr of Halfenhaw, youngest and the only human son of Earl Magnus and the fae princess, Astrid. It was unusual for a fae woman to give birth to a fully human child but not unheard of. At least her other three sons were fae—if only halflings.

Dagstyrr's name meant *day of battle storm*. It was a fierce name for a human. His reputation was just as daunting. Dagstyrr of Halfenhaw was a renowned warrior and sea captain who traded up and down the coast in his father's ships. Perhaps it was trying to keep up with his fae brothers that led him to strive for excellence in everything he did. It was this tenacity that led Rella to believe that he was never going to give up on them. That meant she must resign herself to rescuing his brothers as well.

She slipped from the shadows and followed him. For such a big man, he stepped lightly over the cobbled streets and garbage in the gutters. His chainmail shone like quicksilver in the sun, and his white cape snapped in the breeze, giving her the impression he was made of light, but Sir Dagstyrr was fully human. That was lucky for her. Otherwise, he'd be held captive with his light fae brothers.

The time was now. Rella must make contact with Dagstyrr of Halfenhaw.

CHAPTER 2

Dagstyrr noticed that his shadow of the past six weeks continued to follow him. He'd almost lost his temper today with a man not worthy of his sword: a guard, untrained and useless in a real fight. No doubt the rescued waif would follow him even more closely from now on. The poor creature was no longer trying to hide his presence. Yet he continued to keep his distance, shadowing Dagstyrr as he walked the dusty roads of Hedabar.

The large birthmark circling up the boy's right leg and across his exposed abdomen, then up under the waif's short shirt to finish on the side of his face, marked him as definitely human. Light fae were physically perfect with distinctive blonde hair and bright blue eyes. Not even a scar was allowed to mar their perfection. Those born dark fae used magic to remove any mark they didn't want—or so he'd been told. To his knowledge, Dagstyrr had never met a dark fae. They were many and diverse, often passing themselves off as human. No one talked about them in the Halfenhaw household, though his father had hinted that he'd sailed with some of them.

The boy was very self-conscious of his birthmark, Dagstyrr noted, for he often lifted the tail of his grubby turban to hide where it landed on one side of his face. Yes, he was definitely human. So, what did he want?

As the sun dipped on the horizon, he made his way to the docks. The man he hoped to consult there had a library of rare books. Dagstyrr wanted access to books on magic to help him breach the citadel, but the man was away visiting relatives, and once more, Dagstyrr was left without answers.

His patience was wearing very thin.

The north side of the citadel cast its gloom long and dark across the fouler side of town. Unless Dagstyrr kept to a centerline of the road, stinking mud soiled his boots, and he'd carry that stink with him for the rest of the day. He'd learned to avoid it weeks ago, but his shadow slopped barefoot through the filth.

Dagstyrr stopped and turned. "What is it you want?"

He hadn't meant to sound so harsh, but his voice echoed off the wall, causing the creature to shrink farther into the shadows. Taking a deep breath, Dagstyrr gentled his voice as if talking to a skittish mount. "I'll not hurt you. I just thought if we were to keep each other company, then I should introduce myself. I'm Dagstyrr of Halfenhaw."

"I'm Rell," said the unbroken voice of youth.

"Do you have relatives inside, Rell?"

Silence.

Heaven knew what degradations this poor creature had suffered at the hands of others. No wonder he was shy. That ugly mark alone would make him susceptible to abuse. Coupled with his low station and stink, he must be naturally wary. "I have three brothers imprisoned in the citadel:

Sigmund, Thorsten, and Erik. Erik's the eldest and more fae than the other two. If what the townspeople say is correct, I fear he suffers the most."

"He does," whispered the youth, a tremor in his voice.

A shiver ran up Dagstyrr's spine. He stepped away from the wall and sat on a rock still warm from the sun. "I don't understand," he said, gazing out to sea, not wanting to frighten the boy. Sneaking into the kitchens hoping for a morsel of food was one thing, but surely this boy hadn't penetrated the prison itself?

Dagstyrr needed to know everything the boy could tell him. Then he had to separate fact from fiction. What the boy had seen and what was a rumor. As he'd hoped, the youth followed him but still kept his distance from the rock.

"Erik. He suffers the most. The walls suck his magic from him, and it hurts."

Awareness flashed though his body, urging action. It took all his control not to pounce on the boy. Was he repeating gossip? What could this urchin know of Erik?

Dagstyrr stared, hardly daring to move. "Do you know a way in?"

"Not now," said the boy, backing away, eyes darting from side to side. "Meet me here after the moon has crossed the tower. Leave your armor behind and bring all your fresh clothes," he said, before bursting into a run.

Dagstyrr jumped up to follow but saw it was futile. The youth was fast and almost to the forest, which, no doubt, he knew well. There was no point in running him down. He must be patient and wait for Rell to come to him. But to bring all his clean clothes, what was that about? How many and for what? The boy was a mystery, but if he knew a way in, then Dagstyrr would grant him anything within his power to give.

Hell, he'd have his father knight him. Then he smiled at the image of the great earl knighting a half-naked street urchin.

Aware his heart was beating fit to burst and his hands shaking with restrained energy, Dagstyrr sat again to recover his equilibrium. How stupid to be so emotional, but this was the first news he'd had of his brothers since he'd been thrown out of the citadel by the vizier when it became obvious he had no fae powers. With some shame, he remembered being thrown like a drunkard down the steps. At first, he'd thought his brothers were with him, but no, they'd been taken to the cells—he alone, of all the Halfenhaw brothers, was of no use to the vizier. Dagstyrr was fully human.

He looked to the tower, gauging how long it would take the moon to cross it. About half an hour before midnight, he guessed.

If the price of information was a bundle of clean clothes, he would be happy to pay it. Dagstyrr lifted his head to the great high wall before heading for his room at the inn. It wouldn't do to have anyone think this evening was different from any other. The vizier's spies were everywhere. No wonder the boy was so jittery.

Rella paced the ship's wooden deck. Docked amid the bustle of Hedabar's busy wharf, the tiny ship was a secret jewel among the hard-worked merchantmen filling the harbor. The stevedores struggled with tremendous loads on their bent backs, sweat dripping from their brows. They were almost finished loading, and everything was ready in the cabin. Aft, there was more accommodation—a cage. Rella hoped she wouldn't need it, but a knot in her stomach tested that hope.

This crew had been hired because they had experience in healing addicts. Their captain confessed that they'd never worked with dragon's blood addicts, but for the right price, he was willing to try. The dark fae had access to knowledge forbidden in Casta, but Rella was desperate and would try anything to bring her brother home safe.

This ship, the *Mermaid*, was crewed by fae who were all born dark fae. All that is except herself, and Billy the ship's boy. Billy was human.

The one-eyed Captain Bernst approached her and nodded his approval. They were almost ready. Even if tonight's mission failed, the ship would sail as expected come morning. Otherwise, they'd attract too much attention. After all, the *Mermaid* was disguised as an aging merchantman loaded and ready for her journey.

That would mean remaining onshore as Rell for at least two months without any means of escape or support. Rella shuddered at the thought of living like a human street urchin for so long. The wind snapped a sail, telling her the time had come to leave.

Her new birthmark itched under her gown as if to remind her it was there. With it, she fit in well with the crew. Cook was one-legged; the ship's boy had lost half an arm. Scars and deformities abounded aboard the *Mermaid* as they did on most ships and, more importantly, it marked them as human. No fae, light or dark, needed to show scars or deformities if they didn't want to—except Rella. The Dark Emperor himself had marked her, and no amount of magic could erase it.

A breeze lifted her hair, and she closed her eyes, visualizing the small ship raising its anchor and sailing away with the early tide, the decks heaving with every movement of the ship, and Calstir safely tucked away in the cabin. She'd furnished it with silks and cushions fit for a prince of the light fae.

The human knight was a present from the gods and ripe for manipulation. If this went wrong, he'd be dead by morning, and Rella would be in a cell along with her brother. She brushed away a stab of fear.

The stakes were high. Casta needed a king, and that king was Calstir. She prayed her father would live long enough to give them time to get home to Casta. Otherwise they might be returning to civil war.

Her father was dying when he gave his blessing for her to go and rescue her brother. Rella wanted to be by the old king's side, not half a world away. But her father understood only too well the dangers of him dying without Calstir there to inherit the throne. Rella's cousins, the family Kemara, had three sons, Marvn, Hamel and Lukor, who were greedy and stupid enough to plunge the country into civil war if Calstir did not return soon.

Unless she could spirit him away, tonight would be just another failed escape, and it might be years before anyone attempted to stop the vizier whose strength grew daily. His magic was an abomination that Rella was determined to end once and for all, but not tonight. She'd wait until she had an army to command before taking the Citadel of Hedabar.

That was a problem for another day. One Calstir could help her with once he ascended the throne of Casta.

CHAPTER 3

Dagstyrr couldn't settle down to anything. He'd returned to the inn at his usual time and eaten his supper before repairing to his rooms. Instead of napping, he paced his quarters, every nerve and sinew ready to snap. Even rational thought was becoming difficult, displaced by hope. Could the boy possibly have the key to rescuing his brothers? If so, he needed to be ready to move at a moment's notice.

He sat and took up the whetstone, drawing it along the length of his blade. The reassuring sound prepared him, forcing the calm all men needed before battle.

Was he placing too much hope on the word of an urchin? Was he that desperate? Dagstyrr concentrated on the swish of the whetstone. Damn it. His instructions made no sense. Glancing at the bundle of fresh clothes sitting on his bed, he managed a grin. Perhaps the boy just needed a change of clothes and intended to rob him? If the waif brought a band of ruffians intent on robbery, they'd be in for a surprise. All his pent-up anger at the vizier would be unleashed, and may the gods help every ragtag one of them.

If he were at home, he'd visit the tiltyard or practice fields to wear off the excess energy and clear his mind. He was ready for a fight, but intuition warned him a simple conflict was not what awaited him. The boy knew something, and Dagstyrr was determined to find out what.

Rell had spoken Erik's name with such concern. Sure, anyone in the town could have shown sympathy. His brothers' plight was no secret. The way the boy spoke of Erik, though, the compassion in his voice, made Dagstyrr believe he'd seen his suffering first hand. Or was that just wishful thinking?

The moon traveled across his window, slowly rising to its zenith, which would mark the time to leave. Dagstyrr looked around his lodgings, wondering what terrible privations his brothers had endured. Would they even be capable of escaping when the opportunity came?

If by some miracle he managed to get them out of the citadel, they must head straight for the docks. For weeks now, he'd befriended the captains that regularly docked in Hedabar. There were at least two he'd confirmed would give them passage—they'd said as much. Half a dozen others would too if his purse was full enough. Dagstyrr had studied their routines, and three, including both captains who'd offered passage, would be docked tonight.

The early morning tide was their only hope. If they were still on the island by midmorning, they'd be hunted and caught. So, as soon as they were clear of the citadel, they must head for the docks with every coin he had. Pray a ship was ready to lift anchor and that her captain would have mercy on them. Under better circumstances, Erik, Sigmund, or Thorsten could use their power of compulsion to persuade a captain it would be a good idea. But from what he'd learned around town, his brothers' fae powers would be sadly depleted and unreliable after their incarceration.

Dagstyrr grimaced, remembering the story the townspeople told him of fae prisoners slowly drained of their magic. He put down his blade and started to work a long dagger on the whetstone. Keeping busy was the only way he knew to deal with the waiting.

Later, Dagstyrr filled his purse with gold and secured it to his belt. Then he added his two best long knives to his belt; his two smaller ones he tucked in his boots. His sword, he strapped across his back. He wanted to bring his armor, but had been warned to leave it behind. Never mind. If this worked, Erik could buy him new armor.

The moon reached the point he'd been waiting for. Dagstyrr picked up his bundle of clean linens and took the backstairs down to the courtyard. The wooden steps creaked under his feet, but he gained the yard without being seen. The last thing he needed was someone asking awkward questions.

The light from the tavern shone across the cobbles, but Dagstyrr kept to the shadows, slipping out and under the wall's shade without meeting anyone.

He arrived at the rendezvous point in no time at all. Placing his bundle behind a rock, Dagstyrr scanned the shadows, looking for a sign of the boy. The night breeze brought the forest's scents, reminding him of home. If he closed his eyes, he could almost smell his mother's perfume in the air. Looking up, he saw the moon clear the tower.

Where was the boy? Dagstyrr's nerves were stretched to breaking point. He needed action.

Then a sound alerted him.

He jumped up, peering into the shifting gloom, but the

voice that spoke to him came from a different direction. "Thank you for believing me."

Dagstyrr whirled round. There he was. His turban and rags were clean, and it might be Dagstyrr's imagination, but the boy smelled cleaner too. Clutched in his hand, a bundle of linens. For what? "I had no reason to doubt you, but why the linens?"

"You'll need them later," he said. The boy was shaking, shudders coursing through his narrow frame. Dagstyrr balled his fists. It wouldn't do for both of them to shake like leaves in a storm, but the idea of entering the citadel terrified him. Then he remembered his father's advice: *Only a fool goes into battle unafraid. Recognize it, accept it, but don't let it control you.*

Rell pushed his bundle next to Dagstyrr's, making sure it was well hidden. "You will carry my brother out, and in return, I will show you how to rescue your brothers."

His heart soared. He struggled to keep his voice gentle. "Will my brothers need carrying?" said Dagstyrr, reluctant to promise anything that might mean he couldn't assist his brothers. Then again, without this boy, he couldn't rescue anyone.

"Erik might, but he has the other two to help him. Promise me you will carry Calstir out first–that's the price."

Dagstyrr could see the war waging in the boy's face. He needed Dagstyrr's help but was unsure he could trust him. "I promise."

"On your mother's life. Promise."

Dagstyrr paused. He'd never normally take such an oath, but if it saved his brothers? "Very well, on my mother's life."

The boy cocked his head as if listening to something. "Come, the vizier sleeps," he said, turning and slopping through the filth that continually oozed from the base of the wall. "Quickly now. We must be gone before he wakes," said Rell without a backward glance.

"Who are you?" said Dagstyrr, following in his wake. One thing for sure: this Rell was no ordinary street urchin. The boy had lost his whipped beggar's attitude, and moved with such grace and command it belied everything Dagstyrr knew about him. He watched the boy stride purposefully toward the wall, head high and shoulders straight. When he caught up with him, he wondered whether Rell might betray him. Perhaps he had no intention of helping him rescue his brothers?

The boy stopped before a much deeper puddle of filth, where human excrement and worse flowed from the base of the wall. "This was my first clue of a breach in the wall," said Rell.

"This sewer?"

"Exactly."

"What do you mean?" said Dagstyrr, taking one step back to save his boots from the worst of it. All he saw was a solid wall with foul water oozing from under it.

Rell glanced at Dagstyrr's boots. "Don't bother trying to save them."

"What's your plan?" Dagstyrr had to know before he went a step further. In the silence that followed, Dagstyrr's heart drummed with hope, before settling into a normal rhythm. "Why do you never answer my questions?"

"I have no time for answers." With that, Rell took a short run at the wall, then dove through the muddy water and under the wall, leaving Dagstyrr alone in the night.

Stunned, he stared where the boy had disappeared. The wall looked solid. What was he supposed to do, follow him?

The idea of diving headfirst through that muck turned his stomach.

"Very well," he said, to the wall, not sure whether Rell could even hear him.

In imitation of the boy, he ran and plunged headfirst into the puddle and under the base of the wall. Icy-cold water swallowed him. He kept his eyes and mouth tightly shut as slime and filth clung to his face. Holding his breath, he pushed through a large hole beneath the wall and into the space beyond surfacing into darkness. Wiping the foulness from his face, he looked around, trying to get his bearings.

His hand touched solid rock. It was rough and natural, not hewn. Dagstyrr hauled himself out of the water. "You weren't joking when you said I'd ruin my boots." Dagstyrr's sarcasm echoed harshly around the chamber. They must be underneath the foundations of the citadel.

"Shh, keep your voice down," said Rell. "We have only a short window of time. As soon as the vizier wakes, he'll feel my brother's absence. Another thing you must know: your brothers' magic will be compromised until they..." The boy appeared to regret his candor as if he'd said too much.

"Until they what?" demanded Dagstyrr.

"Until they recover from their imprisonment," he said, turning away.

"I already guessed as much. Why are you helping me?" asked Dagstyrr, a question he should probably have asked earlier.

"We help each other."

"Why not tell me your plans before?"

"You might have betrayed me."

A light flickered not six feet from him, and Dagstyrr saw he was in a natural rock chamber with a river of sewage running through the middle. He was underneath the citadel all right—now to find his brothers. He couldn't help smiling at the thought of his perfectly handsome fae siblings diving into the sewer. "Now I understand why I brought so much clean linen. You could have trusted me," he whispered.

CHAPTER 4

The boy lit two torches and thrust one towards Dagstyrr. Was it his imagination, or had the boy conjured fire? He was so used to his fae family doing so that he no longer noticed, but Rell?

Impossible! A warning crept up Dagstyrr's spine. He pushed it aside, turning to reason instead. The boy couldn't be fae. If he were, he'd be in here with his brother. All fae were born perfectly formed—yet this boy was severely marked. Rell's brother was light fae, so he couldn't be dark fae, unless...

The idea was absurd, yet warnings flashed through Dagstyrr's mind. If the boy was not human, then he could only be light fae or dark fae. If his brother was light fae, then so was Rell. A shiver of apprehension shook him as understanding dawned.

Born light fae, Rell had chosen to turn dark! He was the type of creature Dagstyrr's mother had warned him against all his life.

Rell's next action dispelled any doubt that he was fae. With a wave of his hand, Rell carved an opening in the solid wall and stepped through. He was indeed a dark creature of legend to be shunned by all. Even the fae feared light fae turned dark. It was unnatural.

Dagstyrr moved like lightning, his arm easily wrapping around the boy and trapping his magic hands to his sides so he could not use them. Lifting the struggling youth off his feet, Dagstyrr thrust his face close to the boy's ear and whispered, "What are you?"

"This isn't the time, human. If you want your brothers out alive this night, we have work to do and very little time in which to do it," said Rell, his voice steady and gentle.

"Do not think to compel me, or have you done so already?"

"I cannot compel such as you."

"Why not?"

"You are human, but protected by your mother's magic."

"Not at this distance, I'm not."

"Always. She fed you her protection with her milk."

Dagstyrr's mind was reeling. How could this creature of dark myth know so much about him? It was true. His mother, a light fae princess, had insisted on breastfeeding her youngest child herself against all convention and thus imbued him with her protection against magic. Otherwise, his light fae brothers would have killed him with their childish pranks before he was out of the cradle.

"How can you know?"

"Let's save this for another time."

He let Rell slide slowly to the floor. The boy was correct. Now was not the time for questions. As Rell's feet touched down, Dagstyrr's hand rested on his chest. Another surprise. "You're a girl!"

"Yes. Now let's get on, or we'll lose this window of opportunity. It is short. Come."

Rella dipped her head to hide her blush. His hand on her bound breasts had sent fire racing through her. No one had ever had such an effect on her before. Unable to look him in the eye, she said, "Rella. You can call me Rella."

If Dagstyrr hadn't already worked out that she'd chosen to turn dark fae, then he soon would, and she didn't want to deal with his reaction in here.

"This way," she said.

Dagstyrr's mind was racing, but he determined to focus on their mission. There would be time for answers later. "How far?

"No questions," said Rella. "Once we cross this threshold, my strength will wane. Leave your sword here. It will only get in the way. We have little time, so listen carefully."

Dagstyrr nodded. Beyond the stone threshold, a floor of silvered liquid spilled before them. It was not of the earth. So, once they stepped onto the shimmering surface in front of them, she'd no longer be grounded, and her powers would be impossible to harness. This was why she needed him, a human.

"Your job is to carry Calstir. I cannot. To use magic in here would mean death."

"Your brother?"

"Yes, my brother. Your brothers are well enough to help each other, but they'll be moving slowly, so we need all the time we have."

"Understood."

Dagstyrr understood all right. Tonight was his one

chance to get his brothers out of the vizier's prison, and dark fae or not, he'd follow her to hell and back to rescue them.

They stepped onto the shiny surface that continued up the walls and onto the ceilings. Row upon row of cells greeted his eyes, each with withering fae creatures lying inside.

Behind bars and padlocks, each cell appeared open on the outside wall, but for a shimmering membrane of softly undulating energy. Dagstyrr could see the town outside clothed in moonlight. By the gods! Had his brothers seen him circling day after day? His heartbeat quickened. *They know. They know I haven't deserted them.*

He stopped at a cell containing a half a dozen winged creatures. Like small humans no bigger than his forearm, they huddled together, pain distorting their features. In the cell next to them, another winged creature. Her huge leg muscles spoke of strength, but the despair on her face as she huddled in the corner said she'd almost given up. Just seeing them brought real anguish to Dagstyrr, so fundamental was their agony.

The next cell contained an ancient mountain elf, his white beard falling to the floor as his elongated fingers clutched his gnarled head.

"Don't look at them," whispered Rella. "Their suffering weakens all who see it. You need your strength. Quickly, this way," she said, moving swiftly across the floor.

He followed her up the stairs. An astringent smell grew stronger as they moved farther into the prison. Looking up, Dagstyrr saw levels of cells stretching to the open sky. Only it wasn't open. It just looked open.

The walls and ceilings were made of a magic-sucking substance, solid from the outside, and yet appearing like some strange glass inside. It cut the fae prisoners off from the sky and earth they needed to replenish their energy. It was a particularly sadistic level of cruelty.

Three floors up, Rella stopped, then ran like a fairy nymph across the floor, feet barely touching down. She was no longer trying to hide her fae nature from him.

He ran after her, his boots making no noise on the soft shimmering floor that moved like quicksilver under his feet, yet wet nothing. She stopped again and stepped onto the lowest bar in front of a cell. Dagstyrr's heart clenched when he came to her and saw what lay within.

A man was prostrate on a cot. He was light fae. His golden hair draped over the pillow and fell to the floor, his eyes closed in pain, and his skeletal hands were clenching a ragged blanket to his stomach. Pitifully thin, his high cheekbones made a skull of his once exceptional features. "Calstir, wake up," whispered Rella.

The man's eyes fluttered at her voice, but he couldn't open them. She turned to Dagstyrr, "Open the gate. I cannot. If I use magic, we'll be caught."

Dagstyrr tested the chain and padlock on the cell. They were well made. Thrusting his knife into the lock, he twisted.

Nothing.

Desperation spurred him to try harder. This was no ordinary lock. Looking around, he saw that the other cells had much smaller locks, easily opened. The vizier must prize this man above all the others, which meant he must be a very powerful fae indeed. Dagstyrr strained against the lock, slowly gauging the moment when the metal started to give, then twisted, putting his shoulder into the movement. A sharp ping echoed around the prison. Both he and Rella turned, ready for a fight.

"Don't worry, the vizier sleeps, and so does everyone

else. Now is the time when he feeds on us. Help me," she said, turning and entering the cell.

Feeds! Horror shivered through Dagstyrr, but he daren't slow them down with questions. There'd be time for questions later. Then he understood. She'd said, "us," so he was right. Here was the most despised of all creatures, a light fae turned dark. He wasn't sure whether his brothers would appreciate her help, but he did. Not being fae, he could take people as he found them, and he was in this creature's debt.

Dagstyrr stepped into the cell with its liquid glassy floor, walls, and ceiling. It was eerie. Her brother opened his eyes, and their blue light pierced Dagstyrr's soul. His mother's eyes were of the same bright, light fae blue, and held the same force of nature behind them. Rella's did not.

Calstir. The name invoked a memory deep in Dagstyrr's past, but he had no time to think about it. He bent to lift the man and found to his surprise that Calstir was heavier than he looked.

"Now you understand why I needed you," said Rella.

Dagstyrr unceremoniously hefted the man over his shoulder and swayed out of the cell. "Now for my brothers."

He saw conflict war on her face. She wanted nothing more than to run with her prize out into the night. He understood but hoped she could see his determination and wouldn't waste time arguing. He saw her resignation just before she spoke. "This way."

She led him down some stairs and along a corridor to the last cell. Erik lay on a cot, eyes closed in pain. Sigmund and Thorsten sat perched on stools, their arms tight around their bodies, heads bowed in misery.

"Sig, Thor," whispered Dagstyrr.

Sigmund sighed. "I can hear Dag, almost as if he's right here."

"Mmm, me too," answered Thorsten.

Erik's eyes fluttered open, and a grin split his face. "He *is* here, you fools! I told you he'd work it out," he said, straining to lift himself on his elbow.

Sigmund ran to the cell door, thrust his hand through the bars, and grabbed a knife from Dagstyrr's belt. Forcing it into the lock, he snapped it, then pulled away the chains. The door to the cell swung open with a clang.

"Whatever you do, don't use magic, or we'll be caught," said Dagstyrr. "Come on. We don't have much time," he said, relieved to see his brothers were in better shape than the man draped over his shoulders.

"Who's that?" asked Sigmund, pointing to Calstir. "And why is he so important you save him before us?" grumbled Thorsten.

Erik struggled to his feet and used the bars on the cell to propel himself outside. Then he fell to one knee. "On your knees, brothers. The bundle hanging off our little brother is our lord, Prince Calstir."

Immediately, his brothers followed suit. Their befuddled minds were reacting to fae royalty, unable to grasp the urgency of the situation.

"Get up, you fools; there is no time for this. Anyway, her brother is unconscious," said Dagstyrr. "Are you well enough to follow?"

"Her brother?" said Erik, staring at Rella's brown eyes and marked face, horror slowly replacing the confusion on his face.

"Yes," said Rella defiantly. "There is always a price to pay. Is there not? Now move. I intend to get out of here alive and within the few minutes left to us."

Dagstyrr's mother had tutored his brothers in the ways of the light, but Dagstyrr was seldom around when she did.

One lesson she had drummed into them all was to fear a light fae turned dark. They were an abomination. Power-hungry madmen bent on bringing destruction to all. Dagstyrr looked at Rella and found that hard to believe.

"Sig, Thor, assist Erik. You won't like the way out. It's narrow and...well, you'll see," said Dagstyrr as Rella pulled him with surprising force toward the other end of the corridor.

His brothers hauled Erik up between them, an arm over each of their shoulders. They half dragged him along.

Prince Calstir was as big as Dagstyrr, unconscious, and a dead weight. Dagstyrr's knees threatened to buckle several times. The stairs were especially tricky to navigate without dropping his princely load. Rella could not have done this alone without using her magic.

Dark! He remembered Erik's expression when he realized Rella had turned dark. Right now, big brother Erik was probably coming to terms with the fact that such a creature existed. *By the time we get out, he'll be ready to destroy her.*

Dagstyrr knew he might have to protect her from Erik. He owed her that much, at least.

With luck, Sig and Thor wouldn't be so quick to understand. The promise of freedom was hopefully clouding their minds enough to let it slip by them. Of course, Erik would soon bring them into the picture.

What had she meant about there always being a price to pay?

Rella's plan was working so far. It was a nuisance having to rescue Dagstyrr's brothers, but how could she not? The seconds ticked by along with the beat of her quivering heart.

Time was her enemy as she led the way through the maze of corridors, but she dared not use magic to help the men with their burdens. One hint of magic other than the vizier's inside the prison and alarms would sound throughout the citadel. The dragons would be released. All would be lost.

Sweat covered Dagstyrr as he struggled under Calstir's weight, but he was strong and didn't waver, even when his legs almost buckled on the stairs. She'd chosen well.

The stone threshold beckoned. Rella let her feet fly along the hateful surface of the prison, barely touching down. She could be as light as a feather when she willed it. It wasn't magic, just her nature.

At last, her feet grounded on the rough stone surface. The energy-sucking floor was behind her. She turned, urging the others on. Dagstyrr led the way with one hand out to balance the load over his shoulder. He staggered the last few yards.

Now they were on natural ground. Rella helped Dagstyrr ease his load to the floor. Cradling her brother's head, she gently laid him full length and listened to his heartbeat. There it was, weak but steady. The human leaned against the wall, trying to catch his breath. She rewarded him with a smile.

Just then, his brothers burst through the narrow opening, pushing Erik ahead of them. "Dag, catch him," said Thor.

Dagstyrr just managed to catch his eldest brother and drag him from the opening before Sigmund and Thorsten fell through behind him. The two brothers bent with hands on knees before collapsing to the ground.

Gratitude released their tension, and Rella could see the beauty of their fae features shine through their exhaustion.

Dagstyrr laid his eldest brother next to Calstir, understanding his need to touch the ground. He was a good man, this human.

"We have no time to waste. We must get outside and away from here."

"Lady, this is not waste," said Sigmund. His deep breathing let the energy from the natural earth seep into his being. The sky was the first energy choice of the light fae, but in a fix, any natural substance would suffice.

"We leave now," said Rella, with a hint of desperation in her voice. It worked. The brothers stumbled to their feet.

"Right, where to next?" said Thorsten.

Rella saw Dagstyrr smirk. "You won't like this, brothers."

"What do you mean?"

Rella produced the rope she'd hidden weeks ago. "He means you're going to get dirty, really dirty."

Sigmund looked askance at the pool of sewage. "Not…"

"Yes, halfling. You're going for a swim," said Rella, unable to completely hide her smile.

Dagstyrr, now fully recovered, wasn't even trying to hide his.

"I thought our little brother was riper than usual," said Erik, pushing himself to one elbow. "If Lord Calstir can do it, so can we," he challenged.

"Erik. Really?" said Thorsten, coming to realize what was required of them.

"Well, it's your choice, halfling; stink, or stay. No one's forcing you, but this is the *only* way out," said Rella, tying a rope around Dagstyrr's waist.

His stomach rippled with suppressed laughter as reality dawned on his light fae brothers. Rella felt his energy, warm and kind, as her fingers skimmed his shirt. There was no malice in this man, despite his amusement at his brothers' dismay.

Forcing herself to draw away from him, she realized that, despite the foul-smelling sewer permeating his clothes and hair, she could discern his human scent underneath. It filled her with a feeling of peace—that was strange.

Forcing those thoughts from her mind, she worked quickly to secure the rope around the unconscious Calstir.

"Dagstyrr goes first. He'll pull Calstir through with him," she said. "This rope is long enough to reach to the other side. The rest of you can use it if you need to." She knew light fae could rarely swim without using magic, and given the state they were in, she doubted they could gather enough energy to use magic.

Erik sat and removed his shirt. Ripping it, he covered Calstir's mouth and nose. "Lord Calstir mustn't inhale this muck."

"Go, now!" said Rella, giving Dagstyrr a gentle push.

He slipped into the filthy water and then eased the unconscious Calstir in beside him.

"He cares," whispered Rella, knowing she'd indeed chosen well.

Erik was getting to his feet. Rella needed to be next through the sewer. Erik was dangerous, and she couldn't be alone with him. He'd kill her without a thought. Light fae turned dark were an abomination to him. His light energy tutor would have trained him to kill first and ask questions later if he ever encountered light fae turned dark—just as she had been taught.

Rella positioned herself on the edge of the pool, ready to dive in. How long had it been since Dagstyrr had sunk below the surface? Not long enough. She must give him time to get out on the other side. She waited what seemed an age, her eyes on Erik.

"Give me time to get through before you enter. The

opening is small," she warned. "It's easier if you dive. Use the rope to drag yourself along," she said to the brothers before diving into the foul water for the last time.

She needed to get Calstir away from here before Eric plucked up the courage to follow and kill her.

CHAPTER 5

Dagstyrr pulled the fae prince from the stinking sewer. A breeze cut through his wet clothes sending his teeth chattering as he laid the unconscious man on the ground. Not a sound could be heard in the still night as clouds gathered in the sky. The grass had never smelled so sweet.

"Breathe deep," said Rella, pulling herself from the pool. The shadow of the wall hid them from the moonlight.

Dagstyrr took her advice; after all, she'd done this many times before. It helped.

He untied Erik's shirt, revealing Calstir's handsome fae features, then he felt for a pulse. "He's alive."

Rella nodded then knelt beside him, opening a small purse at her waist.

She produced a package well secured in waxed leather. From it, she took what looked like a handful of raisins and pushed a couple into her brother's mouth before lifting his head to help him swallow.

The prince coughed, then opened his eyes, turning them accusingly on his sister. "I said, no."

"It is necessary," she said, pulling him to his feet.

"No more, Rella. Do you hear me? I'd rather die. Please understand."

Rella took a deep breath. "I understand. We must go."

Dagstyrr wasn't sure what was happening between Rella and Calstir, but the prince's lack of gratitude toward his sister rankled with him.

It started to rain. Not a soft summer rain, but a spring deluge bounced off the filthy puddles around them. "Go," said Dagstyrr. "I'll wait for the others."

As the words left his mouth, he wondered where they would go. Did they have an escape route? They started to pull off their clothes just as Erik burst from the sewer, followed by Sig and Thor.

He pulled each of his brothers from the filth, then glanced at Calstir, who'd exchanged his rags for clean clothes and now ran with Rella towards the docks.

Of course they had an escape route. Rella had planned meticulously.

Dagstyrr smiled ruefully at their retreating backs. She'd used him mercilessly, but she'd saved his brothers, and for that, he'd always be grateful. Still, Dagstyrr was surprised at his own sense of loss when he thought of the waif who'd been his shadow these last weeks. He'd probably never see her again, which should be no bad thing, given Erik's reaction.

The rain was cleansing the stink from their bodies. Sig was even using the pounding water like a shower to clean his hair. When the others started to imitate him, Dagstyrr moved quickly toward his bundle of clean linen. "Here, change your clothes. Then we must run. I don't know how much time we have, but it's not long."

"What's the plan?" asked Thor.

"We head for the docks," said Dagstyrr pulling a clean shirt over his head. "And we pray at least one of the captains I've been buying ale for these last months is ready to sail."

Erik turned his bright blue eyes on Dagstyrr. "You haven't secured an escape route?"

It was just a question, but it stung like an accusation. "There was no time, but at least two ships that have promised passage are docked. Until you were out, I couldn't commit to anything. The vizier pays his spies well."

"Of course. Then let's get to the docks," said Erik, taking charge as usual. Then he turned looking for direction, but stumbled like a drunk. Sig moved first and caught him, pulling his brother's arm over his shoulder.

"I'll lead the way," said Dagstyrr. "Thor, help Sig with Erik. Time is our enemy."

Rain streamed down their backs, removing the stink of the sewer as they ran along the base of the wall. For once, Dagstyrr welcomed the rain, even when he felt his hose turn soggy in his ruined boots.

Thor looked at the wall. "The vizier's illusion is the best I've ever seen. One day I'm coming back here and giving him a taste of hell."

"Hurry," said Dagstyrr, shocked at the vehemence in his brother's voice. Light fae rarely expressed hatred or any other strong emotion.

Then they heard it. A sound like a thousand cats crying seemed to grow from the wall itself.

The alarm.

"Faster. Run!" shouted Dagstyrr. "The vizier is awake." He was no longer afraid of who knew they'd escaped—only of being caught. His brother's freedom was too close now. They could not lose it.

CHAPTER 6

Rella was stumbling with Calstir up the gangplank when the alarm sounded. Fear raised the small hairs on the back of her neck. "Lift the anchor!"

All around their little ship, other vessels scrambled to weigh anchor and set sail. Loaded or not, no one was going to be caught in Hedabar with the vizier's men on the rampage. The captains would rather sail empty.

The little wooden ship came alive as men scrambled to set sails.

Captain Bernst greeted Rella with a grim smile. "Ye only just made it, lass," he said, turning to Calstir. "This would be the prince?" Bernst sounded cautious.

"Fear not, Captain. I am in control of myself. Have you followed the special instructions my sister gave you?" asked Calstir.

"Aye, I have, but it doesn't look necessary," said the captain, raking Calstir with an experienced eye.

"Oh, it will be, believe me," said Calstir, turning his eyes away from the penetrating gaze of the *Mermaid*'s captain.

"Well, you say when. The stern's been turned into the

strongest cage possible at sea. The cabin is ready for your comfort when the worst is over."

"Thank you, Captain," said Calstir.

"They'll use wards as well, Calstir," said Rella, embarrassed, but needing to remind Calstir of her agreement with the crew.

All movement came to a halt on the small ship as the dark fae crew awaited the prince's reaction to news of the wards. Rella's cheeks burned in the fresh night air. She understood the depths of humiliation she was asking her brother to endure. Subjection to being warded by dark fae was something no light fae would allow, least of all a prince of Casta.

"After the citadel, 'tis but a trifle." Calstir waved a regal hand in the air as if he stood in his father's throne room rather than on the swaying deck of the *Mermaid* about to leave port.

Beneath the sound of the alarm, Rella sensed rather than heard the sighs that followed Calstir's pronouncement. Activity resumed on deck. She watched the other ships sail out to sea like an armada running from a fight. Waiting for Calstir and Rella, the *Mermaid* had lost the advantage of her mooring place and would now be the last to leave.

"This way, Prince, if you please." Captain Bernst gestured toward the caged room at the back of the ship. "We'd best be off."

"Of course," answered Calstir, stepping aside to allow the crewmen to lift the gangplank. Then he followed the captain toward the stern.

The sound of running feet echoed between the stone warehouses lining the wharf. At first, Rella thought she'd imagined it. How could she hear them above the sirens? But, yes, there they were.

"Dagstyrr!" shouted Rella above the din as the little ship's head swung out to sea and the wharf slipped away.

"Who?" asked Calstir, pausing.

"Dagstyrr of Halfenhaw. The man who carried you from the citadel! He and his brothers are going to be caught. None of the other ships has waited for them," said Rella, unable to keep the desperation from her voice.

Leaning over the guardrail, she saw the four men burst from the dark alley onto the deserted wharf still lit by torches no one had thought to extinguish in their haste to leave Hedabar.

Seafoam splashed her face as the *Mermaid* changed course to leave the confines of the harbor, but Rella's eyes focused on the four figures trapped on land.

"What will he do to them?" She'd told herself their fate was no business of hers. She'd given them a chance, a better chance than they had before. Now it was up to them. Wasn't it?

Calstir returned to her side. "He'll feed the human to his dragons, and return his fae brothers to prison, without hope."

"No! I'll not let that happen," said Rella lifting her arms to aid the brothers, but she couldn't help them. With her magic tamped down to practically nothing, lest the vizier sense her presence, all she could do was watch. It would take days to ramp it up enough to lift four men off the docks.

The vizier's guards marched onto the wharf. Knowing their prey was caught, they were in no hurry.

Rella watched, impotent, as Dagstyrr pushed each of his exhausted fae brothers into the water, commanding, "Swim!"

Better to drown than suffer whatever lay before them in the citadel, she supposed.

Then he dove like a bird into the foaming waters and came up next to Erik, who was flailing his arms. She watched as he shouted commands to his brothers.

"Calstir, they can't swim." Ice gripped her heart as she watched the four struggling for their lives. The vizier's bowmen lined the pier and began loosing arrows into the brine as the brothers' heads dipped below the surface. Dagstyrr could swim, but he was being dragged down by the weight of his siblings. Each time he dragged one to the surface, another dipped below the dark water. He wasn't giving up, but his task was impossible.

"Better to drown than be caught," said Calstir, echoing her thoughts as the small ship moved farther and farther from the land.

Rella rounded on him, fury driving her actions. She set her dark eyes on her brother with all the dark magic she could muster. "Save them." Her voice was so deep and terrible that Calstir flinched.

Horrified that she'd used her dark magic for the first time to compel her brother, she shuddered. Would he forgive her?

Rella watched him raise his hand, and bright blue battle magic flashed across the dark skies. Even after all those months in the citadel, his magic was strong.

All motion on the docks ceased. Men stood in awe at the spectacle of Calstir's magic swirling above them. Rella watched her brother contain it and direct it toward the four drowning brothers. Instantly, all four brothers lay retching on the deck, seawater pouring from them. All Rella could see was the accusation in her brother's eyes as Captain Bernst escorted him to the caged room.

Using his magic so soon had weakened him. He was having trouble walking without Bernst's aid.

"I shouldn't have needed to compel you!" she yelled to his back.

Calstir turned his head. "I needed to know how far you would go to get your way. Would you manipulate me? Now I know."

"You would have let four innocents drown, just to see how dark I am?"

"I would not have let them drown. I owe these men my life," said Calstir dipping his head and entering his new cell.

Rella ran after him. "Do not test me again, brother. I may be dark, but I am still fae—Princess Rella of our house." Rella pulled off her turban and let her hair fall to the deck in a river of pale gold. The captain and crew gasped as one. Turning dark had changed her eye color and given her a disfiguring mark, but her hair was still a light fae spectacle.

Lifting her chin, she said, "We will talk about this later."

Captain Bernst locked Calstir in the cage and turned to Rella. "What of them?" he asked, looking past her to the Halfenhaw brothers.

"We have no more cages. I don't know how bad things will get. Put three more hammocks in the prince's cell. We'll know the worst by tomorrow."

"Only three, Lady?"

"That one is human," she said, pointing.

"Really? He doesn't feel human," said Captain Bernst.

"It's complicated," said Rella. "You must trust me on this," she continued, not sure she understood herself where Dagstyrr was concerned.

CHAPTER 7

They were on a wooden deck. His brothers were puking seawater over the planks, but they were alive. That was all Dagstyrr knew. He had no idea who or what had helped them, but it was up to him to find out. He was in better shape than his brothers.

As he surged to his feet, he felt strong hands grip him. "You're all right, lad," said a strange one-eyed man with a gentle voice.

Wiping a hand over his eyes, Dagstyrr strained to look around him, just as the deck moved violently beneath him.

"Just a change of tack—you'll get used to it," said the man holding his arm.

"I'm used to longships, not barques. What is this ship?"

"The *Mermaid*. And I am her captain."

"Who dared to use magic to save us?" said Dagstyrr, not sure they were out of danger yet. They had yet to clear the harbor.

"Prince Calstir himself, boy."

Dagstyrr saw the prince raise a hand in greeting then

step into a cage. Strange, but who was he to question a prince.

Relieved, Dagstyrr dropped to his knees by his brother's side. Erik was lying on his back, staring up at the morning stars quickly fading in the pre-dawn light. Thor still had hold of Sig's shirt, and they both shook uncontrollably.

Dagstyrr pried Thor's fist from the back of Sig's shirt. His brother's hand was feverishly hot. Dagstyrr felt that same heat sear his palm when he put it to Sig's forehead.

Erik's fists were clenched at his sides, and his eyes carried the glassy look of fever. He hadn't been stargazing. Something was wrong with all three of his brothers. Raising his hand to his own forehead, he felt it cool and healthy. He was okay; what was wrong with them? Jail fever?

Looking around, he saw her hair first. Its golden light glistened like a beacon in this nightmare. Fae hair had a quality all its own, and Rella's was exceptional even for a fae princess.

Then he noticed the crew's reaction to her display. His mother would never have allowed anyone other than her family to see her hair unbound or unbraided, and neither should Rella.

"Lady." Dagstyrr stood and pulled a cloth from a mesmerized seaman's grip. Draping it over her head, he said, "My brothers are sick. You should go to your cabin in case you catch the fever."

"It's not ordinary fever," she said, turning dark doe eyes on him. "They are addicted to dragon's blood, and now they've missed their last dose."

"What?" Dagstyrr tried to make sense of what she was saying. His brothers would never take powerful drugs, least of all dragon's blood. It was abhorrent to them. Dragons were related to the fae, like mermaids or unicorns. Everyone condemned the trade in dragon's blood. "Nay, Lady, you are mistaken. They have jail fever," he answered, but in her gentle voice and sad eyes, he saw pity and knew she spoke honestly.

Turning to his siblings lying in agony on the deck, he felt his gut twist. "How is this possible?"

Calstir stared at them, his face a passive mask from inside the cage. "The vizier slowly slips us minute amounts in our food until we're addicted. He takes great delight when he tells us and offers us more. We all refuse at first. We'd starve before eating dragon's blood. So he leaves us alone for a day or two. Then, no matter how much we try not to, in the end, we beg for it," he said, turning his face from Dagstyrr.

"Then why are you not in the same state my brothers are in?" said Dagstyrr

Rella pushed her way between Dagstyrr and the cage. "He will be; believe me. Come, we must get them inside the cage before they lose control," she said, pulling at his sleeve.

Several of the *Mermaid*'s crew helped lift each of the now shivering brothers. Rella opened the cell door, and Dagstyrr followed them in. There was barely room for the four hammocks and four buckets. Of course, they'd only expected Prince Calstir, not the three Halfenhaw brothers.

Dagstyrr watched them expertly lay his brothers in the hammocks, and then to his horror, they wrapped them in canvas and strapped them in. They were like giant insects wrapped in cocoons.

"It is for our safety, Dagstyrr of Halfenhaw," said Prince Calstir.

"How long?" whispered Dagstyrr, seeing the glassy look in their fevered eyes.

"I don't know, but as my sister said, I will soon be joining them. They will be well cared for, but let me warn you, no matter what you see or hear in the next few days or weeks, do not enter this cell."

"Why not?" said Dagstyrr.

"Because we will say anything, do anything, promise and threaten anything to get what we want. We are fae. We will use all the magic at our disposal to escape and find what we crave."

"My brothers won't."

"Make no mistake, human, we all will, even myself."

"How are we supposed to stop you? You are a prince of the fae; your magic is inescapable."

"The *Mermaid*'s crew was well chosen. They know what they're doing and are well prepared. I need your word that you'll stay away," demanded Prince Calstir.

Dagstyrr looked at his brothers. Pain and fever showed plainly on their tortured faces. If what the prince said was right then, yes, he must stay well away, but all his instincts warned him to keep watch over his siblings.

A prince of the fae was a powerful and dangerous creature. How much more so when that prince was a dragon's blood addict?

"You are not as ill as they are. Yet, you were imprisoned longer. Shouldn't your addiction be worse, much worse?" questioned Dagstyrr, trying to make sense of it all. Was that a look of shame that flitted across the royal visage? "Well, why are you not shivering and helpless?"

"Do not challenge me, human," said the prince. Dagstyrr felt the blow of compulsion in his words buffet him like a sudden gale. Then he saw the look of confusion on the prince's face when that gale met a solid wall of resistance.

"I learned to deal with light fae arrogance in the cradle, Prince. How could I not, else my siblings would have had a slave instead of a brother?"

"My apologies," answered Calstir with a small bow of his head.

"So, why are you not ill, as they are?" Dagstyrr nodded towards his brothers, whose glassy eyes showed their spirits were engaged in a battle only they could fight.

Calstir's face betrayed his conflict. Royalty was usually much better at hiding their emotions. What secret was he trying to protect?

The prince turned toward him with a sigh. "You saw my sister give me medicine when we exited the citadel. There is no more. But you are correct that my recovery will be longer and harder than your brothers', and I feel its beginnings already. Leave me now."

Rough hands pulled Dagstyrr from the cell, and Calstir was helped onto his hammock and wrapped up in a cocoon. Then the four were left to their particular hell. Dagstyrr watched as the crew placed wards on the cage itself. Every member added his own dark magic to the soup of spells sealing the light fae into their prison. One by one, men crawled over the cage, adding whatever darkness they felt would protect them from the maelstrom the light fae would unleash inside.

A touch on his sleeve drew him away.

"So, Lady, the crew are dark fae too," said Dagstyrr.

"Not just the crew, Dagstyrr, the ship herself," said Rella, gently guiding him to the bow.

"You've sacrificed a lot to save your brother," he said, and that was an understatement. For a fae princess to turn dark was unimaginable.

"I couldn't ask anyone else to do it," she answered, steel in her voice.

"I wish you'd confided in me," said Dagstyrr.

Rella laughed gently. "No, I don't think so. You'd have run from me as you've been taught to do all your life. I'm the stuff of nightmares. I understand that."

Dagstyrr recognized the truth of her words. "I wasn't sure whether I'd ever meet a dark fae." He turned to look directly into her eyes. "You are the answer to my prayer, not a nightmare. Without you, my brothers would still be rotting in the citadel. I am not ungrateful, and neither will my parents be."

"Our brothers still have a long journey ahead of them," said Rella, turning to the cage at the stern.

"My brothers' lives are in your hands. Will they recover?"

"Yes."

"What of their future?"

"You refer to their addiction to dragon's blood."

"Aye."

"They didn't take it willingly. Indeed, according to Calstir, until the prisoners unwittingly consumed enough in their food to become seriously addicted, they had no idea what they ate. The vizier is like a cat with a trapped mouse, watching them refuse their food until they succumb, not to hunger, but to the dragon's blood. They will do anything he asks after that. They become his creatures."

"How do you know?"

"I've spent many illicit hours talking with Calstir, planning his escape."

The picture she painted in his head tore at him. Knowing them as he did, he couldn't imagine the shame his brothers bore, especially the proud Erik.

"They will be shunned."

Rella rounded on him, forcing him to look her in the eye. "No. That must not happen. It will not happen. They will be cleansed and forgiven. Remember, it was not their choice." Her hand went instinctively to the mark flowering on her cheek.

He ignored the gesture. The four in the cage might be forgiven if enough pressure was brought to bear on the court, but he doubted she would be. Rella was marked as light fae turned dark. She'd paid a terrible price for their survival. "Still, the stigma will follow them for the rest of their lives," said Dagstyrr, knowing light fae were not the forgiving type.

"Not if I can help it," said Rella, staring across the choppy waters of the open ocean.

Dagstyrr understood she was thinking of her brother. How could Calstir ever expect to rule with this staining his reputation? Dagstyrr turned to stare across the waves with her. His hands rested on the bulwark, its handrail smooth and worn beneath his fingers. This woman had sacrificed more to save her brother than any other family blighted by the vizier. She was strong and capable, yet he couldn't help wondering if the sacrifices she'd made were too great.

Determined to return Prince Calstir to his throne, she'd said nothing about her position. Never in all the history of the fae had anyone turned back to the light after embracing the dark. Dagstyrr thought it impossible, a one-way street. She was a light fae princess like his mother. Now she was doomed to spend the rest of her days as dark fae, reviled by all who knew her and cast out to live any way she could.

At what point do you say, *Too much*?

"When you're ready, there's food in my cabin, but you'll have to sleep on deck," she said, turning and leaving him alone to come to terms with the plight of a prince, his three brothers, and a strangely beautiful princess.

Dagstyrr turned to the cage where Calstir lay wrapped in linens. He and Rella were powerful fae; probably the most potent Dagstyrr had ever met. Why then did he feel the overwhelming need to protect her, and from whom?

CHAPTER 8

Dagstyrr made his way past her small cabin to the bow of the ship. With one hand on the figurehead to steady himself, he let the wind blow over his body, its cleansing scent washing away any vestiges of the prison-sewer stink.

If only it could cleanse the knowledge that sat like a stone burden on his soul. His brothers had consumed dragon's blood and now were being rescued by the dark fae. What they would make of it all when they recovered, he had no idea.

Without Rella's help, he'd still be walking around the citadel like some demented pilgrim. His brothers would still be imprisoned within its walls eating the vizier's poison and growing more dependent on it with every meal.

Dagstyrr shuddered. How in the name of all the gods were they going to tell their mother?

A cry sounded far off, an animal cry like nothing he'd heard before. It echoed the turmoil in his soul. No one else on board reacted to it. Perhaps he was being oversensitive to an animal kill on shore. Sound often carried in bizarre ways across the water. His sailor's instinct noted a gray morning threatened on the horizon, bringing a stiff breeze—nothing to worry about.

The ship's sails suddenly billowed out, and the *Mermaid* ran before the wind, putting distance between them and the cry. Dagstyrr felt the rhythm of the ship as she rode the waves, causing the wind and spray to batter him.

The strange cry sounded again, farther away this time, and he took his hand from the *Mermaid*'s figurehead. Her head turned, and she winked at him. Horrified, Dagstyrr almost lost his footing. He grabbed the gunwale to steady himself.

What was it Rella had said about the ship being dark fae? He'd had other things on his mind at the time, but now he wondered just what kind of magic the dark fae used. He wished he'd attended more of his brothers' fae lessons, instead of going down to the wharfs with his father.

He bowed to the figurehead and left. If the sailors moving about the ship thought this strange, they didn't show it.

For the first time, he considered his position, a lone human with a crew of dark fae. Dark fae could move amongst humans undetected. Local folklore was rife with stories of people tricked into giving them gold or farms, or even a child as the price demanded for a favor. They answered to no one but themselves. Their magic was as powerful as the light fae's, but it came from a different source deep in the earth where fire reigned. Dark magic was blood magic, they said. Or, was that just a story to frighten children?

His father, Earl Magnus, was human. He claimed to know several dark fae, boasted that he'd sailed with them, but Dagstyrr noticed he never talked about them in front of his mother.

He heard his mother's voice, a warning deep in his soul: *Never let yourself be beholden to the dark.* He pushed the thoughts aside. Rella wasn't dark, not really.

Dagstyrr needed sleep. He had no choice but to trust Rella and Prince Calstir to protect him from the crew. He found a place to lie down on some stored canvas before the heat of the oncoming day made sleep uncomfortable. A black-eyed sailor tossed him a cloak. Dagstyrr nodded thanks before wrapping himself in it, and allowed exhaustion to shut down his reeling thoughts.

It seemed only moments later that he was awakened by that strange cry sounding again, but the sun was high and the call much closer. Dagstyrr had been asleep for hours, not moments. He staggered, sleep drunk, to his feet. Finding the water barrel, he helped himself to a drink before pulling a bucket up from the sea and sluiced water over his head to help him waken up.

The crew was tense. Dagstyrr could see it in their every move. They went about their business as usual, but their eyes kept darting to the skies. No, this crew was different. They were strangely quiet. Even an experienced ship's crew gave and received orders regularly while they were at sea. Captain Bernst never gave an order, yet all was well —strange.

Rella emerged from her cabin, holding the doorway open. "Come, there is food and wine," she said. Her hair was respectably braided, and her nut-brown eyes were soft and inviting. Her blue silk robes rippled in the breeze, wafting exotic perfumes toward him.

Dagstyrr wiped at the water dripping from his chin, suddenly aware of the salt and grime clinging to his clothes and skin. Even his Samish leather boots were coming apart at the seams. He must look a mess. "I'd rather eat on deck. I'm not dressed for a lady's chamber," he said with a small bow.

Her laughter brought his head up fast. "Sir Dagstyrr, we've seen each other in worse condition. Come."

"Still..."

"Come." She held out her hand. Smells of freshly cooked food assailed his palate. Hunger was a good persuader. Ducking under the lintel, he found himself in a small space, but one fit for a princess. Silks of every hue decorated even the ceiling, and the smell of exotic foods perfumed the air.

"I know you have many questions, Sir Dagstyrr," she said, modestly lowering her eyes. "I will endeavor to answer them. There should be no secrets between us now."

Rella spread her hand in invitation. "Please sit." She poured wine into silver goblets. Dagstyrr drank it down, the cooling liquid refreshing and not too sweet.

A feast was spread out before him—roasted meats, new baked bread, cheeses, and fruit. He sighed gratefully after the first mouthful and then ate heartily.

After assuaging his initial hunger, he stopped. The woman in front of him was intoxicating. Even the mark staining the side of her face couldn't tarnish her ethereal beauty. Her dark eyes contrasted with her pale blonde hair, making him want to stare at the unusual combination. "I do have questions."

She leaned over and refreshed his wine from a silver ewer. "Finnish eating, and then we'll talk."

Dagstyrr ate. If Rella was genuinely dark, could he trust anything she said?

CHAPTER 9

Again, that strange cry sounded, and this time, it brought Dagstyrr to his feet. It was close, very close. He could hear shouts from the deck as the crew hurried to change tack. "What is that?" he said, stepping out of Rella's chamber and onto the deck.

"It's the vizier's dragon. It follows us," said Rella, at his elbow.

"A dragon, if one truly exists, would have caught up hours ago."

"Yes, but this one's blind," answered Rella, a catch in her throat.

"Blind. Then how did it find us? And how do you know so much about it?" It was time for answers.

"He smells the dragon's blood coursing through our brothers' veins," she answered.

"I'd have thought they'd be free of it by now. It's been some time since their last dose, and they're all suffering withdrawal," said Dagstyrr, thinking there must be something else drawing the dragon toward them.

Rella paled, turned without a word, and re-entered her

chamber. Dagstyrr followed. She wasn't going to avoid his questions this time. He gripped her elbow and spun her toward him. "It's time to explain a few things, and don't try any of your tricks. Remember, I grew up with fae."

~

Rella gasped. No one had ever touched her so roughly in all her life. His touch was both frightening and strangely compelling. This human confused her.

Not taking any chances, she pulled a ball of energy into her hand, ready to release it if necessary. His face was close. Anger emanated from him like a red mist.

She'd used him to rescue Calstir, but she'd helped him save his brothers in return. A fair exchange, she thought. Also, she'd demanded Calstir save him and his brothers from the sea, but that part was purely selfish. If they'd died because of her, she'd have borne the guilt for the rest of her life. Still, why was Dagstyrr so angry with her?

His face pushed closer, eyes boring into her. Rella felt her breath stifle. To her horror, she was panting like a wanton inviting his touch—which she was not. He was not for her. She turned from him to dispel the effect his proximity had on her.

"How do you know so much about the vizier and his dragon?" His hand gripped her chin and turned her once more toward the anger flashing in his eyes.

She felt her ball of energy slip from her hand and dissipate across the floor, singeing the hem of her gown. Horrified at her lack of control, she fought to show him only serenity. To challenge him now could be dangerous for both of them.

"This is the patriarch of all the dragons. The vizier

blinded him. He uses his sense of smell to find his way in the world," she said, struggling to remove all emotion from her speech. "That is how the vizier controls him. If he doesn't return after carrying out the vizier's orders, a member of his family is blinded as punishment."

"And dragons put family above everything else," said Dagstyrr, quoting his mother's stories.

"Quite so."

"Many ships left Hedabar last night. Don't say he's following the scent of the blood in our brother's veins. We've already established that can't be correct."

"Dragon's blood pellets." Even as she stated the truth, she felt the pull of the small pouch containing the dried poison she'd secreted in her chamber. Twisting from his grip, Rella slid behind a curtain.

What a fool she'd been. The pellets were keeping the dragon on their trail. She must lose them now. She dug in the pocket of Rell's pantaloons, until her hand closed around the pouch. She'd lied about there being more in case Calstir was unable to go without; men in his condition had died in the throes of withdrawal. Now she had no choice. They'd all die if the dragon caught up with them.

The worn leather of the pouch felt heavy in her hand, and she could feel the potency of its contents like an exotic poison beckoning with promises never to be fulfilled. She'd carried the hateful thing for days. Now she must be rid of it once and for all.

Calstir had prepared for what was to come, and he was strong. She hoped the Halfenhaw brothers were also strong. With a prayer in her heart, she dashed from the cabin, pushing past Dagstyrr, who quickly followed on her heels.

She worked her way down the ship, past the cage, and towards the stern. An unnatural wail of pain sounded from the cage as she passed. They, too, sensed or smelled the pellets. She didn't know which. Sparks flew from inside the cage, sending three of the crew to renew the wards protecting the ship from the four inside.

Dagstyrr was on her heels. He pulled up her arm with the pouch gripped tight in her fist. The look in his eye said he understood what it was. His large hand closed around hers. "I can throw farther."

Rella nodded and released the pouch, both sad and relieved to have the poisonous energy leave her hand. Her throat was too dry to speak as her legs started to tremble. She had never consumed any dragon's blood, but it was the most addictive substance on earth, especially for the fae, and she'd been carrying it around for days. The tortured sounds came from behind her as a reminder of the hell those four were suffering. She knew how dangerous a cargo was contained within that cage.

Despite never having taken the forbidden substance, she felt its loss. It was just a taste of what the addicts were going through.

Rella watched as Dagstyrr leapt upon the gunwale. Holding fast to the tiller, he threw with all his might—the small thing arced through the air before dropping to be swallowed by the sea.

He stepped down, and she joined him to watch the skies for the monster that was sure to appear. Just as she thought they'd escaped, a black shape broke from the clouds.

Dagstyrr's arm went around her shoulders, protective and solid, but even his strength couldn't save her from a dragon. The ship's crew froze in silence. Sound would attract the sightless beast.

∼

To Dagstyrr's ears, every creak of wood and rope on board sounded an alarm. Thankfully, there was no noise from the cage.

The beast's massive size took his breath away as he watched him sweep across the sky. His vast black wings beat the air buffeting the small ship. The head of the dragon moved back and forth, searching with his snout for the purse of dragon's blood. Horns, black and sharp as pikes, curved away from his head like a pair of recurved bows. Dagstyrr's heart tore when he saw the fire that raged where the dragon's eyes once had been.

The beast roared his frustration, spewing a plume of fire from his maw, causing the water around their craft to boil momentarily. When it did, the dragon's eye-sockets went blank, dead, and useless.

The monster turned, his long black tail whipping behind him, barely missing the ship's mast. Something had caught his attention. Without warning, he rose with such an incredible turn of speed that Dagstyrr gulped. Flipping in mid-air, he dived, wings flat by his sides. The dragon entered the water exactly where the purse had entered.

For a few moments, no one onboard dared to move. Then the voice of Captain Bernst echoed in Dagstyrr's head, *Hold. When it comes up, hold fast and not one sound.*

Dagstyrr was shocked that the captain had such abilities. This was highly developed fae magic. It explained the lack of shouted orders usually heard on a sailing ship. Pulling Rella closer, he ducked down, gripping a railing with his other hand. Silently, the rest of the crew grasped whatever was near. Then they waited. If it surfaced too close to the ship, they'd be sunk.

Seconds stretched to minutes, and the tension onboard grew almost to a breaking point. Dagstyrr prayed that whatever had quieted the men in the cage would continue, and give them all a chance to evade the beast.

The sea had calmed completely after the dragon's dive, and still, there was no sign of it.

Suddenly the massive head burst through the surface just beyond the stern, sending water pouring over the gunwales. For a moment, Dagstyrr looked straight into the black sightless face of the monster, but far from being afraid, he felt overwhelmed by compassion. The dragon's scales were dull and damaged, his horns were scorched, and pain etched a web of weariness over his ancient face.

There and then, Dagstyrr made himself a promise: *I am going back to the citadel. One day I will set you and everyone else there free.* He knew it was madness, but how could he not want to free this noble creature? No one, human or fae, could look into that face and not want to put an end to the suffering it represented.

The ship still rocked violently from the beast's emergence from the foam-flecked sea. Water poured off his back and drenched their vessel. The dragon shook the vestiges of seawater from his body and circled in the sky above them.

No one on board moved or said a word to attract attention—one person would make a tasty snack for a dragon of this size. Just as it appeared to be moving away, it returned and hovered over the small vessel. Dagstyrr felt the crew brace for what was to come, but the last thing he expected was the pain surging through him.

Letting go of Rella, he gripped his head, trying to make sense of the heat filling his skull. *YOU!* The deep dragon voice rumbled through his brain. *I will spare your puny ship, but you must do as you promised. Return to the citadel. Set us free.*

"I will!" shouted Dagstyrr. "Take it off. Take away the

fire." Hands covered his mouth, dragging him along the deck.

I will be waiting for you, Dagstyrr of Halfenhaw. If you do not come for us, I will seek out all your family to ten generations and feast upon their crunchy bodies, the dragon's voice thundered.

Then he was gone.

The crew stepped away, but the looks on their faces told him they knew he'd conversed with the dragon. Dagstyrr, a human, had done what none of them could.

The crew went about their work, leaving Dagstyrr sprawled on the deck. Captain Bernst made his way over. "What did you promise it?"

"What makes you think I promised him anything?"

"I know dragons. That one could smell us, yet he let us go. You felt his fire," said Bernst bending his face close to Dagstyrr's.

Dagstyrr sighed as the enormity of his promise to the dragon took root and chilled his blood. Sympathy had fueled his rash promise, but how, by all the gods, was he to follow it through? "I didn't involve you, your crew, or Rella if that's what you're afraid of," said Dagstyrr, getting to his feet.

"Oh, but we are involved. What did you promise?" The crew started gathering behind their captain, waiting for an answer.

Dagstyrr defiantly repeated, word for word his promise to the dragon, though he'd had no idea the dragon could hear him at the time. As he spoke the words aloud, he felt again the compassion that had prompted him in the first place. "How could I not?" he finished.

"How many generations?" said the captain.

"I didn't say anything about generations," said Dagstyrr,

starting to understand that this man did know about dragons after all.

"You didn't have to. How many?"

"Ten."

"He doesn't believe you can do it or he wouldn't have demanded ten generations. Oh, he thinks you're honest and willing, but he doesn't believe you can set them free. We'll be ready when you are," said the captain.

"You won't be involved. I told you that." Dagstyrr knew nothing of dark fae. Was this some strange code of honor forcing the captain to offer himself and his crew? "What do you know of dragons?"

"I know when you mind-spoke to him, he believed you spoke for all of us. We will be with you when the time comes," said Bernst, turning from him and setting the crew to man the sails.

Guilt gnawed at Dagstyrr. Had he involved the whole crew in his rash promise? Strangely, Captain Bernst appeared resigned to it. Perhaps he wanted to rescue dragons? It was undoubtedly a way to make a name for yourself if you succeeded.

Dagstyrr took Rella's elbow. "Come, let's talk in your cabin." He led a strangely subdued Rella the length of the ship to her cabin at the stern.

"Captain," said Dagstyrr over his shoulder, "will you join us?"

CHAPTER 10

The captain's presence filled the small cabin, his leathery skin and rough clothing an affront to the pale silks adorning the walls. "Sit down, Captain," said Dagstyrr.

With a wry grin twisting his face, the captain sprawled out and took a cup of wine from Rella, which he quaffed in one swallow. "Now, youngster, what questions might ye have for me? I have no objection answering, as long as the wine keeps coming." He took the ewer from Rella and filled his cup before resting his one-eyed gaze on Dagstyrr.

"This is not a game, Bernst," said Dagstyrr.

"Ye're right there, lad. Not a game at all. Now, what's your plan to best the vizier and free those dragons?"

In the silence that followed the captain's question, the reality of his position hit Dagstyrr. What a fool! It had been Rella's plan that had saved his brothers, not his. All he'd done was provide muscle. It was going to take a lot more than brute strength to defeat the vizier, and he didn't dare take his brothers. They were just what the mad vizier of Hedabar wanted.

It was all very well feeling sorry for a wounded creature, but impulsive promises were the mark of inexperience. Dagstyrr hadn't known he was making a promise to anyone other than himself, and he said so.

"If I hear you right, lad, it's wrong to break a promise to anyone—except yourself?"

Chastened by the absurdity of his argument, Dagstyrr sat and stared the one-eyed captain full in the face. "You must think me the biggest fool that ever lived, but how was I to know dragons can hear your thoughts?"

"Nay, lad, I've known worse," said Bernst getting to his feet. "But from now on, ignorance is no excuse. It's extremely rare to hear a dragon speak, and no fae that I've ever heard of can do it. You're a rare man, Dagstyrr, but you've got a lot to learn. The best teacher anyone could ask for is right there," he said, pointing to Rella. "With at least a month at sea ahead of us, you should take advantage of her and learn all ye can."

Following Captain Bernst's departure, Dagstyrr took the time to compose his questions. The last thing he wanted to do was to insult Rella, but he had to understand everything he could about dragons. He knew nothing about dark fae, or about the way Bernst and the dragon could talk in his head. He'd never experienced that before. How did it work, going from light to dark? What were the consequences, besides mutilation and scars? All he had to go on were stories made up to scare children.

More importantly, he needed all the information he could find on the vizier if he was to defeat him. This strangely beautiful fae princess was his only hope—or his downfall, he thought ruefully as her intoxicating perfume wafted over him.

∽

Rella busied herself about the small cabin as Dagstyrr brooded. He sat on a cushion, back against the wall with one knee drawn up, his deep blue eyes staring into the middle ground while he, no doubt, contemplated his fate.

Guilt squeezed past her defenses, and she almost apologized to him. This new tangle with the dragon was her fault for carrying the pellets. Dagstyrr must be furious with her. The tension in the small space grew. How was she supposed to know he could dragon-speak?

Eventually, it was Dagstyrr who broke the silence. "Why does it hurt?'

Rella turned, confused. "Why does what hurt?"

"When the dragon spoke to me, I thought my brain would boil in my skull, yet when Captain Bernst did the same earlier, it didn't hurt at all."

Rella knew he'd need more than simple answers. If he was to survive this quest, he required all the knowledge the fae had at their disposal, both light and dark. "Everyone can hear Captain Bernst. Human or fae, dark or light, it makes no difference. The gift belongs to the captain. He can reach into our minds and speak as though he'd spoken aloud. It's a rare and precious gift for any leader."

Dagstyrr could undoubtedly understand the advantage. "Can he hear our thoughts?"

Rella smiled. "No, and that's the main difference between the dragon's ability and Captain Bernst's. With dragon-speak, the listener is the one with the gift. Our legends tell us all dragons converse using only their minds. This is why we call it dragon-speak, and yes, the dragon can hear you as well as speak to you. To a dragon, it is normal to communicate that way. That is what I've been taught. However, until today, I thought it impossible," she said.

Watching the effects of her words dance across his handsome face, Rella wondered whether she could convince him to renege on his promise. After all, the dragon was a captive. It might be a hundred years or more before he was let out again.

"If this is my gift, why did it hurt so much? I thought my head was going to explode."

"According to legend, there is one story of a child stolen by a dragon thousands of years ago. The dragon was a female who'd lost her child to a dragon slayer. She stole the slayer's children, but when she spoke to them, they died in agony, all except the youngest, a male infant. They say the youngest child let the dragon in, and so he lived. He showed no fear of her and crawled over her sleeping form to snuggle between her wing and her warm body at night to sleep. His first words were dragon-speak. He grew up knowing only the dragon mother. He thought he was a dragon. One day, he saw a beautiful human girl and fell hopelessly in love with her. He spoke to his dragon mother and asked her who he was and why he wanted the girl so much..."

"I can guess the rest. You think I'm descended from the boy and this girl?"

"That is what we believe. Every hundred years or so, we hear word of a human dragon-talker. You are very rare, indeed."

"So, why would such a gift come out in me so many generations later? No one I've ever heard of on either the human or fae side of my family has had this ability."

"Do you know of anyone in your family who has met a dragon?"

"No. Like most people, we thought they were all dead or living far away."

"So, how could anyone know whether there are any more dragon-talkers in your family?"

"I don't know."

"Remember, it is only a legend. It may be that we too spoke to each other using only our minds at one time. I think it is related to the gift Captain Bernst has but quite different."

"It may come in useful."

"How?" said Rella, trying to keep the dread from her voice. Was he seriously going to try and free the dragon?

"If I can 'speak' to this dragon, then perhaps I can speak to them all. Do you have any idea how many the vizier has enslaved? There must be more than one. The dragon talked of 'us,' and I'm sure he wasn't referring to the addicts dining on his blood."

"You cannot be serious!" Unable to keep her composure, Rella sat with a thump across from him. "If you set so much as one foot on Hedabar, the vizier will have you put to death. The last human he punished lasted four days in agony before he died. His crime was shorting the citadel on grain supplies. What do you think the vizier will do to you?"

"I wasn't thinking of announcing my arrival," he said with a grin.

Rella's stomach somersaulted. His deep blue eyes, coupled with that devilish grin, were awakening desires she'd rather not acknowledge right now. He was not for her on so many levels. He'd been brought up with the perfection of light fae all around him. His idea of a desirable woman must be far removed from the street urchin he'd first encountered. Besides, he was human, and she a princess of —of nowhere.

She swallowed her thoughts. "Even now, he'll have your likeness posted in every doorway, tree, and wharf on Hedabar. Every ship that docks will take your image with them when they sail."

"And he'll offer a substantial reward, no doubt," said Dagstyrr. "I wonder what I'm worth?"

"Do not joke about such things," she snapped. How could he be so cavalier? Unless he changed his attitude quickly, he'd be dead within a six-month. She must keep her distance from him. There'd been enough heartache in her life recently. "Don't forget the vizier's nature. He's more likely to threaten torture and death than offer a reward."

"Can the vizier dragon-speak?"

"I doubt it. I've never heard of anyone who can, besides you," said Rella. "Why don't you ask the dragon? We are still but a short distance from him."

"You mean he could be listening to this conversation now?"

"I've no idea. Perhaps Captain Bernst can give you a better idea of how far the gift will reach. Remember, though: it is a different kind of mind-speak from his."

"Or perhaps I can just try and communicate with him now?" he answered.

Rella could see it was the last thing he wanted to do. A memory of the pain inflicted by the dragon passed fleetingly across his face. All the same, this obstinate knight was not one to be challenged. Were she to demand he not, he would surely go his own way. She sighed. "It is up to you."

"I am in no hurry to feel that pain again, but how else am I to plan this campaign? If I had direct contact with the dragons inside the citadel, it would be a great advantage." She saw his plan take root and knew it was only a matter of time before he returned to Hedabar and attempted the impossible.

As enthusiasm blossomed in him, an aching seed of heartbreak planted itself in her soul. She watched as subtle changes transformed his expression from one of despair to one full of hope and promises. The beauty of it transfixed her. His energy changed with each thought passing through his stubborn head until his presence in the small chamber dominated everything, even her. That, she would not allow. She couldn't. His was an impossible quest, and besides, she had a journey of her own to finish.

Calstir must return to Casta. Then what? There was no longer a place for her at his court. She would be an anathema to all light fae, especially the highborn lords and ladies of the court. With her marks evident to all, they would never understand the choice she'd made. They'd never trust her. Oh, no doubt some of her friends would support her, but that would only damage their positions until eventually, under enormous pressure, they too would have to rebuff her.

If she was to have any life of her own, she had but one choice: to fulfill her promise to the Dark Emperor, the most powerful dark fae in existence. She shuddered at the thought, remembering his cruel mouth and dead eyes. He would welcome her to his court as his queen. He'd made that much plain. It was the price she had to pay, but could she do it?

"Is the vizier human?"

His voice brought her back to the task at hand. "No one knows. The vizier must be either human or dark fae; I suspect dark fae. Perhaps Calstir can enlighten us. He was in the citadel longer than your brothers and met with the vizier several times."

"I met him only once. When we first landed and were invited to the citadel to dine."

"That is how he ensnares people. No visitor to his shores can refuse those invitations without giving offense. The food is heavily laced with dragon's blood," said Rella.

"Then I'm thankful I was thrown out before dinner."

"He must have thought all four of you were light fae. Light fae are his preferred captives, but he'll take any fae at all. You saw the variety of dark fae in the cells the night we rescued our brothers. However, he wouldn't waste his time on a human."

"I saw no deformity or scars on the vizier, but his robes could have hidden them. In truth, I wasn't looking for marks. I might have missed something," said Dagstyrr.

It was like a knife in her soul. She was marked, terribly marked. She couldn't hide the anguish his words brought, but she quickly recovered. "I'm sure there is a sign if he is indeed dark fae," she managed to say with a steady voice, though she could not look him in the eye.

His warm hand covered hers, bringing solace with that one simple act. His hand was large and callused, with all the small scars one would expect on a human warrior, yet she was not repulsed by it. She turned her small hand in his and held on. For just a moment, she allowed herself to enjoy his touch.

"I'm sorry if my words offended you. I didn't think. We humans are not so sensitive to marks and scars. I have plenty myself. Please forgive me. I wouldn't distress you for the world," he said.

Rella pulled away. She didn't need his pity. "I have studied the vizier from afar and tried to make sense of what he's doing. There is no doubt in my mind that he's trying to gain power from the light fae. Which..."

"Which would indicate he is not light fae," said Dagstyrr. "Human then, or more likely dark fae. How else could he use magic to imprison the dragons and the light fae?"

At that moment, Captain Bernst returned and joined in the conversation. "Don't think all the dark are marked or scarred. It doesn't work that way." He sat and helped himself to Rella's wine.

Puzzled, Rella stared at him, trying to make sense of his words. "What do you mean?"

Bernst sighed, looking distinctly uncomfortable. "Not all of us are marked. We are fae, born as physically perfect as any other. The only difference between us is that we lost our ability to heal instantly."

A chill flooded Rella, leaving her temporarily mute.

"What do you mean?" asked Dagstyrr. "I thought the marks and deformities the dark fae carried were a choice. To help them pass as human."

"Nay lad, these marks are the result of our arrogance," said the captain, his gruff voice reverberating off the wooden planks beneath them.

"I don't understand," said Dagstyrr. "You have only one eye. Most of your crew are marked with some injury or deformity of some kind."

"Mmm...Let me try and explain. You've been brought up with three brothers, each of whom had enough fae blood to be considered light fae. What was the difference between you and them in the tiltyard?"

"Father wouldn't allow them to use magic at practice. They were faster, that's all."

"Aye, that's right, lad," said Captain Bernst. "They were faster. What else?"

Dagstyrr thought back to their time growing up in Halfenhaw. He could see his big brothers almost dancing in swordplay, fearless, leaping higher and moving so swiftly his eye had trouble following them. His memories brought with them an ache of longing to be home, which he pushed aside. "They were fearless."

"Exactly!" said Bernst. "That is the arrogance of fae. We have trouble fearing any physical exercise because we are so incredibly fast and accurate. At one with the earth itself, we are elementals. Part of our very being is made of the same substance as the earth itself, the air too, and fire and water. Rock is our brother and can sustain us in times of need. A stream talks to us, the trees are our kin where the dryads live, and we go to them for the ancient wisdom. We move through the air as if we are air itself, which is why we're so fast. If need be, we can burrow into the earth and lie there for days or years without moving. We are fae!" The captain's voice rose to a crescendo, and his fist banged on the table.

Dagstyrr dared to break the silence that followed the captain's impassioned speech. "Which is why our brothers were held in a prison of pure energy."

"Aye, but that was energy with no soul, no grounding in the earth or the skies above," said Captain Bernst with a shiver, before knocking back the rest of the wine.

Finding her voice at last, Rella asked tentatively, "How does that explain my mark?" Her hand strayed to her cheek where the brown mark that started on her leg ended.

Sobered by her words, Captain Bernst looked around the small cabin as if for a quick escape, then appeared to think better of it. "I'll not pretend to know what reasons Himself had for it. I'm thinking that you asked for a mark of some kind to make you look human. Am I right?"

"I couldn't land at Hedabar as Princess Rella of the light fae, could I?" Furious, Rella wondered just what the Dark Emperor's reasons had been for insisting on this huge birthmark. It was enough of a deformity, not only to mark her as human but to mar her beauty in the eyes of everyone, human and fae.

Rella saw compassion darken the eyes of Captain Bernst. She'd been tricked, and he knew it. It was the price she'd paid for her brother's deliverance. Rella had made the bargain willingly. No one had coerced her. The Dark Emperor wanted her back at his court as his creature, and he'd made sure she had nowhere else to go.

All this time, Dagstyrr listened thoughtfully. "What I think you're saying is that their remarkable abilities lull them into a sense of infallibility, but when they misjudge, they can heal, yet they must bear the scars forever, like a human."

"Aye, lad," said Bernst, quaffing yet another cup of wine. "Our arrogance."

The ship's steady movement rocked Rella as she watched the compassion in the eyes of the men in her cabin. Or was it pity? Either way, she'd had enough. "I must ask you to leave me. I need rest," she said, the timbre of her voice bearing all the autocracy of a full-blooded fae princess and brooking no argument.

~

Dagstyrr understood dismissal when he heard it. Putting one hand under the captain's elbow to help him rise in the small rocking space, Dagstyrr followed him out onto the bright, sunlit deck.

Dagstyrr turned at the open door. "I'm sorry," he said, immediately regretting it. The pain etched across her face shamed him. She'd taken it as pity, which he knew no fae could tolerate from a human.

"Don't pity me."

"I don't. It's just that I wish I could do something about it," said Dagstyrr, knowing he was pushing his luck.

"Why? This was my choice."

"But you hate it. I just wish it wasn't so."

"I said, don't pity me, human!"

He ducked as a flagon of wine flew with remarkable speed at his head. Only the lessons of his upbringing saved him. He'd seen the signs and moved before the jug left her hand.

"So, the lady has a temper," he laughed, but in his heart, he prayed she had steel behind that temper, for she was going to need it. Whatever the Dark Emperor had in mind for Rella, he doubted she'd comply gracefully. Especially now that she knew he'd deceived her.

CHAPTER 11

The ship sailed on peaceably for the remainder of that day and the next. Dagstyrr was grateful for the rest. There were no disturbances from the cage, and Rella stayed steadfastly in her cabin admitting no one but the ship's cabin boy. The next morning, the sounds of sailors shouting and running awakened Dagstyrr. Were they under attack?

Throwing his blanket to the deck, he reached for his sword only to find it wasn't there—it was back in the cave under the citadel. Jumping up, he soon realized they weren't under attack at all. The commotion was coming from the cage.

Bernst's voice echoed in his head: *Stay where you are, lad. Let us deal with it. Keep her away!*

Turning, he saw Rella, roused from sleep and starting to run toward the cage. He reached out and grabbed her around her waist before she could accelerate past him. "Let the crew deal with it."

"Don't order me!"

"Please, Rella, it's the captain's orders, not mine."

Her fists pounded against his encircling arms, showing her frustration. Dagstyrr understood. She was reacting to her brother's pain, but it was up to others to help him now. He gently carried her to the relative privacy of the bow. She pushed herself upright, her hands on his shoulders. "If I put you down, do you promise to stay with me and let those better equipped deal with our brothers?"

The fight went out of her at his words. Her instincts were brave and right, but the crew was better able to handle fae addicts. They'd done it before, though not with dragon's blood addicts. It is why she'd hired them in the first place.

"Aye, I won't fight you. I'll wait with you."

He let her slide slowly to the deck ready to pounce should her words prove false. However, his instincts had been right. She understood. After all, she'd hired them for their experience. Later, when the worst was over, he and Rella could do their share of nursing the recovering addicts.

Dagstyrr watched her trembling hand reach for the gunwale. Surprised that a fae princess would show such vulnerability, his instinct was to put his arm about her, but he knew she'd not tolerate it. His own heartbeat thundered under his linens, as the cries from the cage slowly subsided.

Her deep brown eyes were a striking contrast to her bright fae hair. With a blush staining her cheeks, she drew him like a siren to the rocks.

"What are you staring at?" she said, now fully recovered.

"You," he said, thinking, *Yes, a siren*. Where she led him there was danger, but he was captivated and didn't want to be released.

"Did your mother never teach you it is rude to stare, especially at the aff...?" Her hand went instinctively to her cheek where the mark ended its twisting journey. She turned her face from him and gazed out to sea, from which the breeze brought her scent wafting over him. He ignored it, knowing this was a crucial moment in her acceptance of who she was now.

"The 'afflicted'? Is that what you were about to say?" Despite the pain she was trying so hard not to show, he couldn't let it be. Putting his hands on Rella's shoulders and turning her swiftly into his arms, he held her close enjoying the momentary shock in her eyes. "I'm human, remember?" he whispered in her ear. "No human is physically perfect. In fact, we appreciate those little imperfections in one another that make us unique—a contrast to any perfection we might be gifted with."

She stiffened in his arms. "I am not human, and this mark is no little imperfection. I care not a whit what you think."

"Then I'll do the caring for you. You've given up so much to rescue Calstir, far more than I for my brothers. You needed me, and you used me. I've no complaints. It brought us both what we wanted, but what kind of life does that leave you with, Princess?"

"You know nothing, human. Calstir will explain my appearance to the court. They will accept me or answer to him. Believe me, they do not want to cross him," said Rella, a shadow dulling her eyes.

"Is he so terrible?"

"Of course not. Calstir is their prince, soon to be crowned king," she said, as if that explained everything.

"You were not with Calstir when he arrived in Hedabar. Was it your father's illness that prompted you to rescue him?"

"Yes."

"You have no other brothers, cousins, lords who could have taken up this quest?" Despite being full-blown fae,

Rella had trouble hiding her emotions. Her skin grayed in front of his eyes, and her eyes darkened to almost black. Was that temper or deep sadness he saw?

"Let me guess. They considered you expendable. Oh, they would have presented the situation to you perfectly. You would be the noble sister sacrificing to bring back her brother, the new king. After all, you were a perfect choice. Who would suspect a girl capable of breaching the vizier's citadel? If you succeeded, they had their king. If you failed, I'm sure there's a noble cousin waiting in the wings to take his place. No doubt they hinted you would sit beside Calstir on the throne—a constant reminder of all he owed you," said Dagstyrr, letting all the bitterness of her situation sound in his voice. "But they didn't reckon on this," he said touching her marked face with his fingertips. "Did they?"

"Yes, that's about it, and before you tell me how stupid I was to believe them, know this: I'm not a fool. No one expected me to succeed. They expected me to be caught or die trying. They knew I couldn't sit back and do nothing knowing Calstir was in that place, but they underestimated me," she said.

"Ah, so that is why you went to the Dark Emperor," said Dagstyrr.

"I couldn't land in Hedabar otherwise. There is another family who would have candidates for the Throne of Casta," she said, her temper bringing color flooding back to her features. "The problem is they will fight among themselves instead of uniting to bring order." A smile touched the corner of her mouth but went no further. "Are they in for a surprise."

Dagstyrr's estimation of Rella took a leap. She'd known and gone ahead anyway. Tragedy seemed to wrap around her like a heavy blanket as she gazed out across the steel-gray ocean. Everything she felt showed in her body in little nuances of posture and color. She was unlike any woman he'd ever known, and he was starting to care deeply about her. "What did he promise you?"

"Who?" she answered, barely paying attention.

"Calstir."

"*Prince* Calstir to you, human."

"Very well. What did Prince Calstir promise you?"

"It doesn't matter, does it?" she said, capturing his gaze with her flashing eyes. She moved slowly, eating up the small space between them. Pushing her body against him, threatening in true light fae style, she looked up at him fearlessly. "Calstir would've promised anything, wouldn't he?"

"True," said Dagstyrr. Calstir was drug-addled prisoner in the worst hell imaginable, Rella his only chance of getting out.

"Anyway, by the time he saw me, I was already dark fae. Oh, I've no doubt he'll think whatever he cooks up for my future will be in my best interest. He is a kind man, but deep down in his soul, he is royal light fae to the last vestiges of his being. I *am not stupid*, human!"

Waves of energy buffeted him with every word, like slaps to his face. Dagstyrr wanted to reach out and hold her to him, comfort her, tell her he'd protect her, but if he did she'd run from his arms and might never trust him again. He stepped back and dipped his head in courtesy. "I never thought you were, Princess Rella. Forgive me, I am only human," he said softly, a smile quirking his mouth.

She rolled her eyes. "Come, let's eat, as long as there are no more questions," she said.

"I thought I was supposed to ask you questions. According to Captain Bernst, you are the authority on the citadel and the dragons."

"Very well, that you can ask about, but leave my private life alone."

Dragons. The reality of his own situation came flooding back to him. How was he to rescue dragons when he couldn't rescue his brothers without her help? He knew he must talk to the dragon again, but didn't relish the pain that came with it.

CHAPTER 12

Over the next few days, between Rella and Captain Bernst, Dagstyrr almost felt like he was back with his tutors. The crew explained the process his brothers were going through, and how Dagstyrr could help as long as he obeyed their instructions. They also explained what dark fae could and couldn't do. Sadly, there was not much they could teach him about dragons except for reciting old legends. Prince Calstir and the Halfenhaw brothers had more accurate information about the vizier and the citadel than Rella. Once they were better, Dagstyrr must question them.

He couldn't help feeling the key to beating the vizier forever was the dragons. Compassion drove his need to free them, but his desire to destroy the vizier was pure revenge. He'd never forget the nightmare Rella had led him through the night of the rescue, and so many were still living it. Visions of dying fae still haunted his dreams, and he swore he could occasionally smell that weird astringent scent that permeated their cells.

Worst of all were his memories of the dragon's blank

eyes and the roar of pain invading his head. He knew he'd feel that pain again and again before this ordeal was over. *Can't you speak to me without killing me?* he whispered in his mind.

I will try, came the answer, searing through his head. Dagstyrr gripped the gunwale, screwing up his eyes and bowing to the pain. Long-distance communication was possible, it seemed, but not comfortable.

Ok, with as few words as possible, can you read my thoughts? He tensed, ready for the pain of the dragon's answer.

Not yet. Not so bad that time.

Very well. Am I right in thinking that you can only hear me when I "speak" my thoughts directly to you?

Yes.

But eventually you will be able to read my thoughts?

Yes. Dagstyrr started to relax. As long as the dragon confined his answers to one word, he could manage the flare of heat rushing through his head. Dagstyrr left the gunwale and sat on some coiled rope with his back against a trunk. *Are you alone?*

No.

That one simple word managed to convey immense sadness, even over all these miles, and so without thinking, Dagstyrr asked, *How many?*

He heard the dragon sigh. No pain was attached to the sibilant sound. *One hundred and sixty-eight dragons, not counting hatchlings and eggs.*

So many? whispered Dagstyrr, trying not to convey his shock at the dragon's answer. *What is your name?*

You would not be able to pronounce my name. You may call me Drago.

Drago. That means "dragon" in my language. Why don't I just call you dragon?

You can, but there are many of us. You wouldn't want us all to answer at once. Dagstyrr sensed rather than heard a low laugh accompanying the dragon's words.

True, very true. My brains would be fried.

As long as you call me Drago, the others will not answer you, nor will they converse with you on any level. We want you alive, human.

Why is it everyone has started calling me human? You know my name. I am Dagstyrr of Halfenhaw. I'm going to need your help when the time comes, said Dagstyrr, suddenly very serious. *I will also need as much information as you can give me about the vizier. For now, answer me one thing. Is he dark fae?*

There is nothing fae about him. He is like you, Dagstyrr of Halfenhaw.

You mean he's human? This was not the answer Dagstyrr had expected. How, by all the gods, had a human set up so abominable a thing as the citadel? Those were questions for another day. *You know it is going to take time to gather those I need to help you. The* Mermaid *and her crew will assist, but first I must return Calstir and my brothers to their homes. They are not part of my promise to you. I will return to free you as soon as I can, you have my word.*

Whatever you do, don't enlist the help of any dragon's blood eaters. They will not be welcome.

I don't intend to, said Dagstyrr. *Talking to you doesn't hurt so much now,* he said, realizing the dragon's voice was no more than a hot breeze in his head instead of the roaring fire it had been at the beginning of their conversation.

You have relaxed and let me in, said Drago. Dagstyrr could almost hear him smile. *Never forget, Dagstyrr of Halfenhaw, I can kill you with a thought any time I want. You, the crew, and all your families unto ten generations.*

You had to go and spoil it, didn't you? There was I, almost becoming fond of you, said Dagstyrr.

Drago's laugh echoed lightly in his head. *Only contact me when necessary, and don't be surprised if I don't answer right away. Remember, as my eyes become yours, so your eyes become mine.*

You mean the vizier will see the change?

Not if we're careful.

I understand, said Dagstyrr, knowing now what risks Drago was taking in conversing with him.

∽

Rella stood just inside the door of her cabin, watching Dagstyrr converse with the dragon. "He is more powerful than he knows," she whispered.

"Aye, he is, for a human," said Captain Bernst, leaning against the wooden structure with one raised hand cupping the fancy carving etched around the door.

"Human or not, he must be watched," she said. "There is nothing more dangerous than someone who has yet to understand their own power."

"For certain. Look what he's dragged us into already. Release the dragons from the citadel? If only it were that simple."

"If we'd known there were still dragons alive, we'd have rescued them years ago," said Rella, sadly. "I only became aware of them after Calstir's capture."

"Aye, and anyone else seeing them, hasn't lived to tell about it."

"But we lived to tell the tale. You can thank Dagstyrr for that."

"He promised to rescue a dragon without understanding the circumstances, and we are all part of that promise, whether he understood it or not."

"I get the feeling he'd do it anyway, despite any consequences," said Rella.

"Aye, he's a rare one."

They watched together as Dagstyrr's eyes flashed fire while he spoke to his dragon friend. "He's a bumbling human. I bet he doesn't even know we can see him talking to the dragon," said Rella.

Bernst sighed. "At least he's learned how to talk to the dragon without torching himself. I was worried he'd be killed, and the rest of us still bound to rescue the dragon."

"Do you think the distance between us and the dragon makes it easier, or do you think he has learned to converse safely?" said Rella.

"I'd say the second. According to legend, the distance makes no difference. As you well know."

"The legends were written back in the time before light and dark—not at all reliable," she said.

"You'd be surprised. Sometimes the most unbelievable part of a legend is the only true part, the dross surrounding it made up to placate the sensibilities of subsequent generations."

"Perhaps, but you and I must protect him until he understands the power he wields. Also, I insist that whatever he asks or demands in the dragon's name, we must first see Prince Calstir safely home to Casta. That was our agreement."

"I suppose," said Bernst, walking over to Dagstyrr and squatting down to observe his talk with the dragon.

Rella thought he made a fearsome sight. A true warrior if ever she'd seen one, even poorly dressed and slumped on the deck. His powerful body and the way he carried himself would prevent most from challenging him. However, when he spoke to the dragon, even fae would think twice. All around him, wisps of smoke threatened the deck as fire flashed from his eyes.

Bernst turned to Rella. "Poor bugger's no idea."

∽

A few days later, the weather was still cooperating with them. The sails billowed like fat-bellied merchants letting the *Mermaid* fly across the choppy sea. Rella ducked back into her cabin. They were coming close to light fae shipping lanes, and the *Mermaid* had to don her new disguise. It was time for Rella to put on her armor.

This human was about to see who he was dealing with. Whether he was a dragon-talker or not, *she* was still the leader of this expedition.

She dragged the blue and white cushions from the top of her trunk and lifted the lid. Inside, her armor lay cushioned on bright blue silk. It sparkled white and silver—the uniform of the Personal Guard of the Royal House of Casta. She lifted a greave and ran her finger down the intricate silver decoration. Dare she wear it?

In deference to the dark fae, she'd packed it away, not wanting to flaunt her rank or remind them who she once was. Rella wondered whether she'd ever be allowed to wear it once they returned to Casta. However, as part of the ship's disguise, she must wear it until they were past these narrow straits. No one would question or approach them when they sighted her on deck in full regalia.

She'd impress Dagstyrr one more time, even if he was only a human. Why did she even think that? She didn't care what he thought.

Rella went through the ritual of washing and braiding her hair before starting to don her beautiful armor. Underneath she wore dark blue padded silk supposed to enhance the blue eyes of the guard. She no longer had blue eyes.

Her white leather boots stopped just short of the brown mark disfiguring her leg. Then the armor itself—gleaming white enamel embossed with sparkling silver. A short white leather kilt and a helmet of sky blue with silver detailing, including the royal coronet of the House of Casta, completed her ensemble. With her sword at her side and her knives secreted about her person, she turned to the mirror. All she could see was the horrible disfigurement poking out above her greave and splashing across her face. She was marked as consort to the Dark Emperor.

Rella closed the cheek guards of her helmet. Now the mark could only be seen it if you looked for it. Taking a deep breath, she left her blue-and-silver shield wrapped in her cloak at the bottom of the trunk and prepared to appear on deck.

∼

Dagstyrr sighed as he felt the dragon leave his mind. Blinking at the bright light reflected on the sea he saw the sun was now low in the sky. They must have been talking longer than he'd thought. The crew stood around, staring at him. Every man was silent, his eyes glued to Dagstyrr. Even the captain crouched not five feet from him.

Dagstyrr groaned. "What have I done now?"

"Don't know. You tell me, lad. Made any new promises to

dragons lately? Any that might involve us?" Captain Bernst indicated the crew with a sweep of his arm.

Dagstyrr could smell the stench of fear coming from the crew. He needed to reassure them and quickly. "No, of course not. I've learned my lesson where promises to dragons are concerned."

"But you don't deny you were talking to him, for we could all see he was talking to you."

What did Bernst mean? Did dark fae have some power to hear when he spoke to the dragon? "What makes you think I was talking to Drago?"

A wave of snickers and whispers behind hands washed over the crew. Dagstyrr rose to his feet. What was going on here? Why were Captain Bernst and the crew staring at him like this? Then he knew. "I called him Drago, that's how you knew. You tricked me."

"Oh no, lad, that's not it at all," said Bernst. "You should know that when a dragon-speaker converses with his dragon, his eyes shine like his dragon's. Your dragon has no eyes."

Dagstyrr tried to visualize the image the crew had just witnessed. "You mean, you see fire where my eyes should be?" He was trying to downplay the horror of it.

"Exactly. So you'll forgive us for being a little curious about it. No doubt we'll get used to it soon enough, but you should guard against letting anyone else see it. Do you understand what I'm saying? Many lords would pay handsomely to have a captive dragon-talker in their court."

"Of course," said Dagstyrr, understanding all too well. One word from any of these men and Dagstyrr would be hunted down like a stag at the solstice. "I'll be more careful in the future."

"Oh, not on our account, lad. 'Tis a wonderful thing to

see a man converse with a dragon, and that dragon's fire shine in his eyes like beacons," said Bernst.

Dagstyrr laughed, not sure whether Bernst was taking the piss or not. "I'd like to see that myself, but in the future, I must make sure I cover my eyes," he said, with a short bow to the crew, who returned his nod and went about their business in twos and threes, heads together, whispering. "Captain, I apologize for upsetting your crew."

"You're learning, lad. Don't be too hard on yourself, but sailors are a superstitious lot. They haven't quite decided whether a human dragon-talker among them is a good sign or a bad," said Bernst, flashing his fingers in the age-old sign against evil.

He's just as superstitious as they are, thought Dagstyrr, and he wondered just how safe he would be on this ship if they turned against him. Well, he'd have to prove himself, because once he'd delivered his brothers home safe, and then taken Rella and Calstir on to Casta, this ship and its crew were all he had to rescue one hundred and sixty-eight dragons, not counting hatchlings and eggs.

"You'd best get ready for some changes around here," said Bernst.

"What do you mean? Are my brothers ready for me to help them?"

"No, lad. I mean the *Mermaid*. We're approaching shipping lanes that won't welcome us as we are, so we have to change. These lanes are restricted. Light fae only."

Dagstyrr had heard of these lanes. Everyone other than light fae had to take the outside passage, which was more dangerous. These waters were surrounded by light fae colonies and they were jealously guarded.

CHAPTER 13

G rowing up within a light fae household, Dagstyrr had seen many strange things in his life, but nothing like this. The ship's hull elongated and appeared to lower into the water. One mast dissipated altogether into a soft mist with the sails still attached. The one remaining mast grew, acquiring an extra spar and a sail of momentous proportions. The deck shrank from side to side, and everywhere, subtle changes occurred so quickly it was hard for Dagstyrr to keep up with them. The noise was horrendous. Any ship within miles would reckon the *Mermaid* was breaking up. In a way, she was.

He glanced at the cage where the four addicts had lain in their hammocks side by side across the deck. Now, the cage had narrowed and changed its shape, and two hammocks were positioned behind the other two. Calstir and Erik were in front, Sig and Thor behind. Dagstyrr saw Erik's eyes open and his brother watch the ship changing as if it were part of another reality he was living. "He thinks he's dreaming," said Dagstyrr.

"That is how he'll remember it, right enough," said

Bernst, appearing at his side. "We're nearly finished. Just don't move from this spot, or the decking will snap your ankle."

"Aye, aye, Captain."

"Good lad."

Unable to move, Dagstyrr watched the tortured expression on his brother Erik's face. "The noise probably woke him," said Dagstyrr, trying to imagine waking to see the ship going through this change.

"Not a lot to do about that. Can't ask the *Mermaid* to change without a few creaks and groans."

"Creaks and groans? More like a forest being uprooted," said Dagstyrr. The *Mermaid* was now a sleek longship. Like his father's that plied their trade from Halfenhaw to the ice frontier beyond Casta and south to the warm lands of Demenos. They were fast vessels, and he knew how to sail one. Dagstyrr had taken the tiller many times and labored on the oars as a youngster, until he'd grown as strong and broad as his father. The *Mermaid*, however, was different. Her oars dipped and pulled her along at a fast pace, but there were no rowers.

The ship's boy, Billy, struggled past him, trying to balance on decking as it constantly shifted. He went up to Captain Bernst and whispered in his ear, pointing to Rella's cabin with his one hand. Just as Dagstyrr was about to go and see what was happening with her, she emerged. The creature that stepped onto the deck was no Rella he'd ever seen before. Gone was the fae princess so ashamed of her state that she hid in her cabin most of the time. Here was a full blood light fae warrior princess of the House of Casta. The sun danced off her armor and helmet as she strode proudly along the deck of the longship. Her shoulders were squared and her head held high, white leather kilt swinging in rhythm to her pace. All eyes were on her as she looked down on Dagstyrr from the elevated platform at the center of the ship.

She was magnificent. How on earth was he ever going to persuade her to become his woman?

Well, now, *that* was a new thought. One Dagstyrr had been toying with ever since their first night aboard. But for the first time, he openly admitted it to himself. Any doubts he had about wanting to make her his woman disappeared as he watched her take command of the *Mermaid*. He wanted her, and he'd lay down his life for her.

Even Captain Bernst looked for her nod before calling out his instructions to the crew. Dagstyrr watched the breeze catch the long golden plait hanging down from the top of her helmet, a sky-blue ribbon twined through it.

The crew hoisted the royal pennant of Casta and brought an ornate chair so that Rella could sit in full view of any passing ship. She looked like a goddess, serene and majestic sparkling in the sun.

Dagstyrr thought of Rell, the stinking waif who'd followed him around the citadel day after day with bare feet, rags, and a filthy turban. This proud princess had lived like that for months, letting the *Mermaid* leave port and return as scheduled so that no suspicion would fall on the ship. She was the bravest woman he'd ever met, and she hardly knew he existed.

Dagstyrr wandered to the prow, where he greeted the spirit of the *Mermaid*, as he did every time he sought refuge from the rest of the ship. "That was a magnificent change."

Thank you.

"You've changed your figurehead too." She was no longer a siren, but a sea serpent.

Longships always use fierce figureheads. This is the most common. I defy anyone to tell me apart from a few dozen others.

"I bow to your wisdom," said Dagstyrr. "My father has at least two with sea serpent figureheads: the *Knucker* and the *Viper*."

I know them well.

"You do?"

I have been sailing these waters since long before the fae split into light and dark. Nowadays, I sometimes sail with a human crew, sometimes with dark fae. I enjoy the company.

Dagstyrr smiled. "Never light fae?"

Never.

"Until now."

She is dark, and they are dragon's blood eaters. I'd rather not have the addicts aboard, but she's all right, and they'll be gone soon.

"They are not addicts by choice," said Dagstyrr, feeling the horror again, yet jumping to the defense of his brothers.

If they were, I'd not tolerate them for a second. Rescuing those in the citadel is good. The vizier is a poison on the land.

"Do you know of my promise to Drago?" asked Dagstyrr.

I do. It was made without foreknowledge. Drago shouldn't hold you to it.

"But he will, and who could blame him?" said Dagstyrr.

Indeed. Not I. I remember him when he was young and free, a magnificent flyer, with fire that could light up the night sky. Drago and I used to race down the twenty-one waterfalls of Demenos. He always won. Now? Well, you saw the state of him. What scares me is he's growing bitter, very bitter.

"Who would not? It is beyond description. He and his kin are being kept alive in the worst conditions imaginable, and for one reason only: to produce a drug that the vizier uses to control the fae. I just don't understand why."

You saw the dragon nests? The shocked figurehead turned to him.

"No. I have seen how the fae are kept, and I have felt Drago's pain. He is not living in some gilded nest, believe me. I doubt many hatchlings survive," said Dagstyrr, sadly.

I cannot imagine his pain, she said.

"Face forward, or some ship might see you," he added, pushing a hand against the cheek of the carved serpent. The figurehead turned to face forward. "Are you with me then, when I go to free Drago?"

Of course, I am. Whether I like it or not, I am part of the promise he extracted from you.

"I'm sorry," said Dagstyrr. Would the weight of his promise never ease?

Don't be. I'd be going anyway. I'm one of the few dark fae old enough to remember when dragons roamed free over all the earth.

Dagstyrr didn't like to ask what kind of creature the *Mermaid* was, or her age. He turned to look at Rella sitting regally in the middle of the ship so that all who came close would notice her first and give them a wide berth. The silver decorations on her armor and helmet flashed in the sunlight, and Dagstyrr realized this was light fae spectacle as he'd never seen it before. He tried to imagine a whole cohort of warriors like her. They would strike fear into the hearts of all who went against them and lift the spirits of those who fought with them, for fae warriors were not only dazzling to look at, they were deadly.

You want her for yourself, said the *Mermaid*.

Dagstyrr considered denying it, then thought better of it. "I do, but look at her, and look at me," he said scrutinizing his boots with their uppers coming away from the soles, his shirt stained and worn from being washed in seawater. "Not even a decent pair of boots to dance with her," he said.

You are worthy of her, Dagstyrr of Halfenhaw.

Dagstyrr laughed. "You are the only one who thinks so."

The important thing is: do you think so?

"I think of nothing else. Except freeing dragons, of course," he added quickly. Then he sighed enjoying the luxury of opening up to another being. Perhaps because she was a magical ship and not a person, he found it easier. "Sometimes, I see her vulnerability, and I long to take her in my arms and hold her safe. To tell her no harm will come to her while she has me by her side."

I'm thinking your thoughts are not always so pure. I know mine wouldn't be if I were in love with her.

"You're right. I just didn't want to make a *Mermaid* blush at the terrible, lascivious thoughts running through a poor human's brain."

The serpent lifted its head a fraction and laughed, and the sound bounced on the waves like an echo.

~

Rella sat as still as a statue, watching the fresh breeze dance across the water. This might fool others from a distance, but no one on Casta would be fooled for a second. She'd turned dark, and it was written on her face for all to see.

She knew Calstir thought he could convince people that it was a subterfuge necessary to free him, nothing more. He would maintain that his sister was as pure and light as ever, but Rella knew better. The look on Erik Halfenhaw's face when he first saw her in the citadel told her the impossibility of ever being accepted.

Terrified to think otherwise, she'd convinced herself that Calstir was right. That people would see the mark as a sign of love and sacrifice, not a betrayal of the light, not of dark fae walking the halls of Casta Palace. Her alternative was the Dark Emperor; bile rose in her gorge at the idea of being his Queen.

Then again, Dagstyrr didn't seem to notice her mark anymore, just as Calstir had predicted. However, Dagstyrr was human—a flaw if ever there was one. She heard his laugh up at the bow. He was talking to the *Mermaid* again. Whatever did those two have to talk about?

Captain Bernst commented that he'd never seen the *Mermaid* take to anyone the way she had to Dagstyrr. He was special. Rella knew that. He had gifts aplenty, he was loyal, strong, kind, thoughtful. But he wasn't fae, not even dark fae.

Out of the corner of her eye, she saw a flash of red on the horizon, a ship bearing down on them fast—the first of many they'd encounter in these straits. A long day lay ahead. It was a barque selling spices up and down the waterway, probably going as far as Hedabar. She needed to warn them.

"I know what you're thinking, Princess, but ye cannot risk telling them," said Captain Bernst. "Anyway, I know that ship. She's a human crew manning a light fae vessel. There won't be any light fae on board."

"You can't know that from this distance." Rella ground out the words, furious that she was so transparent.

Ignoring the captain, she waited until they were closer and lifted her hand in greeting. A scurry on board the deck of the red-sailed barque, and three light fae emerged from below, their long golden hair declaring their heritage.

"Bring us in line with the other ship, Captain," said Rella. "And keep us parallel with them, but not too close."

Bernst rolled his eyes and gave the order. Then signaled the other ship.

The light fae male was dressed in Royal Casta blue and silver, the two women in plain silver. They were courtiers. "Greetings, your Royal Highness. Is Prince Calstir with you?" The woman who greeted her was more anxious than she should be. Something was wrong. Then Rella remembered them. They were from the family Argan.

"Of course. He sleeps rocked by our ocean, and dreams of home." Rella smiled across the sea to the other ship.

"Then he'd best get home soon," said the man.

Fae did not speak so bluntly, especially to a royal princess. Something was terribly wrong. Rella stood. "Your advice is always appreciated, Lord Ash, but I detect a note of concern. With the court of Casta in the hands of nobility such as yourself, I cannot imagine what harm can come to it. Unless...Is my father..."

"Our condolences, Princess Rella. We thought you would know."

So, her father was dead. The weight of her grief descended like a thick blanket. She wanted to hug it to her and mourn her father as was her right. But she was to be denied what every other soul took for granted. These people were fleeing the unrest about to erupt at court. She had no time to grieve. "I have no doubt my brother will build a suitable monument to his memory, Lord Ash. He was a great man."

"He was. Let me see Calstir," demanded Lord Ash.

Rella took one step and faced Lord Ash directly across the water. "You forget yourself, sir."

"There are rumors, my Lady," said Lady Elise, rushing to intercept her brother's boorishness. Lady Elise stood tall and elegant. "Prince Calstir's cousins are spreading the story of his incarceration in a terrible place of death. Yesterday, we heard from another ship that he is indeed dead, and now your cousins are preparing to take over the throne."

This was Rella's worst fear come true. She put her hands on her waist and laughed. "Then they are in for a nasty surprise when we sail into port. But tell me, Lady Elise, why is it that the Argan family is leaving court instead of fighting to maintain loyalty to their prince, my brother?"

"We seek the truth, Princess. Forgive us," said Lady Elise with a curtsey.

"I will see Calstir," said Lord Ash, pushing forward. "I'll not be party to tricks and subterfuge. If the royal cousins take control...."

"Yes, yes, yes, I understand exactly what you mean, Lord Ash," said Rella pacing back and forth, one hand on her sword hilt and the other raised as if to shade her gaze from the sun. They must not see her mark.

Damn, she should have allowed this sanctimonious prick to land in Hedabar. It would serve him right. "You would like to take up your place in court, no matter who sits on the throne. I understand. So, you leave on an urgent business trip. Let others fight and argue about the rights and wrongs of insurrection. Correct?" Her eyebrow lifted, and she was gratified to see a blush steal over the face of Lady Isa, the youngest of the Argan family.

Aware of movement along the deck of the *Mermaid*, she had no choice but to carry on and pray those in the cage were quiet. "If my brother were dead—which he is not— chaos would reign in Casta, which is why you are fleeing the court. I have three male cousins with equal claim to the throne, a recipe for disaster. In truth, I don't blame you for wanting to avoid the court under such circumstances. My brother, *King* Calstir, and I will return and restore order. A bride is what the throne needs, not a war," she said, purposely eyeing both sisters. Let them think on that.

There was a scuffling behind her on deck. What were they doing? Didn't they realize she was fighting for their lives? The three fae on the other ship were dangerous creatures, and Rella hadn't tested her new magic or her fighting skills since she'd turned dark. She had no idea whether she was as fast and strong as she ought to be.

"My Lady, behind you!" shouted Dagstyrr.

Rella turned, ready to scold him, then saw Dagstyrr helping Calstir onto the silvered chair. He looked terrible. Somehow the crew had him awake and dressed, but unable to walk unaided. Dagstyrr had "walked" him along the deck as if they were both drunk and holding each other up. Both Dagstyrr and Calstir sweated under the effort of getting Calstir onto the chair.

"A little too much grog, my Lady," said Dagstyrr, with a smile and an empty hand indicating drinking, before sitting hard on the deck at Calstir's feet.

She noticed Captain Bernst on the tiller, his eyes fixed on Calstir. Was he trying to influence her brother? The ship's boy ran up and put a silver goblet in Calstir's hand. Calstir raised it in salute to the other vessel.

Rella turned in time to see all three fae courtiers bow low to Calstir. This might just work. At this distance, the shake of his limbs and the glaze over his eyes would be imperceptible.

"Lord Ash, how nice to see you. How are things at home?" said Calstir. A shiver ran up Rella's spine. Her brother would never speak like that. She threw a glance at Bernst. He was influencing her brother, no doubt speaking in his head repeatedly until Calstir's addled brain repeated it.

Rella grabbed Dagstyrr's forearm. "Get him out of here," she whispered.

"Mmm, easier said than done. Better if you get rid of that ship," he answered quietly, with a smile for the sake of the Argan family.

Rella glanced at Calstir. Dagstyrr was right. Calstir was fading fast. Short of carrying him across his shoulders, there was no way Dagstyrr could get him back to the cage or into the cabin.

The Argan family was looking distraught. Rella could only imagine the thoughts going through their heads. They'd been caught. Now, they'd want to come aboard the *Mermaid*, ply Calstir with all the court's machinations and make good their standing with him. It could take days.

"We're off to Halfenhaw. I have all four brothers with me, and I've been promised good sport in the forests," said Calstir.

Lady Elise stepped forward. "Halfenhaw, how lovely! I remember the forests well, and Lady Halfenhaw, a jewel. Four brothers, you say? I understood there were only three."

Dagstyrr was used to these insults from fae nobility and enjoyed unnerving them.

He stood, spread his arms wide, and smiled at her. "I'm the fourth. Dagstyrr of Halfenhaw, fully human and proud of it. Do you take exception, Lady Elise? If so, Calstir and I can get back to our drinking and not spoil your day any further."

Calstir laughed, and of his own volition, Rella was sure. It worked. The Argans were wrong-footed and now was the time to get rid of them. "Why don't you turn that vessel around and go back to court?" said Rella. "You can give them the good news. Prince Calstir is alive and well, and on his way home." Rella allowed just a little compulsion in her voice, an insult to show them just how angry she was.

"Go home, my good Lord Ash. I'll enjoy your company when I return," said Calstir, and remarkably, Rella could tell it was Calstir speaking not Bernst. He was annoyed enough to break through his pain. That meant he was starting to heal, at last.

CHAPTER 14

Dagstyrr watched the other ship maneuver carefully in the narrow strait. It was no small feat for a fully laden barque to change direction, but they managed it. He couldn't help but wonder what exactly it was loaded with. The Argan family's worldly goods? By the time they were out of sight, Calstir was unconscious and slumped on the chair, the goblet long since fallen from his hand. Rella was stiff as a statue, her eyes never leaving the deck of the barque as it made its way home to Casta.

He knew what she was thinking. What kind of reception would she find in Casta? If those fae courtiers were typical, she'd get no quarter there, despite what her brother told her. The *Mermaid* was due to dock in Halfenhaw in just under two weeks. There, Calstir could fully recover before going on to Casta.

Dagstyrr was determined to accompany her to the court. She needed at least one person to fight in her corner. Perhaps he could persuade Sigmund and Thorsten to come with him, if they were well enough. He wouldn't ask Erik for obvious reasons.

The crew carried an exhausted Prince Calstir back to the cage, renewing the wards that protected them and kept the cage invisible to those not on board.

"Does he realize our father has gone?" said Rella, her voice tense and full of sadness.

"I don't know," said Dagstyrr. "Perhaps we should talk to him."

"That's my duty. I'll make sure he knows."

Dagstyrr followed her to the cage. He could see she was exhausted. Having to deal with Calstir's addiction when they should be grieving the death of their father together as brother and sister was going to be hard. He suspected Calstir was never easy to deal with, particularly while in the throes of his withdrawal.

The prince was lying prone in his hammock. His arms tightly bound within the canvas to prevent him from using his magic. His long, fae hair hung to the floor of the cage, and his eyes were closed tight.

"Calstir?" said Rella.

"Our father is dead. I am king now," he whispered from the cocoon.

"You heard."

Dagstyrr watched Rella's fingers tremble on the bars before she gripped them tight. Her whole future lay in the hands of this addict. "My sincere condolences to you both," he said.

"No congratulations, human?" said Calstir, terse and prickly, a dangerous state for such a powerful being.

He heard Rella's fast intake of breath. She was very worried about how their father's death was going to affect him. "Forgive me, your majesty," said Dagstyrr, with a bow.

"Oh, don't worry about it. I am hardly majestic. Let's stick with prince until we reach Casta, and I can show people they have a king. A very fit king, ready to show them all he can do."

"That's a wonderful idea, brother. We must concentrate on getting you well. Then you'll prove how wrong Aunt Kemara is," said Rella.

"You can do nothing to help me, sister. I must win this battle all by myself, especially if I am to convince the court to accept *you*. Now go, I need my rest," he said dismissively.

Dagstyrr put his hand on her shoulder and guided her away from the cage.

Rella was trembling from head to toe. "Well done, lass," he said as the other ship dipped out of sight.

"I'm not your 'lass,' nor will ever be, human. Let's get that straight now."

The fearless warrior princess was back. Dagstyrr smiled, refusing to be baited. "Come," he said, gently touching her elbow, "the night is falling. Let's light the lanterns and get off this deck. Allow me to arrange supper for once."

She took a deep breath and rewarded him with a small smile. "That sounds like an excellent idea. I need a cup of Samish wine, and I must thank you for what you did today."

"No thanks necessary. Whether we like it or not, our lives are bound together for the time being. You might as well get used to it," said Dagstyrr, with the most disarming smile he could muster.

∿

Rella's muscles ached from the tension she'd carried all day long. She stored her uniform in the trunk, and then she bathed in warm water scented with rose water and peppermint leaves, and enhanced with a small healing spell. It worked. As the warm, magical water relaxed her muscles, the aches disappeared, but not the worry.

She had a backup plan if the court would not accept her, but it was a last resort. Rella hoped she'd not need it, but she'd do anything now to avoid fulfilling her promise to marry the Dark Emperor. She was sure of that. Why had she ever imagined she'd be able to become his queen? She'd been desperate, that was the truth of the matter.

Now her fate revolved around her brother. Was Calstir strong enough to persuade the light fae nobles to allow her back at court? Then she remembered Erik's face at the citadel, and she shuddered.

Their time at Halfenhaw would be a good test. Dagstyrr's mother, Princess Astrid, was known for her diplomacy and open-mindedness, as well as her great beauty. When Astrid fell in love with a human lord, she'd married him, much to the consternation of her light fae family and suitors. Astrid was the first light fae to mate with a human in over a thousand years. She'd left the court never to return yet she appeared quite happy with the arrangement.

Rella's bathwater was cooling. She stepped out and toweled herself down before throwing on a loose blue silk robe. Just in time, for she could hear Dagstyrr's promised meal being ferried into the tiny space used for entertainment.

Rella walked out from behind her curtains to the most delicious scents of highly spiced food. Rice dishes of yellow, white, green, and orange proclaimed the liberal use of saffron, herbs, and cloves. Heavier scents of garlic and cumin rose in the steam from dishes of meat and vegetables of various kinds. Warm bread still wrapped in cloths graced the center of the low table. Rella sat back on her cushions and poured two large glasses of Samish wine. The food smelled so good she'd start without him if he didn't appear soon.

She needn't have worried. Dagstyrr's head dipped under the doorframe, and he smiled at her. "You needn't have waited."

Raising her glass, she said, "I didn't." The first sip of wine burst like ruby velvet on her tongue. Just what she needed.

Dagstyrr sat carefully across from her, unused to the low Casta seating. His presence filled the small space with a different spice. Pure male strength and hunger were the same, whether fae or human. He really was an impressive specimen. Warmth emanated from his weather-darkened skin, allowing him to look good even in the rags he wore as if they were the finest of garments. His dark hair was too long, and it curled in silky ribbons around his face and neck. A striking foil to his deep blue eyes—not fae blue, but still blue.

She watched him tear some bread and dip it in the sauce. He filled his plate quickly, and she followed suit. There was something very intimate about sharing a meal like this. They ate in silence, savoring the spices and wine. Neither had eaten since morning, and the food on offer was of the best.

At last, with a deep sigh, she leaned back and succumbed to the feeling of comfort surrounding her. Dagstyrr reached across and refilled her glass with wine. Then he too sat back, obviously sated and as comfortable as she was.

"Bernst says we can start letting them out of the cage tomorrow," said Dagstyrr.

"Really? It's not too soon?"

"Only for short periods, and never more than one at a

time," he answered. "That way if something goes wrong we'll only have to grapple with one of them."

"Of course. Captain Bernst has done this before. He says they have to earn the right to leave the cage."

"Yep," said Dagstyrr, finishing his glass and pouring another. "That's what he told me. I suppose..."

"What? What do you suppose?"

"I suppose we should allow your brother to be first out tomorrow," said Dagstyrr. "He did well today."

Rella thought for a moment, sipping her wine. "No, I think we should start with Sigmund or Thorsten."

"Why?"

"Calstir did well today, but Captain Bernst helped him talk, and you virtually carried him to the chair. No, he's been incarcerated the longest. He'll probably take longer to heal than the others."

"Then, what about Erik? He's the eldest and the strongest light fae. Sigmund and Thorsten are light fae too, but they are limited in their powers," said Dagstyrr

"Exactly. Erik was the worst of your three brothers when we rescued them. Let's see how the other two do before risking Erik or Calstir. They could as easily harm themselves as us."

"Are you telling me Sig and Thor are expendable?"

"Of course not. Just that they are less addicted, so their recovery might be faster."

"I hope so," said Dagstyrr, knowing how it would break his mother's heart to see her sons like this.

"Tell me, Dagstyrr, how did you manage to conjure up this meal? It is far superior to anything we've had since we came aboard."

"I'll tell you if you answer one question for me," he said, drinking down his wine.

"Very well, if you want to play questions. But I go first."

"Naturally. He smiled across at her, and the lantern light caught a flash of very white teeth.

Rella moved uncomfortably as visions of those white teeth nipping at her flesh disturbed her. *It must be the effects of the wine*, she thought, regaining her composure. "I think you like games."

"Who doesn't? So, what is your first question?"

"I already asked. Where did you get this meal?"

"I made it. All the ingredients were in the galley, and with a fae cook to speed things along, all it took was the recipe," he said, eyes twinkling.

"You know such recipes?"

"Ah, that's another question. My turn, I think. How did you know Calstir was in the Hedabar Citadel? And before you answer, I know you knew he was there before you set foot on the island. Otherwise, you'd have landed in your true light fae form and you'd be incarcerated with him," he said, looking remarkably sober.

This was a subject Rella had avoided up until now. With Dagstyrr's ability to read people, he must have guessed it was something she didn't want to talk about. Furious that she'd walked into his trap, she determined that she would not give him the satisfaction of knowing he'd irked her. Recipes indeed. How could she have walked so blindly into a game she knew could lead to dangerous revelations?

She gazed down into her cup of Samish, drawing her finger around the rim as if lost in thought. All her instincts were telling her to attack him, but she refused to let him know she'd been caught. He'd used her natural prejudice against her, a move worthy of a light fae courtier. She'd never have walked into this game with a fae, light or dark.

But he was human, and that was why she'd underestimated him. She'd not make that mistake again.

Forcing a smile, she looked up at him. "Very clever, human."

"Well?"

"When royalty sail, we sail ships manned only with light fae," she said. Dagstyrr nodded in her direction. So, he already knew that much. "Calstir sailed with a human ship's boy. The vizier obviously wasn't interested in the boy, who escaped and made his way to Casta. So, for the first time, there was someone outside of Hedabar to tell the tale."

"Would the vizier have let me leave the island?" he said, and she saw the truth dawn on him.

"Oh, no, Dagstyrr, my turn," she said with a laugh as if this was the best game in the world. He could never know it was tearing her apart, making her relive her decision to turn dark. She pulled herself away from that nightmare and said, "First, I need more wine. I hadn't realized I was expected to entertain tonight."

Dagstyrr filled her glass, a frown marring his forehead. Either he didn't like her answer or, her attitude. Or, he didn't enjoy the prospect of having to answer a probing question from her. So be it. Rella took her time drinking the wine, dipping some bread in the cooling sauces. "This really is delicious."

"I'm glad you like it."

He sounded almost sad. He would never win this game at court. In the Casta Court, you never allowed your emotions to show. If they were false, you were considered ill-mannered, and if real, weak. "Where did you learn to cook?"

Dagstyrr threw back his head and laughed. "My, you are a high fae princess, right enough. My mother would have done just the same thing in these circumstances. Pretend you don't care. Pretend that what you've been forced to reveal is of no consequence."

"Forced? It is easy enough to refuse to play a game. It is not so easy to force anything from me, as you will learn."

Dagstyrr smiled. "You would not lose face here. Not in front of a mere human."

"Quite right!" She laughed. "With no one here to witness it, it didn't happen. That's what my nanny taught us, and she is never wrong."

"Well, I know nothing of highborn fae nannies, but I know you well enough to recognize the red tinge of fury in your neck and face," he replied.

Rella forced herself to relax. This human was unpredictable; she liked that. And he was far too observant. Soon he'd be gone, and she couldn't help admitting to herself that she'd miss him. Still, it was as well he'd soon be put ashore at Halfenhaw. "We have a busy day ahead. These straits will be filled with ships. Thankfully, there will be few who'd recognize me as anything more than a royal escort. Most will see the pennant and me on deck and give us a wide berth. You will have to deal with Sigmund and Thorsten by yourself."

"I'll have the crew to help me," said Dagstyrr, starting to tidy up the plates. He called the ship's boy, and together with another crewmate, he made quick work of clearing the cabin. "Do you want me to leave the wine?"

Rella leaned back on her cushions, unable to resist raking her eyes up and down the very male length of him. The wine was really very good. "You haven't answered my question yet."

He laughed. "My father, Lord Magnus taught me to cook."

"I know he's human, but I cannot imagine the ferocious

Lord Magnus of Halfenhaw in an apron," she said, laughter bubbling from under her defenses.

"It's true, I can assure you. Father finds fae food a little bland and overly sweet. My best memories are of spending hours in the kitchen with him concocting recipes full of exotic flavors." He looked wistfully into the middle distance. "My mother complained of all his spices and strange vegetables, but I think she secretly liked the taste of cilantro. I've seen her pinch some from the herb garden when she thought no one was watching."

"Well, I concur. Earl Magnus's recipes are marvelous. I hope I'll be treated to more of them at Halfenhaw."

"No doubt. Father's venison sausage is particularly good. Just make sure you get a spicy one," said Dagstyrr.

"I've always enjoyed venison sausage. I hope I get the opportunity to try some."

Dagstyrr heard Billy outside the cabin, giggling at Rella's statement and repeating it to the cook. The boy was spending too much time with adult sailors.

"I hope so too," said Dagstyrr, lifting the bottle with a question in his eyes.

For a second she was ready to have him stay. His company was comforting and easy. "No, take it away. I'm going to need my wits about me tomorrow."

"Very well. Goodnight, Princess Rella," he said, ducking out the door to her cabin.

"Goodnight, Dagstyrr of Halfenhaw," she whispered and immediately felt the loss of his presence.

CHAPTER 15

Dagstyrr finished off the bottle of Samish wine before falling asleep on deck. His one answered question, about how they knew of Calstir's capture had given him a lot to think about. He hadn't really needed her to answer his question about the vizier allowing him to leave Hedabar. He knew now he'd been just as captive as his brothers, just too foolish to realize it. The vizier couldn't risk Dagstyrr spreading word of his atrocities against the fae.

He awoke early the next day. A cool breeze swept across the sea, raising small waves that the *Mermaid* cut through like the serpent she was imitating. On either side of them, land swept up in treed hills toward white mountaintops. Sheer granite cliffs fell to the choppy waters on both sides, giving nowhere for ships to land or people to rescue ships that got into trouble. Which explained why the considerable traffic plying these waters wasted no time on niceties. The sooner they were out of it, the better.

Dagstyrr dipped his head in a barrel of salt water to wash away the night. Grabbing a fresh bread roll from the passing ship's boy, he shouted after him, "You and I must talk, young man!"

"What about?" answered the boy, puzzled.

"Later," said Dagstyrr, waving him away. He didn't hear Captain Bernst coming up behind him.

"So, you've worked it out," said Bernst.

"That Billy was the one to escape Hedabar and tell Rella what had happened? Yes. I still have to work out the rest of it," said Dagstyrr between mouthfuls of breakfast. "I don't suppose you'd like to help me with that?"

"Dark fae don't talk about one another. Ask me a direct question, and I'm likely to answer it, but I don't tell tales about others. For this story, you must ask the princess or Billy."

"Who will we take from the cage first?" said Dagstyrr, changing the subject. He'd get no more from the captain.

"Sigmund, I think," said Bernst. "Expect him to be reluctant at first, wanting to return to the safety of his hammock. In a few days, he'll get used to being outside, and he'll want to stay outside, but we must keep to the schedule I've devised. They go and come when we say, not when they want to. Understood?"

"Understood, Captain." Talking to the ship's boy would have to wait. Dagstyrr's spirits were high now that real progress was being made with the addicts. With luck, his brothers would be well enough to walk off the *Mermaid* on their own two feet.

∼

Rella watched Sigmund leave the confines of the cage on trembling legs, his arms tight across his chest as if he'd fall apart if he didn't keep holding on. A stupid grin below glazed eyes showed he was doing his best. Bernst had told Dagstyrr to stand back and watch this first time.

"By the gods, I hope my parents never see this," whispered Dagstyrr.

"I hope so too," said Rella from her chair, shocked at his condition.

"We cannot bear to see Mother hurt, and this would tear at her heart. My brothers know that. They fear her finding out. So I know they'll do their utmost to recover quickly."

"She is their guide through the world of magic. They must be so very proud of her heritage. I imagine they would happily die rather than disgrace her like this," said Rella, with sympathy. Thankful that her father would never see Calstir in such a condition.

The tension on board was multiplying. Rella's anxiety about meeting more fae ships and having to converse with them stiffened her every muscle until she looked like a statue. Bernst had told her it was unlikely, but she couldn't seem to relax until these straits were behind them.

All the others were focused on the first addict allowed out of the cage, fully prepared to swarm him if necessary.

"Dag? Dag, is that really you?" slurred Sigmund.

Ye gods, he was so thin. Sigmund's blonde hair hung in rat's tails down his back, and his bones poked through his shirt. With his heart near breaking, Dagstyrr stepped toward his brother, only for Bernst's voice to shout in his head, *Stop! Remember what you agreed to?*

Dagstyrr halted midstride. "Hi, Sig. How are you feeling?"

"Good, yeah, good."

"I've got to tell you, brother, you don't look so good," said Dagstyrr, remembering his instructions to never lie, and never to accept a lie from the addicts.

Sigmund started to tremble harder. "I think I'm going to puke," he said, before turning to the offered bucket and spewing out what little there was in his stomach.

"It hurts," said Sigmund.

Dagstyrr had to turn his face away, lest Sigmund see the tears threatening in his eyes. With a swallow, he turned back. "I know, brother, but you'll be better soon. Once we're home, Mother will make sure we get some meat on those bones of yours."

"No. No, not Mother."

Dagstyrr saw the panic rise in Sigmund.

"Never. Never let her or Father see me like this. They mustn't know. I cannot bear the shame."

That's a good sign Dagstyrr. If he can feel shame, he is not too far gone, Bernst's voice echoed in his head.

"They are bound to find out, Sig, but by then you'll be much better. Mother and Father are stronger than you think," said Dagstyrr, fully understanding Sig's reluctance to shame their parents.

"No, they must never find out." Sigmund's head went back, and a feral cry emanated from his throat, sending waves of his pain out into the world.

The crew stepped forward ready to intervene, but somehow Sigmund held it together. Trembling like a leaf, he stared at Dagstyrr. "Promise me, Dag. Promise me, they'll never know."

Bernst threw Dagstyrr a warning look. He was right to do so, for his every instinct was to lie to his brother. Help ease his pain just a little. But he knew better. "I can't promise that, Sig," he said, sadly.

"You must. Yeah, you must. It's the only way. We won't tell her. She'll never know." His pleading was pitiful, but it soon changed to threats when Dagstyrr faced him with sad determination. "We'll make you. Erik will make you. You can't stop us. We're fae, you're only human. You'll never stop us. Hah, that's it. Soon, Erik will deal with you." Sigmund turned toward the cage, trembling. "I've got to go now."

Two crewmen stood in his way.

"Dag, tell them. I've got to go now."

"Why don't you sit with me a while, Sig? It's been a long time since we've just sat and talked. I miss you," said Dagstyrr. It was true. He did miss his brothers. He'd give anything to have them back as they were. His brother's head began to twitch.

"Can't, gotta go now."

Bernst stepped up to Sigmund. "Just turn around and say goodbye to Dag, Sig. Then we'll get you back inside."

"Need medicine," said Sigmund, his head twitches worsening.

"I know. You've done really well. Just turn around and say goodbye to Dag, ok? Then we'll get you some medicine," promised Bernst.

Dagstyrr watched in horror as his brother turned his head, tears streaming down his snotty face. "Bye, Dag," he managed.

"Good lad," said Captain Bernst, with a nod. The crew reacted quickly, lifting Sigmund back into the cage and wrapping him in his hammock. The crew took time to replace the wards, and then peace reigned.

Later, a similar scene was played out with Thorsten. Dagstyrr's nerves were stretched to breaking point. He couldn't imagine they'd be well enough to walk off the ship when they reached Halfenhaw. Both Sig and Thor were worried about their mother finding out, and with good reason. It would break her heart. Then she'd go looking for revenge. But she must never set foot on Hedabar.

Dragon's blood was the most addictive, hateful, poisonous drug known to light fae. Dragons and fae were distantly related on a magical level. If what Dagstyrr knew about it was true, the effects might stay with them forever. The poison could call to them even years after they'd stopped taking it. Worse, they'd be able to smell its presence miles away, and they'd run to it like moths to a flame. That they hadn't taken dragon's blood knowingly would be little comfort to their mother.

Dagstyrr sat staring out to sea, his heart heavy. He prayed his brothers' recovery would be complete. Otherwise, they could never be fully trusted. How was Erik to take his place as earl with this shame hanging over him? Would men follow him?

A large hand on Dagstyrr's shoulder announced Captain Bernst. "Ye did well today, lad."

"You think so? I nearly cracked. You do know that. I wanted to take them in my arms and lie my stupid face off. Anything to give them some comfort."

"I know."

"I thought Sig was bad. I'd hoped Thor would be in better shape. He's usually stronger, but if anything, he was worse. Trying to bribe me with his woman, that's not him. He loves Zigi," said Dagstyrr. "And what for? To not tell Mother! As if she won't know the second, she sets eyes on them."

"They are past the worst. Now the hardest part for you and Rella begins. Working with them day after day, listening to their nonsense, is exhausting," said Bernst.

"I can believe that," said Dagstyrr, remembering his exchanges with Sig and Thor.

"They'll be better by the time we reach Halfenhaw. Not well, mind you, but a lot better than today."

"How?"

"The work we did today was only the beginning. The more we bring them out of the cage and talk to them, the quicker their recovery will go."

"What did Sig mean when he asked for medicine? I thought you didn't use drugs."

"I don't. However, if we leave addicts to suffer withdrawal completely on their own, they die. So, we use a combination of magic and natural herbals. This is dark fae magic from the forests and rivers, we call it medicine because that is what it is."

Dagstyrr laughed. "Erik will hate that."

"I know."

"It doesn't seem right. Humans are taught that the old stories of dark fae are not true, that they don't exist. Light fae are told the stories and taught to fear the very idea of dark fae. Yet neither knows the truth. Why don't you show yourselves?"

"It suits us the way things are. We blend in with humans well enough, and the light fae leave us alone, pretending we don't exist."

"But why?"

"When we split from the light fae it was because they were losing their connection to the living earth. They put too much store in their ethereal beauty, courtly manners, always striving for perfection. The one we called the Dark Queen saw the dangers there. We are all elementals. We need the earth, water, wind, fire, and all the weird and wonderful things that grow there."

"I see."

"Do you, lad? When we split, the light fae cursed us. Called us dark, took away our ability to instantly heal, but we relearned what all fae had forgotten. From the forests and the creatures dwelling there, we learned true healing. That is what I'm using on the addicts."

"You have dark eyes and hair."

"Aye, well, that's a bit of camouflage. We live among humans. We like it that way, and we don't want them to know we're different. They might not like it, in fact, I know they wouldn't."

"Is it true you intermarry with them?"

"We do."

"Why?"

"You should know that, lad. We fall in love with the delightful creatures, of course," said Bernst, smiling.

"My mother fell in love with my father. I've heard her call him many things, but never a creature," said Dagstyrr.

"Princess Astrid is a very rare creature herself. She's the first light fae to marry a human in hundreds of years. Many wanted to kill Lord Magnus. There were even some who tried, but he bested them all. Eventually, Princess Astrid went to Calstir's father and begged him to put a stop to it, and he did."

"My mother is from a small principality on the northern edge of Casta. She gave up her right of inheritance to marry my father, that is what swung the deal."

"Aye, she was the last of her line. Which is why there was such strong objection to her marrying a human, but she is very persuasive."

"I'd like to have been a fly on the wall during that conversation," said Dagstyrr.

Captain Bernst threw back his head and laughed, his big belly dancing with each exhalation. "I was that fly, young Dagstyrr. Well, not exactly a fly, but I was there right enough listening to every word. Unseen behind a screen in the royal anteroom."

"Why?"

"The Dark Queen had sent me as envoy to Casta. I just sat quietly until everyone forgot I was there. You'd be surprised what you can learn if you know how to stay quiet and still. All I know is, she's a very persuasive woman, your mother. And you are right, giving up her principality to Casta swung the deal."

"My parents will look after them, no matter what has befallen them. They love us. However, since their rescue, all my brothers can focus on is the shame."

"Very true, but Princess Astrid is not some Crystal Mountain fae ready to crack and break at the first nasty thing to enter her world."

Dagstyrr thought of his mother. He imagined her standing before him. "You're right. She is by far the strongest woman I've ever known. I think it's disappointing her that they fear the most."

"There, now, that's the truth of it. Don't listen to your brothers. They'll do everything they can to manipulate you, and they're clever. Cling to what you know in your heart to be true," said Bernst.

"Thank you."

"Just remember, every sodding word that comes out of their mouths is there to trick you. Don't let it," said Bernst, turning away.

"My parents will have the finest doctors and healers brought to Halfenhaw as fast as possible," said Dagstyrr.

"I hope not," said Rella.

Dagstyrr hadn't heard her approach. "Why not?"

"Because the very best healers are the Crystal Mountain fae. I'm hoping they won't leave their monastery for halflings. If they catch me, it will mean my death."

Dagstyrr watched her stare across the sea rather than

look at him. He couldn't understand the pain she was feeling. As a human, it was beyond him. "Why would they want to harm you? They might be able to reverse what the Dark Emperor has done to you. Their healing powers are legendary."

"All light fae will want to kill me on sight, you already know that. Erik would have done it at the citadel, if he'd been able. But Crystal Mountain fae are a whole other level of dangerous. They will want to capture me, subject me to their tests for weeks or years before eventually sentencing me to death," said Rella her voice so sad it tore at him far more than if she'd screamed or shouted.

"I will not let them near you."

A small laugh escaped her. "You wouldn't be able to stop them. They have studied the magic arts all their lives. They have powerful magic at their fingertips that even Calstir cannot imagine."

Dagstyrr watched a shudder run up her body. She was truly frightened of these fae. His fearless Rella was afraid. He put his arm across her shoulder, and was rewarded when she leaned into him. "Stay by my side, Rella. I promise, I will not let them take you."

CHAPTER 16

Dagstyrr leaned on the *Mermaid*'s prow watching Halfenhaw appear over the horizon. He was exhausted, as was Rella and every man on board. Sig and Thor came up beside him. "Home. I can see the tower," said Sig, whose eyesight was always better than the others'.

"Aye," said Thor. "I hope Erik and Calstir manage to get up to the castle unaided. They're both still very weak."

"If not, Dag can carry them," said Sig.

Dagstyrr turned to his brothers. "You'll carry them yourselves. Princess Rella and I will be going on ahead."

"We're healthy and strong now, Dag. You don't tell us what to do," said Sigmund.

"If you're so healthy and strong, you won't have any problem helping Erik and Calstir should they need it, will you? Things have changed. You no longer command me. Well, you never should have tried. After what I've done for you, you should be down on your hands and knees, thanking me."

Thorsten turned to Dagstyrr. "You're correct, Dag. I, for

one have never been so happy and proud to have a human brother."

Sig hung his head. "I guess. I just wanted to pretend none of this ever happened, to go back to the way things were. Thor's right," he said, looking up at Dag. "I'm very glad you're my brother, and I'm very grateful you're human. I'll always be indebted to you."

"Yes, you will be," said Dagstyrr with a smile. "I'm going to land first and take a horse to Castle Halfenhaw. I need to let Mother know we're coming." He watched his brothers squirm at the idea.

"Don't you think it better if we just turn up?" said Sig.

"Aye, we don't need to say anything right away," said Thor.

"No." He looked both his brothers in the eye. "We are Halfenhaws. We don't lie, even by omission. It will come much harder for Mother if she thinks we tried to hide it from her."

"Thank you, Dagstyrr," said Erik, coming up behind them. "These two are stuck on Mother not knowing. I wish it were possible, but it's not. Let's get this over with. Then we can face the future as a family."

"Right," said Dagstyrr, nodding. Erik had made great strides to wellness these last days. His weight loss was such that clothes hung on his large frame, and when he lost focus, a glazed look still stole into his eyes. But though physically weak, he was stronger than Sigmund or Thorsten in other ways.

Erik and Calstir had been hardest hit by the addiction and the vizier's drain on their fae powers, yet they fought so much harder than Sig and Thor to get well. As such, their abilities were returning faster, and Bernst assured Dagstyrr that as soon as they touched ground, their powers should start to return to normal. He was proud of his big brother Erik.

"I'll send down horses, and Mother's sedan chair for Calstir. Calstir should lead. Let Mother and Father greet him before she lays eyes on you three," said Dagstyrr.

"Why do you say that?" chorused Sig and Thor.

Dagstyrr lifted his eyebrow and leaned back against the gunwale. "Take a look at yourselves, and then imagine what Mother's first instincts will be when she sees you."

"I see what you mean," said, Sig, sheepishly. "She'll have us all three tucked up in bed and be spoon-feeding us within minutes. I won't be surprised if she does the same to Prince Calstir."

"If she does, just shut up and be grateful. I'll go and see if Rella's ready. It won't be long before we land," said Dagstyrr.

As he stepped toward the cabin, Erik caught his arm. "*Princess* Rella to you, and since when do you enter the cabin of a highborn fae princess unasked?"

"Don't worry, brother. I always knock," he said with a wink, twisting his arm from his brother's grip and making his way to the door of her cabin.

The door opened as he raised his hand to knock. "Don't be so formal, Dagstyrr. Come in," said Rella, so the brothers could hear.

He laughed. "You heard them?"

"They have deep, rumbly voices, every one of them," she said, with a smile. "And I have extremely good hearing."

Dagstyrr began to sit then he saw the whole place was strewn with silks and lacy things. "Couldn't decide what to wear?"

Rella snatched some delicate underclothes from the cushions Dagstyrr usually occupied. "There, is that better?"

she said, irritated. What was it about him that snuck under her normal defenses? "Pour us some wine. I'll get rid of this. I was trying to decide whether to arrive as Princess Rella or as an officer of the Casta Household Guard."

Dagstyrr understood her dilemma. As Princess Rella of Casta, she should dress accordingly when arriving at someone's home. However, if she wanted to hide the mark, her uniform did that best, though not altogether. "Wear your uniform, you look magnificent in it. It's sure to impress my father," he said, pouring two glasses of rich red Samish.

Rella plopped down opposite him and reached across for her wine. "But not your mother?"

Dagstyrr enjoyed the camaraderie that had built between them over the last couple of weeks while they helped each other to work with the addicts. Each night with their brothers tucked up in the cage, they would return to the cabin, exhausted. After a simple meal, she'd fall into bed, and he'd bed down on deck. In the morning they'd rise, ready to do it all again.

The addicts could be violent as well as vicious with their tongues. Being warriors, Rella and Dagstyrr had learned quickly to work together. They were always looking out for each other, deflecting a sly kick or punch when the other's back was turned. "I'm uncomfortable with them being outside the cage," said Dagstyrr.

"I am too," answered Rella. Her dark eyes twinkled in the lantern light.

He smiled, appreciating the beauty of her eyes flashing a challenge. "The problem is, they are convinced that they're quite well."

"It will soon become obvious they are not. I've arranged for Captain Bernst to take the cage up to Castle Halfenhaw along with a half dozen of his more adept crewmen," she said, watching him as if to gauge his reaction.

Dagstyrr whistled. "You do know they think they've seen the end of that cage?"

"I do."

He thought of his parents' reaction to such a device entering the castle. "Father won't want it in Castle Halfenhaw."

"Dagstyrr." She leaned forward, her blue silk top slipping off one shoulder and showing where the brown mark coiled up and around her body onto her face. "They will soon come to understand."

His heart skipped. She was letting down her guard. If only she understood how beautiful she was! But his eyes must have lingered too long on her shoulder.

"Don't look at it," she said, pulling up the sleeve and grabbing a shawl, anger blooming a blush on her cheeks.

Dagstyrr ignored her outburst and sat back on the cushions. "We need to be alert. Anything could happen when my parents confront not only their sons, but your brother as well. My mother is a full-blood fae princess, Calstir's equal, and I honestly don't know how she'll react to all four of them being dragon's blood addicts."

"You and I can manage our brothers if we stay alert," said Rella.

"We'll no longer be within the confines of the ship. A lot could go wrong."

He watched her digest his words. She sat, a little frown marring her perfect forehead, and he saw there was something she was working up to. He drank his wine and gave her time.

"We've talked about your mother's reaction to her sons and my brother, but what will her reaction be to me?" While her voice was strong and steady, her eyes looked down at her wine.

He leaned forward, lifting her chin until her eyes filled his vision. She had to see the truth of what he said. "I have no idea how Mother will react. Like all light fae, she's been brought up to despise dark fae. In our household, their very existence was denied by everyone except my father."

"I am so much worse than dark fae, Dagstyrr," she said, and he saw pain flash in her eyes. "There is nothing more abhorrent to light fae than one of their own choosing to go dark."

"'There is no greater honor than to sacrifice for others.' That is the Halfenhaw family motto. Father will understand, and he will help Mother understand."

"It is you who don't understand, Dagstyrr. Do you know the difference between light fae and dark fae?"

Dagstyrr thought he did. However, there must be something more or she wouldn't look so terrified. Watching her reluctance flit across her face, he wanted to take her in his arms and wipe away the uncertainty and fear, but this was too important to her. So, he racked his memory to try and find something he'd missed. "No, tell me."

She took a sip of wine. "There are the obvious differences, light fae always have blue eyes."

"Aye, a very special blue you never see on humans or dark fae," he said.

"We also have extraordinary long blonde hair of a shade rarely seen in the dark fae or humans."

"Your hair is very beautiful."

"Don't." Rella turned from him.

"I'm sorry," he said. "What are the differences I can't see?"

"I'm getting to that."

"I know you rarely mate with humans. My mother is an exception. I know your magic is bright blue in color, and the dark fae have green magic. I always thought that was because light fae draw their energy from the sky and dark fae from the earth. Light fae never seem to age, but dark fae allow themselves to age appropriately," he said, wanting to get to the crux of whatever was bothering her.

"Yes. However, every so often a light fae decides that they want to taste the dark fae magic. It is a power play, a very dangerous one," she said.

"What do you mean?"

"These people will turn dark, but aim to hold on to their light fae magic. There is an ancient prophecy that speaks of a light fae prince who will come in the future to guide us. He will have both light and dark magic at his fingertips. Such power is unimaginable."

Dagstyrr whistled softly. "That is what tempts them to try it."

"Exactly. However, the prophecy warns against trying it. I cannot imagine the strength needed to wield such power," she said.

"Some have tried?"

"Oh, yes."

"But none have succeeded?"

"The prophecy is clear:

Those who turn dark,
Will be eaten by darkness.
First, you will kill,
Then you will enjoy it,
Then comes madness,
Then, your evil will consume you."

"So, they go mad before they can martial their new magic?" said Dagstyrr beginning to understand her deep-rooted concerns. This explained why she hated her green magic so much.

Rella took another sip of wine. "Oh, there have been those who demonstrate green and blue magic for a short while at solstice fairs—claiming to be born that way. It is usually brought about by powerful spells, and it is just a feeble illusion. However, the real problem with Princess Astrid seeing me is, that we are all taught from a young age to kill any light fae turned dark on sight."

"My mother has never killed."

"Perhaps not, but she is capable of it. You saw Erik's reaction to me. Hers will be so much worse," she said, trying to smile at Dagstyrr, and reaching out a hand to cup his face. "Don't you see? A fight between Astrid and me will mean the death of one of us."

Her touch on his cheek stilled the rising conflict warring inside him. "I will not choose between you and my mother. But know this, Rella, I will protect you, always," he said, his voice deep with pain. Dagstyrr lifted her hand to his mouth and softly kissed her palm before she pulled it away.

"You need to be prepared, Dagstyrr," she said. "To kill them is the only defense we have before they go mad and destroy all around them. For such creatures are powerful, very powerful."

Dagstyrr noticed she did not include herself when she spoke of them. "That is what you fear, going mad."

He saw her attempt to calm herself with every breath before she burst out. " Of course that is what I fear. This was only supposed to be temporary."

"He tricked you!"

"I don't want to talk about him right now. I just need you to understand what to expect from Princess Astrid."

"Don't worry about my mother. I will make her understand. She is very liberal. After all, she married my father," he said, smiling.

Her eyes closed as if willing it to be so. Dagstyrr held her chin. The temptation to bend just a little and steal a kiss from her mouth was almost too much. Instead, he kissed her temple, right on the mark flowering on the side of her face. She gasped and pulled away.

"Now, I think you'd better get dressed. We're almost there," he said, rising and ducking under the doorway before she could chastise him.

Night had fallen, and Castle Halfenhaw was lit up as if for a celebration. To Dagstyrr's horror, he saw a chain of lights leave the castle wall and wend its way down the hill to the moorings, where people were gathering. Riders with torches prepared to welcome them.

Captain Bernst came up beside him. "Don't fret, lad. I suspect the Argan family stopped here and mentioned that Prince Calstir was about to pay a visit, along with the sons of Halfenhaw."

"Well, that's scuppered my plans," said Dagstyrr. "Tell me, Captain, Rella's been explaining about light fae turned dark…"

"Shhh, lad, we don't talk about that," he said. "Enough. Get yourself ready."

"Can you cure such madness?" he said.

"Never tried. Now, let's get this over with," said Bernst.

Dagstyrr thought about Bernst's reaction while he belted on his sword and secreted his knives about his ragged clothes. Presumably, the dark fae would also kill such creatures on sight, but maybe not. Bernst had taken Rella in as one of them. Perhaps they could cure the madness before it affected everyone around them. He still had so much to learn.

"Well, not too much on our plate tonight. Just explain to my mother that her sons and her prince are addicts and her human son converses with dragons, and then we need to stop her and Erik from killing Rella."

"To say nothing of a shipload of dark fae docked at the castle with a cage to house her sons and her distinguished guest," added Bernst, with a wink.

CHAPTER 17

Rella's heart skipped when she saw Princess Astrid and Earl Magnus standing to greet them on the wharf. Magnus was as big as Dagstyrr and looked magnificent. His bright red hair blazed in the firelight as he stood protectively by his wife's side. Dagstyrr's mother was indeed as beautiful as her reputation suggested —a full-blood light fae princess. Rella feared this was not going to go well.

Thankfully, Erik and Calstir disembarked first. Rella watched as Erik greeted his parents then introduced Prince Calstir. Astrid curtsied, and Lord Magnus shook his hand, but Astrid was watching Erik and Calstir closely—too closely.

As the cage was lifted off the ship, Erik tried to move his parents away from the wharf, but Lord Magnus was not so easily distracted. "What the hell is that for?"

"It is mine, Lord Magnus," said Calstir.

"Let's get up to the hall; I will explain everything," said Erik, taking his mother's elbow in an attempt to lead her away, but she was not going to move.

"That crew is dark fae," said Astrid, the tiniest frown marring her perfect face. The very fact she acknowledged that dark fae existed spoke to her discomfort.

As soon as Rella saw her frown, she knew Astrid was extremely uneasy. Light fae didn't show emotions so readily.

Dagstyrr waved and smiled from the deck of the ship, trying to reassure his mother.

"When did you last see your mother frown?"

"When we got word Father had drowned. He hadn't, obviously."

"She knows something's wrong."

Calstir tried to deflect Astrid's curiosity. "Yes, the crew is dark fae. As your son so rightly suggested, explanations should wait until we are alone, Princess. Besides, I have looked forward to visiting Halfenhaw for many years. I hear the hunting hereabouts is second to none," said Calstir, making a brave effort to distract his hosts.

The dark fae crew manhandling the cage along the wharf was suddenly swept aside by Sigmund and Thorsten as they ran towards their parents, shouting. "Don't let them put us back in there!" Only Bernst's quick thinking stopped the cage from landing in the water. Rella saw him use his magic to halt the progress of the cage's slide off the wharf until the crew could regain control, but not before two men fell in the water.

The crew was screaming at the human warriors from the castle to save their crewmates. The warriors were shouting at the crew to get the cage back onto the ship. Sigmund and Thorsten were behaving like lunatics, waving their arms and shouting.

The human warriors were confused. They knew something was wrong but they had no orders, and no idea what threat had landed in their midst.

Dagstyrr ran to the ship's rail and pointed at four of his father's retainers. "You four. Get them out. Now! They can't swim."

Rella watched the chaos unfold about her. Her worst fears were going to be realized. She dare not go ashore.

Calstir turned and faced Thorsten and Sigmund who slowed their race to their parents' side. "Boys, we don't want to frighten your parents—do we?" Rella could just imagine his compulsion buffeting their actions.

"No. It's all right. We don't need the cage any longer."

A low growl only perceptible to fae ears emanated from Calstir's throat. Erik stood behind his brothers, one hand on each of their collars. "Remember what we agreed?"

"Yes, Erik," they chorused.

"Now, before Mother imagines the worst, let's get up to the hall without any more drama."

"I think that's a very good idea," said Lord Magnus, taking his wife's hand and leading her toward their home.

Even from this distance, Rella could see the supreme effort it was taking for Astrid not to demand Calstir's apology for compelling her sons on their own shores like that.

As light and quick on land as any fae, the crew soon had the cage delivered to the castle with six crewmen to guard it.

In a tense procession, Lord Magnus and Princess Astrid led their guest up the hill, Erik brought up the rear, keeping the younger boys in order. Rella hung back, grateful that Dagstyrr never left her side.

"It's time we caught up with them," he said.

"I suppose we must," said Rella. "If Calstir can't persuade one family, he'll never be able to persuade the court to accept me. This is a test."

"Don't think of it like that, Rella. My mother is more stubborn than most. If you don't believe me, ask Bernst."

Eventually, they reached the large hall of Halfenhaw, by which time Princess Astrid was mute with fury. The hall had been decked out magnificently for a true Halfenhaw welcome. The high beams were strewn with boughs of fir and cedar, and strings of flowers cascaded down the pillars, scenting the room with a heady forest fragrance. The tables were filled with delicious foods, and servants stood about with trays full of wine and mead, ready to serve their guests and welcome their sons home. Rella grabbed a cup of wine from a passing servant and then retreated to the shadows.

With a wave of her hand, Princess Astrid indicated the servants should put down the trays and leave. The sound of doors banging shut echoed around the hall, as servants gratefully retreated from their mistress's fury. Earl Magnus managed to seat Prince Calstir and his fae sons together around the fire before turning to his wife.

"My dear, we must listen to their tale," he said.

Rella used her acute hearing to eavesdrop unashamedly. She wasn't safe here. Even with Dagstyrr by her side, the danger from Princess Astrid and her son, Erik, was very real. For if Astrid attacked her, Erik would forget his promise to Calstir and attack as well. The mother-son bond was stronger than any promise he'd made while an addict.

Earl Magnus stood by his wife, one hand resting on the back of her chair, as Prince Calstir and Erik told the sorry tale. Every so often, Earl Magnus's gaze would flick up towards Dagstyrr and Rella, where they stood well back in the shadows of the hall. Otherwise, the human lord looked carved in stone. His red hair caught the firelight, making a halo around his head, but his hand never left his wife, tension freezing his body.

Once the tale was told, Sig and Thor immediately started telling their parents how well they were. That all they needed was to put on some muscle, and they'd be good as new. Their glazed eyes and agitated ticks told a different story.

To Rella's dismay, Princess Astrid agreed with them wholeheartedly and brought plates of food, and cups of mead to all four of them. Rella shot a glance at Dagstyrr, knowing they should not have wine or mead.

He nodded then watched as Rella used a tiny amount of magic to instantly change the mead to water without anyone noticing. She was rewarded with a smile.

Earl Magnus took that moment to leave his wife and, arms extended, walked smiling toward his youngest son and Rella. "Thank you, my boy. I am so proud of you," he said, wrapping Dagstyrr in a bear hug. Both men were very similar in build. Only Dagstyrr's dark hair differed from his father's red.

"Thank you, Father," he said, stepping aside. "May I present Princess Rella of Casta?"

With his calloused hand extended in greeting, Earl Magnus smiled. "It is my pleasure to welcome you to Halfenhaw, Princess, and to thank you from the bottom of my heart for the return of my sons."

Rella extended her arm and grasped Earl Magnus's forearm as one warrior to another. "I couldn't have done it without Dagstyrr, Earl Magnus." She saw father and son exchange an open look of unconditional love. It was like nothing she'd ever seen before.

Just then, Princess Astrid appeared by her husband's side and took her youngest son in her elegant arms. As she held him, her eyes closed, and the pleasure it gave her to hold her son was obvious for all to see. *She has learned to show her love, and she loves deeply*, thought Rella.

Princess Astrid turned to Rella, but before any greeting was out of her mouth, a deep growl emanated from her throat bringing the three fae Halfenhaw brothers to their mother's side.

Astrid had noticed the mark, or maybe the shadows failed to hide Rella's brown eyes. Astrid's reaction was visceral.

Rella drew her sword and crouched ready to pounce.

Dagstyrr jumped between them. "There is always a price to pay, is there not, Mother? Prince Calstir left out some of the less palatable parts of the tale. Princess Rella paid the price of my brothers' escape," he said, nodding toward the three of them.

Rella froze, deep in pain and sadness, now knowing for certain how the light fae at court would see her. Princess Astrid stood, trembling with fury barely able to control the energy sparking from her body. Her bright blue fae eyes fixed determinedly on Rella, seeing her as a despised thing to be eliminated as quickly as possible. To be killed before contaminating anything around her with madness. Behind Astrid, the three Halfenhaw brothers, led by Erik, were crouched, knives in hand, ready to kill.

Dagstyrr drew his dagger, and addressed his brothers. "No! If you harm even a hair on her head, you will have to kill me. Then her brother will deal with you. Mother, give us a chance to explain."

Confusion started the brothers glancing at each other for guidance, but Erik was steadfast. "We stand with Mother. Are you standing against her?" he taunted.

Rella's heart sank. This was worse than she had imagined.

Suddenly, Earl Magnus stepped between Dagstyrr and his fae family. "Dagstyrr, get her to your rooms. *Your* rooms, understand? Now!" he yelled.

Before she could protest, Dagstyrr had thrown down his dagger and wrapped his arms about her, trapping her hands and preventing her from using her magic. Then he whispered in her ear, "Forgive what I'm about to do, but if you value our lives, go with this, Princess. My father knows what he's doing." Then he picked her up and threw her over his shoulder. He opened the nearest door and ran down a corridor. Outside, he yelled for Bernst: "Captain, they need your assistance in the hall!"

"I'm going to kill you for this," she said, through clenched teeth.

"No, you won't," he replied.

They crossed the bailey and mounted the tower stairs. Rella sensed the ancient wards guarding the rooms at the top of the tower even before they reached them. With such wards in place, she couldn't so much as strike him without it backfiring on her—never mind using her magic.

He burst into the room and dropped her on a large bed. "I'm sorry, Rella, but I wasn't going to stand there and see you hurt. If you'd accessed your magic, so would they."

"I could have killed them," she said.

"Exactly, which is why I had to trap your hands and stop you using your magic."

"I suppose your mother taught you that trick?"

"No, Father did," he said with a grin. "You'll be safe here. I'm going to try and help Bernst." He turned and left her.

CHAPTER 18

Dagstyrr ran back to the hall in time to see Sig and Thor being carried out to the cage, and Erik being subdued by four dark fae crewmen. Calstir was standing with his back to the fire, focused and stiff. It was taking all his concentration to remain calm. Was that why he hadn't moved to help his sister?

Captain Bernst was by his side, and Dagstyrr knew instinctively the good captain was "speaking" to him as only the captain could. Dagstyrr went to the prince. "She is safe, Your Highness." Calstir acknowledged him with a cursory nod.

Dagstyrr saw the prince's hand tremble as he fought to control his yearning for the dragon's blood. It appeared the prince was only in control as long as everything remained calm. Any upset, and his iron will to fight the craving would start to flag.

Earl Magnus held tight to his trembling wife while he whispered in her ear. In all his life, Dagstyrr had never seen his mother so close to the breaking point. Raising four sons she'd had many reasons to lose control with them, but she'd always maintained her calm.

At last Erik was restrained and carried out to the cage. Prince Calstir sat heavily in a chair and faced the fire, bringing his hands together, fingers steepled to show he was once again in control. Dagstyrr had to admire the prince's determination to beat this thing.

Earl Magnus led his wife to a chair by the fire opposite the prince and dismissed Captain Bernst with a nod. Dagstyrr watched the captain head for the door before ducking inside an alcove and sliding to the floor. *Just in case, lad. You might need me.*

Dagstyrr stifled a grin but managed to nod in the direction of the alcove. He remained silent until his father took a seat next to his mother. Earl Magnus confined her lethal hands in his great fist, so that she would not be tempted to use her magic or cast a spell. "So, Dag, can we now have the full story?" said his father.

"Only as far as I know it, Father," said Dagstyrr, choosing to remain standing. "As you know, we were on our way to Demenos hoping to re-open trade with them. But after three weeks of foul weather, we'd run short of supplies. Hedabar was the nearest port. We had no intention of disembarking, but an invitation came from the vizier to the Halfenhaw brothers to attend a feast at the citadel. As we couldn't leave until the captain had secured supplies, Erik saw no harm. None of us did."

"That's how they get you," said Prince Calstir, his voice hoarse. "We too ran short of certain necessities and put into Hedabar to resupply the ship."

Earl Magnus leaned forward without letting go of his wife's hands. "Do you mean to say light fae are being lured there intentionally?"

"Yes, Father, and not only light fae. I saw many types of fae held prisoner, even mountain elves," said Dagstyrr. His mother's eyes flashed to his face. She was coming out of whatever fugue had taken control of her at the sight of Rella.

"So, you did not attend the feast with your brothers?"

"I did. However, as soon as it became apparent I was not fae, the vizier's lackeys threw me out." Dagstyrr saw his father suck in his breath. "Which was just as well, Father. Otherwise all four of us would still be there now."

"Dagstyrr speaks the truth, Earl Magnus."

"I didn't doubt him. My sons don't lie," said Earl Magnus.

Dagstyrr raised an eyebrow. "They do now, Father. Until they are well again, they cannot be trusted."

His father stood and faced him with hands bunched at his sides. "I would kill any other man for saying that to my face, and you know it."

Calstir started to laugh. Magnus rounded on him. "What is so funny?"

"I'm sorry. This is inappropriate, Earl Magnus." But he continued to laugh. "Dagstyrr speaks the truth. Even I will lie in this state, so you cannot trust what I say, and I'm saying Dagstyrr tells the truth, and now you cannot trust that either. A conundrum if ever I heard one." The prince struggled to control his giggles.

"No conundrum. Dagstyrr is not afflicted with this disease, and I know my sons don't lie. A disease that makes you lie—I've never heard of such a thing," said Earl Magnus, disgusted.

Calstir sobered quickly. "Not a disease, Earl Magnus, an addiction. Or maybe both. Who knows? You might as well get used to the idea now. It is going to take some time to cure us. Unfortunately, I fear Sigmund and Thorsten may never fully recover. For some reason, they are struggling with their recovery more than most, and they lie all the time."

"Why did your sister turn dark, Prince Calstir?" The first words out of his mother's mouth were cold and hard to hear.

"She couldn't land at Hedabar as light fae, could she?" said Calstir, piercing Princess Astrid with all the power of his bright blue eyes. Such a look coming from Calstir might fell a human or lesser fae, but his mother gave as good as she got, never blinking.

Earl Magnus's hand waved between them, forcing them to break the deadlock. Such behavior in humans was childish, but between highborn fae, it could lead to disaster. They could sit there for days until one of them attacked the other. Families had been torn apart and careers ruined by such silly games. It was a testament to his mother's distress and Calstir's addiction that they indulged in such behavior.

Dagstyrr struggled to stay silent, but he knew this tale was better coming from a fae prince than a human.

"Could no one else in Casta champion their prince? I'm surprised your father allowed her to go," said Astrid.

"My father was already dying. Rella was the only one willing to leave the court at that time. If I failed to return, then one of the cousins would inherit the throne," said Calstir, without a hint of bitterness.

"So, no one expected her to return," stated Princess Astrid.

"Exactly."

"Who arranged for you to run out of supplies near Hedabar, thus ensuring your absence when your father died?" asked Earl Magnus, quick to get to the crux of a matter.

"One of the cousins, no doubt," said Calstir.

"How did Princess Rella know you were at Hedabar? What prevented her from rushing straight there and being caught herself?"

"It's not what you're implying, my Lord. Rella is faithful and true to our family. It was a human, the ship's boy, who managed to sail on another ship out of Hedabar and make his way to Casta. He told his story with the whole court listening, and, for his troubles, they took his arm. It would have been his life if Rella hadn't interfered. Princess Rella saved the boy and took him under her wing. She made sure he healed. With the help of the dark fae, of course," said Calstir, unable to hide his disgust at the mention of the dark fae.

"If she hadn't saved him, there would have been no witnesses, and you would still be languishing in the citadel," said Earl Magnus.

"Aye."

"She must have gone in front of the council to ask permission before leaving Casta and her duties," said Astrid.

"Of course, and naturally, they said yes," slurred Calstir, before coughing and pulling himself together. "She received permission to leave, but she wasn't allowed to bring any of her warriors with her."

"Not even an escort?" said Dagstyrr's mother, shocked.

"Not only did they offer no assistance, but they also reprimanded her for leaving her dying father to rescue her brother. They assured her the mission was impossible. Which, if you knew my sister, only ensured her determination to go. May I have some wine?" said Calstir.

Dagstyrr went over to the table of drinks. *No, lad, only water, remember?* Dagstyrr heard the captain's voice in his head reminding him, though it wasn't necessary. He nodded and poured fresh water into a silver wine goblet.

Calstir took it gratefully and sipped. When he tasted water instead of wine, he looked somewhat embarrassed. Dagstyrr politely ignored him. "You see, Earl Magnus," said Calstir, "I lie even now. You should know we cannot be allowed wine or mead. Water only, as your youngest has just reminded me, again."

He raised the goblet in salute to Dagstyrr.

"There is much to learn, Father," said Dagstyrr. "Captain Bernst and his crew will teach you. They've done this before."

"We served mead to all four of you earlier," said Earl Magnus.

"It was water, Father."

"I suspect that's why we became so...feisty," said Calstir, drinking his water. "What you have to understand is, all we want is...is the poison that made us this way."

"Dragon's blood. Say it!" said Dagstyrr, thinking of Drago.

"Dragon's blood," said Calstir with a sneer, his bright blue eyes fixed on Dagstyrr.

Calstir's inability to hide his contempt for humans or dark fae was verging on the rude. At least he was confining his looks of distaste to Dagstyrr and not Earl Magnus. To insult a lord, even a human lord, in his own hall was unforgivable. Dagstyrr stood his ground as Bernst had taught him to do.

Princess Astrid shuddered. "How did Princess Rella find Captain Bernst and persuade him to take her to Hedabar? Dark fae captains are not known for their generosity. I hate to imagine what price they're expecting from us."

Dagstyrr cringed, knowing Captain Bernst was still in

the hall listening to every word. A glance his way found the captain grinning. He was more used to this attitude than Dagstyrr. "Mother, only Rella can tell you this part of the story," he said, still curious himself as to how she managed it.

"It's true, Astrid," said Calstir, "you can just imagine my shock when she turned up outside my cell one night."

"I'm surprised she survived the encounter," said Princess Astrid.

Calstir sighed. "You have no idea what a poor state I was in, dear Lady."

"Mother, don't press your point. Anyone in those cells would be absurdly grateful to be thrown a lifeline," said Dagstyrr.

Calstir stared into the flames. "Death. That is what we prayed for. Every captive there prays day and night for death. Weeks, months went by, and still, we lived. Too weak even to kill ourselves, and believe me, we all tried." He sipped his water.

The only sound to be heard was the crackle of the logs in the fireplace. Dagstyrr hoped he'd say more. Perhaps then his mother would understand Rella's terrible choice.

Dagstyrr held his breath. Just as he was about to break the silence, Calstir took up his tale of woe.

"You probably wonder why we didn't refuse to eat, starve ourselves to death. As a method of suicide, it's not recommended, but it works," said Calstir, his voice a low rumble.

"The thought had crossed my mind," said Earl Magnus.

"We didn't eat the food for nourishment. We ate it for the dragon's blood in it."

Earl Magnus looked puzzled. "Couldn't the older captives warn the new ones not to eat the food and therefore not become addicted in the first place?"

Calstir threw back his head and laughed, tears streaming down his noble face. Princess Astrid glanced at her husband then her son. Distressed at seeing Prince Calstir behaving like a human tavern drunk, she appeared unsure of how to proceed. Not that anyone other than immediate family could tell she was so affected.

When at last he was under control, Calstir said, "Dragon's blood, the stuff of legends supposed to cure every ill. You can buy it at any fair or market throughout the world, right? Wrong! The real stuff calls to you like a siren to the rocks. The first morsel the vizier fed to us in the banqueting hall entered our pathetic bodies, and we were his. By the time we passed out in our cells, we were addicts. At first, we tried to resist it. But it was impossible. Eventually, we anticipated every meal laced with dragon's blood that passed through the bars."

"I don't understand. What did this vizier gain by keeping you?" asked Lord Magnus.

"A good question," said Calstir, turning to his host. "He drains us of our powers. He milks fae energy from us as surely as a maid milks a cow."

"Then he must be dark fae," said Astrid.

"No, Mother, I have it on good authority; he is human like me," interrupted Dagstyrr.

"How do you know, Dag?"

"Your son is correct. The monster that drains dragons of their blood to captivate the fae is human," said Calstir, sipping his water.

"He has dragons?"

"Oh, yes..."

"But why?" cried Astrid.

"Couldn't someone have stormed the place? There is not a castle or citadel that doesn't have a weakness," interrupted

Lord Magnus.

"And it took Princess Rella to find it, Father," answered Dagstyrr. "Her sacrifice was great, but so was the prize."

"You don't understand, Dagstyrr," said Calstir. "You're human. I'll never forget the shock of seeing those eyes and that mark through the bars of my cell. She used to be so perfectly beautiful. I was proud to have her as my sister."

"You should be more proud now. She is a warrior of great renown, and just as beautiful as ever she was. Don't you know the Halfenhaw motto? 'There is no greater honor than to sacrifice for others'" said Dagstyrr, pointing out the plaque over the fireplace.

"Humph," said Calstir, sipping slowly at his water.

As Dagstyrr watched the handsome prince a shiver ran up his spine. This powerful creature would never sacrifice for anyone.

CHAPTER 19

Scrambling off the bed, Rella paced the flagstone floor, willing her temper to abate. Part of her understood Earl Magnus's order and Dagstyrr's quick action to ensure her safety, but her warrior self still wanted to strike out at him. How dare he humiliate her like that?

Rella looked around Dagstyrr's rooms. No silks or lace here, more wood and leather. A human male's space. The large bed he'd so unceremoniously dumped her on smelled of fresh linen and Dagstyrr.

After some time, logic won out and she calmed down. She even managed a laugh at Dagstyrr's huffing and puffing to bring her up those stairs. He had forgotten the weight of a fae's magic was borne in their bones. She might look small and light, but she probably weighed as much as he did. She was a powerful fae and her magic was gaining in strength every day now. Since leaving Hedabar, she'd let it grow freely.

Besides, she was in no hurry to confront Princess Astrid anytime soon, especially after such a raw display of hatred. The wards guarding this place were Astrid's. Rella could feel the mother-love protections, so strong and vital, surrounding the tower. Taking them down would take time, even for Astrid. Rella would have plenty of warning if she came after her. No doubt that was why Earl Magnus insisted Dagstyrr bring her here. Hopefully, Dagstyrr and Calstir could talk some sense into Astrid.

She liked Dagstyrr's father. He was intuitive and very handsome, and his red hair fascinated her. Only humans had red hair, and even then, rarely. Apart from that, he looked like an older version of Dagstyrr. No doubt human father and human son had a special bond in this fae family.

Rella wandered into a well-appointed bathing room. It tempted her sorely. She stood very still and took stock of the wards guarding these rooms, searching for any weaknesses. As she'd thought, they were strong and would give her warning if anyone, even Astrid or Dagstyrr, were to approach. Besides, she had the feeling Dagstyrr was going to spend half the night talking to his parents.

Unable to resist, she laid her armor carefully on a chest in the bedroom and undressed before turning on the four taps protruding from the wall in the white-tiled room.

How luxurious. Rella hadn't had a shower in months. Throwing her head back, she let the warm water flow over her. She pulled fresh energy from the water, which she knew instinctively to be from a spring. It felt good to replenish her powers from it. Reaching for the soap, she lathered herself down in a woody scent that reminded her of whose shower this was.

With her long hair up in a white towel, she dried herself off, then stood naked in front of a full-length mirror. It was the first time she'd dared to look at herself like this since acquiring the mark. She'd only ever seen bits and pieces of it.

Turning slowly, she saw it twist and turn from its root on her calf up to the small explosion on her cheek. It was huge, but she knew that. Why weren't Dagstyrr and the crew of the *Mermaid* disgusted by it?

Touching her hand to the brown mark blossoming on the side of her face, she remembered his kiss and the heat it had brought. Did he really not mind it? What did he see when he looked at her? Turning once more, she watched her reflection in the mirror. It grew like a living thing. The roots on her calf gave way to a bulb on her thigh then sprouted around her waist, across her back, and over her shoulder to land on her face in the vague shape of a flower. In some bizarre, way she liked it. It wasn't nearly as disfiguring as she'd imagined.

Light fae would never accept it though. They spent their lives amid perfection. Even if she could hide it, she could never hide her brown eyes. Sadly, she removed the towel from her hair and used her magic to dry it. The contrast of her fae-blonde hair to her dark eyes was something Dagstyrr found attractive. Rella didn't understand that at all. The contrast was too harsh. At best, she looked like a human girl with dyed hair and a flower painted on her face. That was how she'd managed to enter Hedabar—as a disfigured human.

Rella stepped into the other room. Dagstyrr must have some garment she could borrow. She found a white shirt that reached almost to her knees. That would do. Looking around the room, she noted his display of weapons covering a large expanse of wall. Another wall displayed his books on dark wooden shelves that reached halfway up to the ceiling.

Rella went over and read some of the titles, surprised to see many fae tutorials there. These were used to teach light fae children how to use and control their magic. It was never as easy as the adults made it look. With three fae brothers, he must have been curious growing up. Tucked at the end of his tutorials, she found a small, leather-bound book of poetry. Opening the cover, she saw a dedication:

> *To my very special boy, Dagstyrr, on the occasion of his tenth birthday, with all my love. Your mother in fae, Astrid.*

Typical light fae speak for, "Happy birthday, son."

Surprised by her internal criticism of light fae, Rella concluded she'd lived away from her own kind too long. It was one thing to identify with others when you were trying to deceive or when you were relying on them for your safety, but Rella would have to return to Casta soon. With her brother by her side, hopefully she'd be accepted. The quicker she was able to put her experiences with dark fae and humans behind her, the better—and that included Dagstyrr.

She took the poetry book and sat on a window seat overlooking the vast forest of Halfenhaw. From its well-thumbed pages, she could tell this was a favorite of Dagstyrr's. As she read, the scent of cedar and fir drifted in on the breeze, refreshing her spirit. These were not the epic poems you'd associate with a ten-year-old boy. These were ballads. Rella settled back to read the tales told in stunning verse. Her imagination took flight at the wonderfully simple, yet exquisitely crafted words used to tell each tale.

Lulled into a sense of relaxed comfort, she replaced the little book and got into the large bed. But once she was there, sleep eluded her. She had to get Calstir well enough to claim his throne. Only then could her fate be decided.

She prayed his confidence in his ability to persuade the court would be proved right.

A tear slipped down her face. Was she delusional to think there was even a chance that the court would tolerate her? Calstir had assured her he could convince them to accept her. She knew he was a very powerful and very persuasive fae. Perhaps she should trust him.

Only he could guarantee peace in Casta. He'd trained for this role his whole life, and putting him on the throne must be her priority. She had no choice but to take things one dangerous step at a time.

∼

Rella awoke to an awareness that she hadn't slept so soundly in many years. A feeling of wellbeing filled her. Then she felt skin beneath her hand—not her own, but hard-muscled skin. She opened her eyes to find herself tucked snugly against a sleeping, naked Dagstyrr.

Vague memories flooded back of her raising a hand of welcome to him when he returned last night. She hadn't meant to invite him to her bed.

Her hand rested on his bare chest as he lay on his back both hands raised above his head not touching her. Ye gods! Her leg was hooked around his. She could feel the hair of his thigh against her inner thigh. What had she done?

Just as she was about to move away, his arm came down and pulled her closer, his other hand landed gently on her head where it stroked her hair. "I'm here, don't cry, Princess, it'll be our secret," mumbled Dagstyrr in his sleep.

What did he mean, "don't cry"? She never cried, he must be dreaming. Fully alert now, Rella thought back to the night before, but she had no recollection of anything.

Trailing her finger along the ridge of a rib, she hoped to wake him gently. If he'd just lift his hands over his head again, she could slide out of the bed.

Dagstyrr lifted his hand off her head and scratched his rib where she'd tickled him. Before he could replace his hand, Rella slid away from him, careful not to let his other hand fall. As she slipped out of bed, Dagstyrr turned in his sleep, dragging all the covers with him. Good.

Beams of sunlight shone through the window. He would be rising soon she guessed, though she had no idea what time he'd come to bed. Gods, was she really thinking about him coming to her bed? Rella crept toward the bathing room, where she found a pale green gown and a note from Princess Astrid asking to see her as soon as she awoke.

Rella turned on the shower and made quick work of making herself presentable. She would see Astrid. She'd even wear the beautiful green apology gown given in true light fae style. Then she'd speak to Calstir and Captain Bernst about getting out of here and home to Casta as fast as the *Mermaid* could take them.

She checked her braid in the mirror, noting the flower shape of her mark yet again. Every time she saw it, she thought of Dagstyrr's kiss. Nothing had happened last night. She was sure of that now. But she'd slept in his arms, clung to him even. What was it about him that made her feel so secure?

On overnight missions, she'd slept with others, but they were fae. They understood the rules. Fae mated for life, so until they were ready to make that commitment, they kept a rein on their passions. Besides, males were cautious around princesses. She'd had her moments of fun, but never taken it too far.

Dagstyrr was different. He didn't know the rules.

Thankfully, he was too honorable to take advantage of her. It was ironic that his presence comforted her like nothing else. With him at her side, she felt she could take on the world.

With a quick glance in the mirror, she opened the door and collided with a large human chest. Dagstyrr stood with an arm on either side of the door, making it impossible for her to leave.

She couldn't use her magic here, or her weapons. Astrid's wards saw to that.

"Good morning, Rella. Did you sleep well?" he said, grinning down on her.

To her horror, Rella felt heat rush through her veins. "Very well, as it happens. Though I was surprised to have company when I awoke."

"It is my bed, and you didn't object last night. In fact..."

"A gentleman would have made alternative arrangements," she said.

"Ah, I've never claimed to be a gentleman. A knight, yes. Human, definitely, I think it was the human in me who came home last night and found the most beautiful girl in the world in my bed, and reaching for me. Who was I to complain?" he said, his dark blue eyes sincere.

"Still, it wasn't fair. You took advantage."

"I can assure you, Your Highness, I did not," said Dagstyrr.

"I know that."

"Oh, then you remember it all, then?"

"Not exactly," said Rella, refusing to be defeated. "Will you please let me go?" She indicated the dress she wore. "Your mother wants to meet with me."

"I'm coming with you."

"The invitation was for me," she said.

"I don't need to be invited into my mother's presence. I'm going with you," said Dagstyrr, heading for the waterspouts.

Turning away as water sounded on the tiles, Rella said, "I'll see you there, then." She refused to argue with him. As she was learning, it was usually a waste of time. Rella hoped that she and Astrid would have finished their business before Dagstyrr arrived.

She crossed the floor of his chamber, breathing in his unique scent. As her hand reached toward the iron handle of the studded oak door, Rella felt her fingers move as if encased in a stiff gel. A time-warp spell!

Too late.

Dagstyrr stood beside her fully dressed, a warm grin making his deep blue eyes sparkle. "I put that on last night as a precaution. I've been known to sleep soundly, and I didn't want you leaving me in the night."

"You held me prisoner?"

"No. I merely protected you while I slept," said Dagstyrr, reasonably.

"How can you post wards or spells? You're human."

Dagstyrr's grin widened. "You've never heard a human girl cast a spell at Samhain or Beltane?"

"That's different."

"No, it's the same. When we humans cast, we do it without power of our own. The spirits of the earth decide whether to grant our wish or not," he said.

"You don't seriously expect me to believe that. Your mother had a hand in this," said Rella, testing the texture of the spell.

"Well, yes, of course she did," he conceded. "Rella, everything I've done since landing is for your protection. I'm trying to make light of things, but you appear determined to see only the dark."

She looked into his serious eyes, so beautiful and so confused. "I was right, though, wasn't I? Your mother's reaction was just as I predicted."

"Yes, but Father and I handled it, didn't we?"

"You did." *But who will handle the whole court?* She wasn't sure Calstir was up to it.

"Are you ready to go?" he said, reaching over and opening the door for her.

After weeks alone in Hedabar, Rella couldn't help but enjoy his protective attitude, but she mustn't get used to it, let it weaken her. They passed down the steps of the tower and into the bailey, then out the gates to a field where Princess Astrid had erected a pavilion in which breakfast was being served.

The sun shone steadily from the east, and birdsong filled the air as they made their way across an open field of wildflowers. With each step, Rella felt the earth warm and welcoming underfoot. Since she'd turned dark, the earth renewed her energy far better than it ever had before. It was something Rella would get used to, but for now, it was a novelty. She'd like to walk the grounds of Halfenhaw alone, in peace, to soak up the gifts of the earth—perhaps barefoot.

She noticed Captain Bernst sitting with his back against a tree at the edge of the field. He understood what she was feeling. She gave him a nod, which he returned.

Earl Magnus's bright hair caught the sunshine as he left the pavilion with a smile to greet her. She'd expected to meet with Astrid alone. Earl Magnus was no doubt there to protect his wife, as Dagstyrr was there for her. How silly. If she and Astrid attacked each other, neither human would be able to stop it, never mind survive it.

"Greetings of the morning, Princess Rella of Casta," said Astrid with a curtsey.

Rella responded with a deep curtsey of her own. "May the morning smile upon you, Princess Astrid, Lady of Halfenhaw," she said, and indicated the dress she wore, thus showing she'd accepted the apology.

Astrid nodded her acknowledgment of Rella's acceptance. No expression marred her perfectly beautiful face. It was all done in graceful, high light fae style. Only after this exchange did Astrid resume her seat at the table. Earl Magnus pulled a cushioned chair out for Rella. Dagstyrr nodded to his parents, then sat beside Rella.

The table was covered with a delicious assortment of pastries, meats, cheeses, fruits, juices, and milk puddings. Dagstyrr casually helped himself before passing plate after plate her way. Rella smiled. You'd think he hadn't eaten in weeks. The breakfast continued in silence until all four were finished eating.

"You want me gone from here," said Rella, opening the conversation.

"We are honored to have Prince Calstir and yourself as our guests, Princess Rella," said Earl Magnus. "However, we understand that his presence in Casta is most urgent."

"He is in no fit state to enter the court at Casta, Father," said Dagstyrr.

"There is also the problem of his healers. You would want them to stay here for the Halfenhaw brothers, do you not?" said Rella. "Whereas I fully intend to take his healers with me. We will have three more weeks journeying in which to work with Calstir before he must face the court."

"Those healers are mixed dark fae," said Astrid, regally. "I'm grateful for what they've done for my sons, but they are not Crystal Mountain healers."

Rella took a deep breath. "Yes. They are the only people on this earth who would help me rescue my brother. I trust them implicitly. I understand it is the fashion to deny their existence, but you have always known of them, Princess Astrid. Your husband has sailed with them many times, I'll warrant."

"Yes, it is sometimes necessary. Humans and dark fae help each other when it suits. However, I warned my sons never to have anything to do with them," said Astrid, throwing a glance at Dagstyrr. "I instructed them all to deny the existence of dark fae or their by-blows, lest their chattering attract dark fae to live on our shores."

"Yet, it is dark fae who have worked day and night to bring your sons to health. It is their ship which brought your precious sons home," said Rella.

"You paid them well, no doubt. Or is their price a fae princess?"

Dagstyrr stood. "Mother!"

Astrid stood and faced her son. "I apologize," she said before resuming her seat like a queen.

"What you don't understand, my son, is that there is only one creature alive capable of turning a light fae princess into that," she said, pointing at Rella, "and he does nothing for nothing."

Rella bit her tongue. She didn't want any mention of the Dark Emperor. She saw Dagstyrr turn toward her and smile before turning back to his mother. "Yes, there is always a price to pay, isn't there, Mother?"

"Where did you hear that? From her, I suppose. Well, what is the price? Tell me that, Princess Rella," said Astrid.

Rella put a hand to her throat scared of what she might say. Astrid understood far too much.

"You can damn well see the price," said Dagstyrr, his voice rising to meet his mother's.

"I think we should all just calm down." Earl Magnus's voice of reason cut across the table.

Once everyone was seated, Earl Magnus himself poured four cups of mead and passed them around the table. "Let's just deal with the more immediate problems first, shall we?" he offered.

Rella sipped the sweet liquor, leaning ever so slightly towards Dagstyrr's warm, protective energy.

"I have commissioned healers from the Crystal Mountain, they are most discreet and should arrive soon," said Astrid. "No need to bother the dark fae any longer."

At the mention of the Crystal Mountain healers Rella's heart skipped a beat. They were the last people she wanted to meet up with. If they found her, they'd want to subject her to their infernal testing. A light fae turned dark must pass their test or die. Rella feared it would mean death.

Then she heard the captain's voice in her head: *Ask her what her payment to the dark will be for the return of her three sons.* A small smile played on Rella's lips. She wished she'd thought of that herself.

Instead, Rella lifted a finely arched eyebrow. "What payment arrangement have you come to with the good captain?" she asked, and was suitably satisfied with the quick look of shock on Astrid's face.

"Don't worry, Princess Rella, he'll be well paid," assured Earl Magnus.

"I'm sorry, Mother," said Dagstyrr, who must have seen his mother's shock as well. "Captain Bernst and the *Mermaid*'s crew were hired to transport one addict: Prince Calstir. I should have thought to make an arrangement with him."

"You had other things on your mind, Dag," said Astrid.

Once again, Rella was struck by the love in Astrid's voice for her only human son. How much, wondered Rella, would she pay for the return of Dagstyrr?

"I will talk to Captain Bernst," said Earl Magnus.

"Then it is agreed, I will leave on the first tide as soon as Earl Magnus has agreed upon a price with Captain Bernst," said Rella.

"What will he ask for, do you think?" said Astrid.

Dagstyrr smiled. "Hard to say. A ship or two I should think. Perhaps, some gold. Don't worry, Mother, he'll not ask you to turn one of your sons to the dark."

"Dagstyrr, don't be so hard on me. We are trained from a very young age to avoid dark fae. If one of our own turns dark, we are taught to kill first and ask questions later. It is the one thing that will bring out the beast in us."

"I've never seen you like this, Mother. Captain Bernst is a puppy next to you," he said.

"You seem to know him well," said Astrid.

"I do. I owe Bernst my life and the lives of my three brothers." Dagstyrr's eyes darkened. "I have not repaid him well," he said, and Rella knew he was thinking of how he'd embroiled the *Mermaid*, her captain, and her crew in his promise to Drago.

"What do you mean?" said Astrid.

Not now. This is not the time to tell her about Drago, whispered Bernst in Rella's head. She glanced at Dagstyrr, one look and she knew he'd heard the captain as well.

"Just that, Mother. I haven't repaid him at all, except for the little gold I held on my person, which was not nearly sufficient." He hung his head. When he raised it again, raw pain ravaged his handsome face. "You have no idea how bad it was."

Astrid stood and went to her son. "I am so proud of you, Dag. We will see the captain well paid, have no fear."

Dagstyrr's eyes turned to Rella.

Astrid sighed, glancing Rella's way. "Very well, and Princess Rella will leave here safely with her brother as soon as the healers arrive from the Crystal Mountain." Everyone could see how much that promise cost her. She would never trust Rella.

"Princess, I have great sympathy for all you and your brother have suffered," said Astrid surprising everyone. "You understand better than most my reaction to your presence. I ask that you and Calstir leave our shores and never return, and I want your promise that you will never contact any of my family again."

Rella saw the battle Astrid waged with her instincts, and admired her for it. Dagstyrr had been right to lock her away in his rooms last night. Astrid was a danger to her, and she did not doubt that as soon as she left with Calstir, Astrid would consider her fair game should they ever meet again.

"Calstir, myself and Dagstyrr will leave immediately," said Rella.

"Aye, we'll sail on the next tide, Father," said Dagstyrr.

"What do you mean? You must stay here. She," said Astrid pointing at Rella, "she is nothing to you. Your brothers need you."

"They'll have the Crystal Mountain healers," said Dagstyrr softly. He stood and put his arm across her shoulders. "I have things to do, promises to fulfill."

At the word "promises," Astrid's energy spiked, causing sparks to tremble down her arms and dissipate in blue energy bursts from her fingers. "Tell me you haven't made promises to her?"

"No, Mother, not to Rella. She and I made a deal. I

carried Calstir out of the citadel, and she saved my brothers. Simple, and over with," said Dagstyrr taking her sparking hands in his, and letting the danger fall harmlessly to the earth at their feet.

Rella noticed that her energy didn't faze him or hurt him. It was all part of the ever-present protection against magic his mother had given him as a babe.

"To the dark fae, though?"

"No, you have my word of honor. I have made no promises to the dark fae," he said, lifting her hand and brushing it with his lips. "You taught me well."

"Then stay."

"I have other business to attend to. Then I will return. You do not need me to heal my brothers, and a man must keep his promises," he said, looking to his father.

Earl Magnus nodded.

"Then sail without her. Take one of your father's ships," said Astrid, determined to get her youngest son away from Rella.

Earl Magnus moved to her side and said to Dagstyrr, "Get her out of here, son. Keep her in your rooms and make ready for the afternoon tide."

"Yes, Father."

"My apologies, Princess Rella. I wish we had met under different circumstances. I believe you and my wife would have much in common if not for these sad events."

"Don't apologize for me, Magnus. You don't understand, but Rella does," said Astrid. Blue energy borne of fear for her son threatened at her fingertips.

Rella outranked Astrid, and she'd had enough of her self-righteous demands. If Rella couldn't persuade one light fae who hadn't lived at court for years that she was safe to be around, how was Calstir ever going to persuade them to accept her in Casta? It was time to show Astrid who she was dealing with.

Since landing in Halfenhaw, Rella's magic was blossoming, and so was her highly tuned ability to control it. She lifted her hand, letting her magic energy burst in small spurts from her fingers in green puffs of dark magic, perfectly under her control. "You're not the only one with a temper, Astrid."

Astrid laughed. "*Now, we see the darkness emerge, Those who turn dark, Will be eaten by darkness,*" she said. Astrid was so upset she misquoted the ancient prophecy, but her meaning was clear. Within seconds, Earl Magnus had his arms around his wife, forcing her hands to her sides and preventing her from unleashing magic. If she released her magic energy now, it would kill him.

"The rhyme isn't true. I have no desire to kill. In fact, I'd say I am more in control than you are," said Rella, sending a puff of green to persuade a rosebud on the table to bloom.

"Of course you would say that," said Astrid. "Magnus let me go. I will not harm our guest."

Only another fae could understand the simple blooming of a rose was far more complex than some dramatic demonstration. It required sensitivity, skill, and control. She saw doubt in Astrid's face. Given time, perhaps Calstir could persuade the court after all.

Captain Bernst chose that moment to approach the pavilion. His worn leather clothes and weapons were in stark contrast to those watching his approach. He walked confidently across the green toward the highly decorated tent. When Rella saw him, she smiled. She hoped he'd ask for Astrid's jewelry. It would serve her right.

CHAPTER 20

Dagstyrr's departure from Halfenhaw was painful. He'd always been close to his parents. Now, the family was in trouble, and he was leaving. Dagstyrr couldn't explain without telling them about Drago, and that would only add to their worries.

Always a price to pay, and service to Drago was Dagstyrr's.

His conscience pricked him whenever he thought of Drago suffering in the depths of the citadel. However, the dragon rescue was a journey from which he might never return. Which was why he had to make sure Rella was safe before he attempted it. The question was, how long would Drago remain patient?

Some unspoken pact drove everyone onboard the *Mermaid* to keep silent about the dragons. It would have been one more disappointment for his mother, and his father would probably insist on coming with him. That was the last thing he wanted. Earl Magnus was the guiding hand of Halfenhaw and was needed now more than ever.

No doubt his father was still smarting over the price

Captain Bernst had extracted from him for the safe return of the three light fae Halfenhaw sons. He had indeed asked for ships, two of them, the *Knucker* and the *Viper*, along with weapons and gold.

Had the *Mermaid* mentioned to Bernst that those two ships were Earl Magnus's favorites?

Earl Magnus had promised to hand them over to Captain Bernst on his return from Casta. Both longships were up north but would be home by then. Bernst would have to crew them himself, which given the gold he'd extracted from Magnus, shouldn't be a problem. To give him his due, his father hadn't bargained, but agreed to pay the price immediately. Dagstyrr watched from the stern as his parents grew smaller on the dock, their hands still lifted in farewell.

Three very tall Crystal Mountain healers stood behind them, white, gauzy garments lifting on the breeze, white hair reaching to their knees. Even their eyebrows were white, yet their faces were ageless with the palest light fae eyes Dagstyrr had ever seen, their crystal-blue gazes missing nothing.

He had no idea how the healers had arrived so quickly at Halfenhaw from the Crystal Mountain. He'd heard one mention "unique circumstances."

Captain Bernst had assured them that the healer monks couldn't use their magic against anyone who was on the *Mermaid*. Her protective magic was very ancient, and she'd use it to shield Rella. Besides, if they could, they'd want to study the *Mermaid* just as they would Rella.

Rella had retired to her cabin as soon as she boarded. Her confrontations with Astrid must have left her a lot to ponder. He knew it wasn't going to be easy for her to enter Casta with brown eyes and that mark on her face. She was strong. She'd be undeterred by small slights from the courtiers, but he knew she expected so much worse.

Because light fae spent most of their lives suppressing their feelings, any demonstration of extreme emotion forced theirs to the surface. When that happened, strong passions fueled their thoughts and actions, and they didn't deal with it well. They relied on their indoctrination to guide them, striking out before asking questions. It would take only one person to crack and physically attack her, and then the ever-so-civilized court would devolve into a mob and tear her limb from limb. She knew it, and he knew it.

If anything was going to spark such a debacle, it was a light fae turned dark.

Even so, Rella trusted Calstir to convince the court she was the exception, and that they would welcome her home. Well, they'd soon find out. Dagstyrr was determined to be by her side when she entered the court.

A white mist rolled down off the wooded hills, and Dagstyrr's home disappeared behind it. With a sigh, he strode down the deck of the ship to reach the prow and greet the *Mermaid*. How quickly, he thought, such things become routine. He would no more think of boarding without greeting the *Mermaid* than he would enter his mother's chambers without greeting her.

With a small bow, he said, "How are you, my dear?"

A light laugh echoed around the prow. *Better for seeing you, Dagstyrr of Halfenhaw. Nice boots!*

"Why thank you. The best cobbler in town fashioned them from the best leather he could find," said Dagstyrr with a laugh of his own. It was good to talk about inconsequential things. The fine breeze ruffling his hair brought no solace with it, only a reminder of what dangers Rella was sailing into.

His mind turned again and again to the memory of her snuggled against him in his bed, her soft skin and the scent of roses clinging to him while she slept. He'd never seen her so vulnerable as when she wept in her sleep.

Your heart is heavy, Dagstyrr.

"I am concerned for my friend."

You haven't told her you love her?

"She has more pressing matters on her mind."

And that means you do too.

"Of course," said Dagstyrr, wondering why he could talk so easily to the *Mermaid*. Truth be told, Dagstyrr didn't trust Calstir. He treated his sister like a loyal retainer, and retainers were expendable to princes.

Stay by her side. Don't let her out of your sight for even a moment. The closer she is to you, the safer she is. If you can, insist she sleep here in her cabin when we dock. That is all the advice I have for you.

"It is good advice. I fully intend to stay by her side. Not sure I'll be much protection against a whole hall full of light fae though."

You underestimate yourself, Dagstyrr of Halfenhaw. Your mother's love runs deep in you and protects you even when you don't realize it.

"Yes, I know it protects me. I learned that from Rella at Hedabar, but I'm not sure how it would work against hundreds of light fae. Besides, it protects me, not Rella," said Dagstyrr, wondering how their conversation had managed to go from boots to fighting light fae in such a short time. "Why is Calstir back in the cage?" he said in an effort to change the subject.

I insisted. He is too unstable to be granted the freedom of the ship. In this confined space, his frustrations are amplified, and he is a very dangerous man. You think of him as an addict, but never forget he is one of the most powerful light fae in existence. If he decides to change things around here to suit his will, he has the power to do so. No, we still need the wards over the cage for everyone's sake.

"I hope he recovers before we reach Casta."

He'll never be the same, Dagstyrr, remember that. However, I have high hopes for him. He is a very determined man.

"I never knew him before, so I'm not able to judge whether he is the same or not. I hope for Rella's sake that he is sufficiently improved before he must face the royal court."

Sometimes addicts can surprise you, and he's a fighter if ever I saw one.

Later, Dagstyrr sat patiently, cross-legged, beside the cage containing the fae prince. Inside, Calstir, no longer confined to a hammock, lounged upon a blue silk daybed, his blonde fae hair pooling on the floor. His eyes were closed, but his hands moved as if he directed something in the air.

Fascinated, Dagstyrr wondered what on earth was happening in Calstir's tormented sleep. Dagstyrr understood the creature inside this cage was probably the most dangerous he'd ever encounter. Calstir could defeat an opponent with magic as if the matter were of no consequence. No emotion would show on his aristocratic face.

This was the being Dagstyrr needed to influence. He could not leave for Hedabar until he knew for sure Rella was safe, and only Calstir could protect her once he was gone.

At last, he saw the prince stir. It was now or never. He had to make Calstir see that Rella was in real danger if she went to court, and that she was far safer staying with Dagstyrr on the *Mermaid*. Rella would defy Dagstyrr but, with Calstir behind him, she might stay put.

"Good evening, Prince Calstir," said Dagstyrr.

The man opened his bright blue eyes and ran a glance over Dagstyrr. "How long have you been there?" he demanded.

"Awhile," answered Dagstyrr.

"I thought I detected strange energy. I wasn't sleeping," he said, moving to a sitting position. "The Crystal Mountain healers were kind enough to teach me some magical meditations. Supposed to bring my energies back to their proper alignment. Speed up the healing."

"I didn't mean to distract you," said Dagstyrr.

"Well?" said the prince, wiping a hand over his long face.

"I want to talk to you about Rella. About keeping her on board once we reach Casta."

"She'll be by my side," said Calstir. "I will present her as a hero."

Dagstyrr momentarily closed his eyes. The man's arrogance was astonishing. "They'll tear her to pieces," he said quietly.

"She's my sister. They wouldn't dare."

"My mother nearly killed her—twice."

"Princess Astrid is a lovely creature, but a bit emotional. Comes from living with humans. The court is quite different," said Calstir, speaking as if to an ignorant child.

Dagstyrr's hands fisted, and it took all his willpower to unclench them. "What if..." He nearly said *you're wrong* which would be a disaster. Calstir wouldn't talk to him at all then.

"What if what?" said Calstir yawning.

"What if someone does take offense? I might be able to protect her from one or two light fae, but certainly no more. If one or two attack her, others will follow," said Dagstyrr quickly, trying to get his point across before Calstir dismissed him entirely.

Calstir threw back his head and laughed. "You. Protect her? You couldn't protect her for a second. Even the youngest page at court could kill you like that." He snapped his fingers.

Dagstyrr knew he was wasting his time, but perhaps he could give the prince something to think about. "You're right, of course. It would be a sad and ignominious end to the man and woman who carried you out of the citadel."

"I'm not ungrateful, Dagstyrr of Halfenhaw, and I did save you and your brothers at the dockside. Many people were involved in my escape, but my sister must be the one to take full credit. After all," he said, moving a royal hand to tap the side of his face, "she's the one paying the price."

"Do you think that will be sufficient to sway the court into accepting her condition?"

"Not all of them, certainly."

"Mmm, it's a pity you can't do that before you present her. Explain her noble sacrifice, and love for her brother and country. Give people time to get used to the idea. Give yourself a chance to present her at just the right moment for the biggest impact," said Dagstyrr, watching Calstir take in every word. He'd sown the seed. Now he must step away, and let the idea germinate. "Sleep well, Prince. I've taken too much of your time."

"I enjoyed it. Come again, bring some wine..."

"I will come again, Your Highness," said Dagstyrr, ignoring the request for wine. It could just have been the prince's habit to call for wine, but he doubted it. The addiction still had a hold. And, unfortunately, Calstir didn't understand the danger that awaited Rella at court.

∼

Rella snuggled in her cabin, listening to the sounds of the ship around her. Since being ousted from Halfenhaw by the quick arrival of the Crystal Mountain healers, Dagstyrr was giving her some space and time to think. She smiled, he sometimes knew what she needed before she did. Which gave her precious time to revise her plans.

Her short time at Halfenhaw had brought one too many shocks. First, there was Princess Astrid's vicious reaction to her. Rella had reeled when she had started to quote the prophecy about madness. Hearing it spoken aloud by a fae princess brought her worst fears to the fore.

Secondly, to find that after weeks of work to bring her magic energies back up after Hedabar, it looked like green pond scum. When she'd transformed the rose it had taken her aback. Thankfully, no one had noticed her shock. Rella shuddered at the memory of the disgusting green color where once there would have been bright blue. Was this the first part of the prophecy coming true?

A treacherous tear slipped down her face, and she swiped it away. She was doomed. The court would never accept her. Even if they paid lip service to Calstir's request to hail her as a hero, sooner or later, in some dark corner of the court, they'd attack.

She must see Calstir crowned, then leave as quickly as she could before the Dark Emperor arrived to exact his payment from her.

Rella recognized Dagstyrr's comforting energy approaching. By the time he knocked and entered, she'd dried all vestiges of tears and greeted him with a smile. "It must be suppertime," she said.

"It is," replied Dagstyrr, holding open the door for the

sailors to deposit their dishes of meat stew and fresh bread on the low table. His bulk and human male energy filled the small space bringing the comfort only he could give.

They ate in companionable silence, but Rella saw a frown mar his brow whenever he thought she wasn't looking. *He is deeply troubled*, she thought.

"I like your home. Halfenhaw is very beautiful," she said, trying to draw him out. "I would be sad to leave it too."

"Oh, we'll be returning to pick up the *Viper* and *Knucker* as soon as we've taken Calstir to Casta," he answered.

"Earl Magnus will be sad to lose those ships, but they are a small price to pay," said Rella.

"Really? I thought it high," he said, surprised.

"I believe your father would pay anything for the safe return of his sons," said Rella, thrown off guard at his stance.

"You brought them out of the citadel. Calstir saved them at the docks. I know we were an inconvenience to Bernst, but he was passing this way anyway. I think the price is high."

"The price is always higher than you think," said Rella, quietly.

"Pardon?" said Dagstyrr, unable to hear her murmur.

"You forget the healing and extra work your brothers gave his crew, never mind the wards necessary to keep us all safe."

"I don't suppose my promise to Drago had anything to do with it?" He frowned and chewed on a piece of meat.

Rella laughed. "Drago has everything to do with it."

Dagstyrr turned, moving closer to her, his blue eyes boring deep into her soul.

Rella wanted nothing more than to surrender to that angry, confused energy and let it wash away the despair rooted in her soul. "Why do you think Captain Bernst wants those ships, gold to pay for crews, and weapons to arm them?"

"Drago?"

"Exactly."

"So it is my fault."

"Don't feel so sorry for yourself," she said. "The price is a small one. Even if your father is smarting at it now."

"He was happy to pay the price. It is me who thinks it is too much. If I fail to rescue Drago, the price will be far greater. Ten generations greater."

"You won't fail," said Rella, pretending confidence she didn't feel. He mustn't sense her despair. It would only add to his troubles. She leaned back and brought out another bottle of Samish wine.

Without thinking, she used magic to open it; energy the color of forest evergreens curled around the bottle and was gone.

He must have seen her distress, for he leaned over and covered her hand with his. "It's only a color."

"I suppose I must get used to it," she said, taking comfort not from his words, but from the warmth of his hand touching hers.

"So, what's the plan?" said Dagstyrr.

"What do you mean?"

"I know you well enough to know you like to plan meticulously. You know the chances of Calstir convincing the court to allow you to stay are infinitesimal. So, what's the contingency plan?" He kept hold of her hand and played her fingers through his. She seemed calmer when he was close to her.

"I keep hoping, but I know it won't happen," said Rella, allowing herself to be vulnerable. "Trouble is, I don't have a contingency plan, at least not one worth pursuing."

"Your brother is very sure of his powers of persuasion."

"He's still under the influence of dragon's blood. He calls for wine and mead, knowing it hinders his recuperation. The effect of strong drink brings back a tiny echo of the euphoria of dragon's blood. It is truly pitiful. I wish you'd known him before all this," said Rella with a sigh. She leaned her head against Dagstyrr's shoulder. His arm came around her as if it was the most natural thing in the world.

"Have you spoken to Drago?" she said, purposely changing the subject.

"No, and I think that's strange. I'm not sure whether he's waiting for me to contact him or whether he cannot reach me now that I'm so far away."

"He can reach you."

"How can you be sure?"

"Talking to the *Mermaid*. She says he will wait for you to contact him. He's afraid that having found a dragon-talker after all these years, his fire will destroy you before you become accustomed to it."

"Poor thing. I admit, I'm not looking forward to the pain," said Dagstyrr. Every time he thought of Drago, his fear lessened, and his sympathy increased. It was only a matter of time before he'd have to test their connection again.

Rella yawned. "Excuse me," she said.

"You are tired. I should go," said Dagstyrr, not moving.

"Don't go."

She felt him relax against the cushions, then tense. "If you want me to sleep here, I will, but I need to know the rules."

Rella's breath caught in her chest. The idea of him beside her night after night was so tempting. She fit so snugly against his warm body. "I want you close. I sleep better when you're near, but sleep is all I am offering you," she said, steeling herself for rejection.

"I understand. Fae mate for life. It is not something to take lightly. I tell you what, I will sleep here on the cushions with you behind the curtains. Near, but not too near," he said.

"Are you sure you won't want..."

"I'm sure I will want." He laughed. "But haven't I already proven I won't take advantage of you?"

"Yes," she said remembering the feel of his leg beneath her thigh, his hand holding her head close on his shoulder.

"Make no mistake. I want you, Rella, but not until you decide you want me too. For it will be for life." Her heart skipped a beat. She knew she shouldn't allow him so close, but her desire to feel secure and safe in his arms was strong.

CHAPTER 21

The next couple of weeks, everyone's focus was on Calstir and his recovery. Except for Captain Bernst and Billy, the whole crew worked with Calstir continuously. Those with healing magic used it, those without saw to the more practical elements of his therapy.

The meditations the Crystal Mountain healers had taught him were working to bring back his magic, and calm his spirit. Yet, just as Rella saw the prince start to emerge, something would irritate him and the addict took over again.

After that first night aboard when Rella and Dagstyrr had fallen asleep in each other's arms, Dagstyrr had taken to sleeping in her cabin on the cushions used for seating during the day. Rella slept behind a curtain on her bed, but if she needed his strength in the night, she only needed to stretch out her hand to touch him. It was enough, for now.

Though some nights she found it hard not to tear down the flimsy barrier separating them.

She dreaded reaching Casta, yet perversely she drove the captain and his crew to get them there as fast as the

Mermaid could manage. If she died bringing Calstir to the throne in Casta, at least it would be for a good cause.

One evening, after falling exhausted into her cabin and sharing a simple meal of soup and bread with Dagstyrr, she caught him watching her. "What? What is it?"

"You don't want to reach Casta, do you?"

He said it as if it had only just dawned on him, and Rella flinched at his perception. That was precisely what she'd been thinking at that very moment. "Of course I do."

"No, you don't. What awaits you in Casta? What are you not telling me?"

"Nothing awaits me in Casta, and I do want to get there," she said.

"No, you don't. There is a little muscle, right there," said Dagstyrr, almost touching his finger to her forehead. "It twitches whenever Casta is mentioned. Tell me."

Rella looked at him—so human, so male—knowing he'd never truly understand. "I promise there is nothing in Casta I fear, apart from the obvious. I don't want to talk about it."

"Very well," said Dagstyrr, leaning back into the cushions.

His proximity brought memories of his touch flooding back. He'd never again kissed her, only that once and almost absentmindedly. Yet she'd slept in his arms and found comfort in his presence. Was he scared she'd shy away if he kissed her again, kissed her properly?

Rella quickly banished those thoughts. If he could read her as well as he appeared to, then the last thing she wanted was for him to know how deeply she was starting to depend on his comforting presence. Soon the time would come to pay the real price, and he must be gone from her before that happened, or she might not have the strength to see it through. She might not be able to do it anyway. In which case she'd become a hunted outcast for the rest of her life.

He took her hand. "Are you sure Casta holds no danger for you, Princess?"

"Don't you think it's bad enough as it is? I will have to face the whole court looking like this. Even if they do accept me, they'll still whisper behind my back. There will be no more young warriors vying to enter my cohort."

"I want you to stay on board with me when we reach Casta," he said, his eyes capturing hers.

"I cannot hide forever."

"No, but you can give your brother time to prepare the court."

"He said something about that yesterday after we meditated together. I didn't pay too much attention," said Rella, feeling her anger mount. "I'd rather get it over with. If they attack me, let them. I'll die for Casta."

"Why are you so determined to 'die for Casta'? I'm not sure whether that would be classed as defiant or stupid."

She slapped away his hand. "Don't you dare call me stupid. You know nothing. Nothing!"

Dagstyrr gripped her shoulders. "Then tell me. I can't protect you from something I don't know about. What is it, Rella? What has you so frightened that you'd rather die than face it?"

His blue eyes sparked with fury, yet she sensed the protective energy in him. The safety of his arms enveloped her even while he railed at her. He trembled with frustration. Rella had never seen a man so angry. If he were fae, light or dark, she'd be dead by now, but Dagstyrr managed to keep his emotions in check, if barely. "Tell me, woman," he commanded, hoarsely.

"Woman." She'd never been called that by anyone. It

was enough to push her over the edge. Tears threatened. She stepped into his embrace, surrendering at last to his strength. Feeling his arms gather her up and his hand push into her hair, so strong, so gentle. "If I tell, people will die," she whispered.

He held her there until the tears subsided and his shirt was wet with her anguish. "Tell me," he whispered in her hair.

Rella took a long, shuddering breath. "It's the price. The price I have to pay."

"I thought the mark and your dark eyes—which, by the way, are beautiful—were the price?" he said, gently stroking her hair.

"Not at all," she said.

"What, then?" Tension had returned to his voice, though she knew he was fighting hard to hide it.

"Do you know where I went for help when no one in Casta would help me?" she said, her voice, at last, starting to sound normal.

"You went to the dark fae," said Dagstyrr.

"But do you know to whom?"

She felt a ripple of shock run through him. "The Dark Emperor?"

"Who else?"

"By all the gods, lass, what promise did he extract from you?"

"For the gift of this mark," she said, touching her cheek, "and these brown eyes, there is a price to pay. You see, everyone thinks these are the price, but these are the gift I needed to enter Hedabar. I still have to pay the price." She rested her hand on his chest.

"Part of the price is that you can tell no one?"

"Yes," she said, quietly, feeling the warmth of him

through his linen shirt, and taking strength from it.

"How will telling cause people to die?"

"Because I have no intention of paying the price." Rella watched the implications dawn on him.

"There will be a terrible battle, and thousands on both sides will die. So you see, I must not tell," said Rella, a small sense of relief coming from having told even this much, yet she dared not say more. If her brother found out, he'd wage war against the Dark Emperor to protect her. A war between Casta and the Dark Emperor would plunge the whole world into a war that would rage for hundreds of years.

"What is he like?"

"Who?"

"The Dark Emperor," said Dagstyrr.

Rella sighed. "He reigns beyond the neutral Wild Forests that surround the edge of the mountains. He claims all the dark fae homelands. His palace is called Thingstyrbol. It is grand but very strange," said Rella.

"How strange?"

"It appears to be built of living things, trees mostly. There is rich, loamy life everywhere. Flowers sprout in odd places, moss hangs down in long strands, and lichens make their homes everywhere. The beams of his hall are all living trees. Many creatures live there, not just dark fae. The dryads still inhabit the trees that make up his palace. The stones of the floor are not broken and shaped, but as they originally formed, and chosen with care to form a cobbled floor."

"Strange indeed, as if he commands the living forest," said Dagstyrr.

"I think he does. Otherwise, how could his palace exist? Nature herself bows to him. Like I said, it is strange but beautiful."

"Beautiful?"

"Sunlight pours from a green canopy of leaves and dapples the place with light of many shades. At night the stars peek through and the moon shadows the corners, of which there are many. Everyone there worships him and understands his many moods. He doesn't hide his pleasure or his anger. With one wave of his hand, he can persuade a snowdrop to bloom or command an army dedicated to his will."

"Formidable," said Dagstyrr. "What does he look like?"

"He's taller than any creature in his empire, and he wears a high crown of dark living flora to emphasize his height. It changes from moment to moment, growing, dying, and spilling small creatures onto his cloak of leaves and feathers. His face is long and thin, his eyes the darkest you can ever imagine—dark and cruel."

"Is he battle trained?"

"I don't know."

"Yes, you do. Think, Rella, you are a warrior, so am I. We instinctively know another warrior when we meet one. It's in the way we move, the way we hold ourselves. Our eyes are always assessing those around us. Think about your audience with him and tell me: Is he a warrior?"

Rella took a deep breath and immersed herself in memories she'd spent months trying to forget. Her hand tightened in Dagstyrr's as images flooded in of the Dark Emperor's fluid movements when he crossed the floor to greet her. She saw again his feet light as air upon the stone, and his hands, elegantly expressive. Then, with a shudder, she remembered the eerie and immutable energy that was the Dark Emperor. She recalled the smell of rotting things, rising up to choke her. Felt her revulsion again as he studied her from head to foot. She couldn't forget the way his hand reached out and stroked her neck, her hip, his eyes constantly assessing her, his mouth too close and breathing into her hair, taunting her, until he smiled and nodded. *Very well, little Rella*, he'd finally agreed.

"Yes, yes he's battle trained," said Rella, her heart thundering in her chest.

"Pity."

"What do you mean?"

"Well, I was hoping for a fat jolly man spending his days dining on fruits and vegetation, with no hint of aggression," said Dagstyrr.

Rella tensed. "You are joking!"

"Of course I'm joking," said Dagstyrr, pulling her back into the comfort of his arms. "Is he taller than me?"

"Yes, by about a foot. Is that important?"

"Yes, he is at a disadvantage there. It's difficult to hide if you're head and shoulders above every other warrior in a battle. It will make him a target."

"I can't imagine him hiding. He is too arrogant. He'll direct the battle from a vantage point, letting his cohorts do the fighting for him until he sweeps in and, using his formidable magic, delivers the coup de grace."

"You can't know that, Rella, but I can tell you've imagined it many times. Now you see it almost as a memory. If you continue to do that it will become a prediction. You are manifesting war for Casta. For the battle you see before you is between Casta and the Dark Emperor's legions. Am I right?"

Silence followed as Rella absorbed his words. Eventually, she sat up and looked him in the eye. "You are right. That is what I see, but it is unfair to say I am manifesting it."

He took her hand in his. "Is it? You think battle is inevitable. Therefore, all your energies go to preparing for that battle," said Dagstyrr, serious now. "Without realizing it, you're manipulating others into position for battle as well. Eventually, they won't be able to help themselves."

"There may be more than one battle, Dagstyrr, but these are fae battles, and you are well out of it."

"I am not out of it."

"Of course you are. You must be. You have to rescue one hundred and sixty-eight dragons, not counting hatchlings or..."

"...or eggs," he joined in.

"I think that is enough for one human, even you," she said with a smile, leaning back against his chest.

"What other battle is your fae mind conjuring, Rella?"

Noticing he used neither "light" nor "dark" with "fae", Rella thought, *Only he understands me, but not well enough. How could he? We come from different worlds.*

"Come on, we need to plan your freedom. You know we do," said Dagstyrr, playing his fingers through hers, while a serious frown marred his forehead.

"Very well. One, if we arrive in Casta and one of the cousins has taken the throne we fight our own people to regain it. Two, if they accept me, which I very much doubt, the Dark Emperor will come to demand payment, and Casta will fight his legions. Three is the best scenario. We arrive in Casta and crown Calstir without a fight. Then I leave, drawing the Dark Emperor away from Casta and the light fae population."

"And you can't tell me what the payment is?"

"No."

"Well, I can guess. It is exactly what I would demand in payment if I were him," said Dagstyrr, his voice deep and dangerous as he pulled her tighter to him.

CHAPTER 22

Their arrival in Casta was greeted by a flotilla of smaller craft gaily waving flags and bunting to welcome them home. So, the Argan family had spread the word. It didn't look as though they had a fight on their hands after all. Calstir's throne awaited him. Rella sensed the relief flooding through those on board the *Mermaid*. The sun glinted off the water, adding sparkle to the shimmering castle and town covering the shore.

Rella wanted to rejoice. Her home was so beautiful it pulled at her heart, but if the court would not be persuaded, this might be as close as she ever got to it. Dressed in her uniform, Rella stood at the prow as they swept into the harbor. She'd used a mixture of flour and a tan-colored spice to hide the mark on her face, but there was nothing anyone could do about her eyes. The Dark Emperor himself had changed them, and no fae could countermand his spell. Captain Bernst refused to even try, and he had stronger magic than any other dark fae on board.

Bernst was right, of course. The minute anyone tried to

interfere, the Dark Emperor would know and come rushing to her side. That was the last thing she wanted.

Calstir insisted Dagstyrr accompany him as protection instead of Rella. She was glad to give her brother time to prepare the court before she ventured into Casta. With her promise to stay on board, she'd persuaded Dagstyrr to leave her side, but not before he'd extracted Bernst's promise not to let her out of his sight.

When she saw Dagstyrr in his bright armor and helmet and his white cloak snapping in the breeze, she felt absurdly proud. As escort to Calstir, he looked the part. No doubt the people of Casta would be shocked at a human being given such an honor, but Calstir planned to tell the court the tale of Dagstyrr carrying their prince from the citadel. That would meet with their approval.

In return, she'd promised to stay on board under the pretext of guarding the *Mermaid* and her crew. Though mixed-blood dark fae were tolerated in Casta, they were never genuinely welcome, and stayed aboard their vessels.

If all went well, Dagstyrr was to return and accompany her to the court. She knew that was unlikely. Yet she hoped that by some miracle, Calstir could persuade them. Rella longed to set foot on Casta, to feel again the energy of her home. Every moment she sat on board, she imagined the Dark Emperor getting closer.

Rella was pinning all her hopes on Calstir. Could he convince the court she was not some mad, dangerous creature to be destroyed?

He alone knew the full extent of her promise to the Dark Emperor, and only he could save her. If planned properly, one battle was all it would take for Casta to beat the Dark Emperor. She should know. She'd trained with Casta's army all her life. But there would be casualties. Would the court think her freedom from a promise made in desperation was worth the cost?

∼

Dagstyrr knew they were taking a chance disembarking immediately, as Calstir was barely ready, but the prince wanted to avoid having a welcome committee board the *Mermaid*, where Rella's poorly covered mark and brown eyes would be instantly noticed.

Music played as the crew positioned the gangplank, and people waved the blue-and-white flags of Casta. A welcome committee stood on the dock, their white robes fluttering in the breeze. Some were genuinely smiling, but not all. In particular, an older woman and three young men had smiles pasted on their faces, but the effort those smiles required was thinly disguised. The cousins?

Dagstyrr turned to Calstir. "Ready?"

With a nod, Calstir rose from his chair and followed Dagstyrr. Rather than allow the prince to descend the gangplank first—as protocol usually demanded—Dagstyrr took the lead. If Calstir should falter, it could be put down to the rough wooden surface and, with one hand, he could grab Dagstyrr's shoulders and right himself without falling ignominiously at the feet of the court.

Calstir's face was beaming by the time he reached the dock, his elegant fingers extended for the courtiers to kiss. Dagstyrr stayed by his side, one hand on the hilt of his sword, watching.

Casta's ministers were first to step forward and bow low. Dagstyrr paid little attention to names and positions. His eyes were everywhere and missed little. The group at the end of the line of courtiers was whispering amongst themselves, perhaps about a human escorting their new king. When they reached those at the end of the line, Calstir smiled warmly. "Aunt Kemara, so good of you to leave your duties to welcome me."

It *was* the cousins.

Lady Kemara stepped forward. "I am happy to welcome you back safe and sound, as are all of the family." At this, the three young men stepped forward.

Calstir turned to Dagstyrr. "Let me introduce my cousins. Lord Hamel, Lukor, Marvn this is Dagstyrr, the man who carried me on his back out of my prison."

The look of disdain on Hamel's face was unmistakable. Lukor and Marvn couldn't even raise smiles. "It is very good to meet your lordships. I have heard so much about you," Dagstyrr said with a very small bow.

Lady Kemara snapped her fingers, and a contingent of Casta household guards immediately pushed their way toward Calstir, but Dagstyrr was ready for them. He stood his ground, making it impossible for them to separate him from Calstir without a fuss. Lady Kemara put her hand on his sleeve. "Thank you, Dagstyrr, but we will look after him now."

Dagstyrr ignored Lady Kemara, eliciting the tiniest of frowns from her proud face. This lady was not used to having her orders disregarded. Dagstyrr understood he'd made four very powerful enemies within minutes of landing in Casta.

The crowd called for Calstir, who raised his royal hand and waved, and was rewarded with another roar of approval from the populace. Dagstyrr leaned toward Calstir and whispered, "You are well liked, my Lord. Shall we go?"

Calstir put his hand on Dagstyrr's shoulder and nodded, thus causing the household guard to fall back. Together, human and king made their way slowly past gurgling fountains and up the hill toward the palace. By the time they reached the entrance, Dagstyrr could see Calstir was nearing the end of his strength. As they mounted the steps he tripped, and Dagstyrr's hand shot out and steadied him. "Sea legs," said Dagstyrr in explanation. The courtiers smiled and nodded understanding. *Thank the gods*, thought Dagstyrr, but he noticed Lord Hamel and his brothers whispering with their mother.

Putting a hand under Calstir's elbow, which brought a gasp from the courtiers, Dagstyrr steered him into the blue-and-white palace. "Which way to your rooms, Your Majesty?" he whispered.

With a barely discernable sigh, Calstir answered, "Through the great hall and up the stairs at the back of the throne." Dagstyrr took the lead despite the looks of disapproval he received and led Calstir through a white marble hall. A blue ceiling studded with sapphires twinkled above them as they crossed the hall. Then they mounted the stairs behind the blue crystal throne of Casta.

At the top of the stairs Calstir paused. "Bear with me, my friends. It has been a long and arduous journey. I feel the stink of Hedabar on my person still, and I would like to cleanse and meditate before we feast tonight."

"Of course, Your Majesty," rumbled the court clearly disappointed, as Calstir turned and entered the most sumptuous apartments Dagstyrr had ever seen.

As soon as the door closed behind them and they were alone, Calstir strode confidently across the marble floor inset with sapphires, all stumbling and exhaustion gone from him. Dagstyrr looked momentarily amazed before throwing back his head and laughing. "You're testing them."

Calstir turned. "I am, my friend. You can observe far more when people think you're weakened and their guards are down."

"Your aunt and cousins?"

"I did notice."

The fact that Calstir now considered Dagstyrr a friend and was unafraid to confide in him spoke well of the relationship they'd built during Calstir's recovery. However, Dagstyrr knew better than to take this friendship at face value. Calstir was a light fae prince born and bred, and now he was king. Humans were as nothing to him, and although he called Dagstyrr a friend, that could change in a heartbeat.

Dagstyrr removed his helmet and sword belt, laying them carefully on a precious Samphire wood trunk by the door. His gaze followed Calstir, who wandered around his rooms, touching a piece of art here and there. *He's missed this place,* thought Dagstyrr.

Although the palace was stunningly beautiful, it was so different from his own home that Dagstyrr had difficulty understanding the appeal of all the cold marble and bright color. He followed Calstir from room to room, each one more elaborate than the last, and filled with the scent of lilies, which graced large glass vases in every room.

Drapes fell in cascades from the windows in white silks, which when moved by the breeze, showed blue flashes woven into the cloth. Brocades in deep blues graced the chairs, sofas, and floor cushions set elegantly about to accommodate the king's every mood.

"Were these your father's apartments?" said Dagstyrr.

"No, these have always been mine. My father's rooms

will have been sealed upon his death. When I have a son, they will be opened and refurbished for the heir."

At last, they came to Calstir's bedroom. Expecting a huge bed fit for a king, Dagstyrr was surprised to find a modest bed set in the middle of the room, covered in silks and linens. It lay underneath a domed glass ceiling, where the sun shone down on the bed and where moon and stars would glisten over the sleeping king at night.

The heady scent of lilies was everywhere, and Dagstyrr was starting to find it oppressive. He lifted his hand to his nose.

"Don't you like lilies?" asked Calstir, pulling one from its crystal vase and breathing in the pungent scent.

"In truth, I prefer roses," replied Dagstyrr.

"Really?" said Calstir, with sudden interest.

"Yes, roses and peppermint," he said, absentmindedly, wondering where he'd experienced that combination.

A flash of contempt showed on Calstir's face, and then it was gone, quickly replaced by his emotionless courtly visage. Dagstyrr chose to ignore it, understanding now where he'd experienced that particular blend of scents: Rella.

I might be good enough to be called friend, but I'll never be good enough for his sister, thought Dagstyrr. Calstir would tolerate him until he had no more value. Then he'd be cast aside. It was just as well Dagstyrr had no ambition to stay.

It was clear to Dagstyrr that this court would never accept Rella. If his mother, Princess Astrid, couldn't accept her, then these proud courtiers certainly wouldn't. As soon as the danger to Calstir's throne from the cousins was in check, Dagstyrr would leave with Rella whether Calstir liked it or not.

The idea of Rella being used as bait to draw the Dark

Emperor away from Casta sent adrenaline flooding through his muscles until he wanted to hit someone. He'd known better than to tell her so, but while he lived, she would be under his protection. Some might think being accepted at the Casta court was a privilege, but not Dagstyrr. He'd much rather he and Rella were far away.

The tour continued as Calstir waved him toward double doors in the far wall of his bedchamber. "Here is what I've been longing for, dreamt of, even."

Grinning widely, Calstir opened the doors to reveal a large room with a rectangular pool and a waterfall pouring down a marble wall into it. The two men stood and breathed in the moist, ozone-fresh air. "I know it is sheer indulgence, but there have to be some perks to being a prince." He laughed, pulling off his cloak. "Come on, I'll race you to the far end and back."

Dagstyrr didn't have to be asked twice. He quickly divested himself of his garments and dove into the crystal pool. The clean water glided smoothly off his shoulders as he surfaced and struck out for the far end. Calstir, being fae, was going to win without much effort. Dagstyrr didn't care —the luxury of the pool was something he'd never experienced before, with water clear as a bathtub, and as refreshing as the mineral rich pools in the Halfenhaw forest. A welcome change from seawater.

Turning, he saw Calstir toweling himself dry. "I want to meet with my privy ministers. Stay and enjoy the facilities. I won't be leaving my warded apartments. Besides, I trust these few absolutely. They have supported my family for generations."

If Calstir was as well as he now seemed, Dagstyrr understood it was ridiculous for him to have a human guard, and if he were about to lay the seeds of Rella's acceptance with these ministers, he'd need privacy. "Very well. You don't seem to need my help. I'll swim for a bit, then return to the *Mermaid*."

"I would have you by my side a little longer, Dagstyrr of Halfenhaw. Tonight I will present my proposals to the court."

"You mean about Rella. They won't go for it, you know," said Dagstyrr, understanding he took his life in his hands talking to Calstir like this.

Calstir briefly raised an eyebrow. "Still, I ask you to stay. It won't be for long. But the decision is, of course, yours," he added with a slight incline of his head.

"Well, I am enjoying your pool. Perhaps I could stay for a few hours," said Dagstyrr, throwing himself backwards in the water.

"Good, very good," said Calstir with a smile. "I will send for you when we're ready to descend to the throne room. Help yourself to whatever you need."

Dagstyrr's relationship with the new king of Casta was shaky, to say the least. He'd seen Calstir in the worst of circumstances, which any proud fae would resent. However, Dagstyrr had also carried him over his shoulders from the citadel, for which Calstir was grateful. Add Calstir's addiction to the mix, and it was a very tenuous relationship indeed.

Calstir could not be trusted.

∼

Rella paced the deck. Her frustration at having to stay on board was mounting. What was Calstir thinking? Why on earth did he want Dagstyrr with him? The household guard was far better equipped to protect him; besides, she was anxious to know her fate.

The crew was loading supplies. Of course, having been declared dark fae, they were not allowed to set foot on Casta. So, lines of human dockworkers climbed the gangplank to drop their loads of supplies into the waiting hands of the crew.

"This is all so insulting," said Rella with a wave of her hand.

"You wouldn't have thought so a year ago," replied Bernst. "I'll wager you've seen this a dozen times and thought nothing of it."

"You're right, Captain," said Rella with a heartfelt sigh, "but now I know better."

"And that makes you angry."

"It does."

"Why?"

"Because it's wrong. Wrong and stupid," she fumed.

"Well, just because you've changed don't mean anyone else has. Best you learn to live with it."

Rella saw her life stretch ahead of her, lived like this, as dark fae. "I will never learn to live with prejudice. I was born and bred to fight for justice. I can't just live with this kind of ignorance."

"Fight whom? For what?"

"Fight for what is right. How can you accept this? Once I'm back in the council, I'm going to make some changes. Then everyone will understand that, dark or light, we are all fae."

"Your brother might have something to say about that," said Bernst, shading his eyes. "Looks like we have company."

Looking out across the docks, she saw Lady Kemara with the three cousins approaching. A royal guard of about twenty men and women escorted them. "An odd choice, but this must be my escort if they have a royal guard with them." Rella smoothed her white leather kilt and wondered whether to remove the paste hiding her mark or not. It had dried and flaked and would fool no one at close quarters.

She wished Dagstyrr were here with her, if for nothing else but to lend moral support. He, more than anyone, understood what she had overcome at Hedabar. Never mind, she would soon be with him again. Putting her hand to her cheek, she decided to remove the ridiculous paste.

The light fae didn't give her a chance. They boarded at a run. Blue light flashing from their fingers, they sent the crew crashing against the bulwark, where they were held captive with ropes of light energy. Before she understood what was happening, she too was thrown to the deck and a strong shield placed over her magic by Lady Kemara.

The three brothers came forward, their faces mocking and cruel. Their blatant aggression and disregard for her high position here in Casta scared and horrified her. Struggling was useless against the light energy shield that damped down Rella's newfound dark fae battle energy. The cousins meant business.

"Stop." Lady Kemara stepped towards them. "Do not sully yourselves with touching this creature, my sons. Not while she dares to wear that uniform."

A rumble of agreement went round the twenty household guards who wore the same colors. Apparently, something had changed in Casta.

Kemara approached until she was standing over Rella's prostrate figure. Rella knew she must move slowly, or she was dead. Lady Kemara might be full of bluster and drama, but she was a powerful light fae noblewoman. Rella could feel the strength of her magic in the shield surrounding her.

If nothing else, Rella must ensure no harm came to the *Mermaid* or her crew because of her.

"Take off that uniform."

"Don't be ridiculous."

"Things have changed since you left, and the old king died, leaving no heir in Casta."

"My father named Calstir heir before I left."

"Calstir had disappeared. We thought he was dead."

"Of course. You thought to put one of your sons on the throne. Let me guess—the weakest one, because it is you who have always wanted the throne, not your boys. Kingship would be too much like hard work for any of them," said Rella, seeing her words strike a chord with her clueless cousins.

"It is only a matter of time before Calstir falls and the House of Kemara rules in Casta," said Lady Kemara. "You had to be the hero and rescue Calstir. All you've done is disgrace your family. Calstir is weak, and you are an abomination. Do you seriously think the council will accept you?"

If Lady Kemara was willing to say that in front of witnesses, then things were far worse than Calstir knew. Rella forced her most radiant smile. "Yes. I do. My brother is strong, stronger than you could ever be. Even now, he meets with the council, and tomorrow he'll be crowned. There is nothing you can do about it. It must irk you after all your careful scheming. I know you didn't expect either of us to live."

"The council will never agree to let you live."

"Tell me, Aunt, who sent Calstir out on the *Konig* without sufficient supplies, and perhaps a suggestion that Hedabar was rich in market stuffs?" said Rella, taking a stab in the dark.

Lady Kemara's face was stone, but Marvn's glance at his

mother told her she'd stumbled on the truth. "How did you know about the vizier?" said Rella.

"We didn't. Rumors had reached us of something happening there. Nothing specific, you understand."

"Calstir will kill you and your brats for that."

"I don't think so. I have already sent my apologies, taking the blame for the horrible mistake I made in calculating the supplies necessary and of course, submitting my family's resignation as suppliers to the royal fleet."

"Mother! How could you?" Lukor looked furious. "We need those revenues."

Kemara stood back, allowing Rella to stand. But she kept her shield in place.

"Take it off."

"No," said Rella, slowly getting to her feet.

"Rella of Casta, you have defiled that uniform. Your cohort has been disbanded, and your name stricken from the archives. You have chosen to become a monster, yet you dare to stand there in that uniform with those brown eyes and defy me? Either you take it off now, or it will be ripped from you," said Lady Kemara, her blue fae eyes bright with malice.

News that her cohort had been disbanded knifed through Rella. She had no choice but to fight for them. Rella drew her blade. "Not a chance. Only the king has the right to demand my uniform or disband my cohort. Who do you think you are? You are nothing but grocers."

"Very well," said Lady Kemara with a sneer, turning her back and nodding to her sons, who advanced on Rella barefisted.

A fight it was going to be. Well, she'd not make it easy for them.

Lady Kemara swirled around and directed her blue

battle magic at Rella's sword, sending it flying through the air. One of the guards caught it, and Rella realized this was not going to be a fair fight. Rella couldn't use her battle magic because of the shield, but even without using theirs, the cousins had their mother's magic to help them when needed.

Rella fought with everything she had, biting and kicking at the men who were so determined to strip her of her uniform. Hamel made the mistake of bringing his face close to hers, and she bit his cheek close to his eye, but not near enough to do real damage. She earned a punch in the face for her trouble. No one had ever gotten that close to her in a fight before, and it scared her.

His knuckles bruised her flesh and bone, yet there was no fae energy behind the punch, just brute force. Hamel was fighting dirty, and for good reason. They didn't want to leave their magic signature on her. Her head whipped around, and she saw this was a battle she could not win. Yet, the warrior inside her would not give in. "Kemara, you sniveling whore, can't you take me on without your dogs to do your dirty work?"

This earned Rella a punch to the gut that knocked all the wind out of her, and her knees buckled even as she registered Captain Bernst's voice in her head. *Don't fight them, lass. All they want is you out of that uniform.*

"I earned this uniform!" she yelled.

"What you've earned is death. Or, if you're lucky, banishment, but not before the whole court witnesses your downfall and degradation," said Kemara, a small smile playing across her lips as she stood calmly on deck.

"Really?" yelled Rella, kicking Lukor's knee. She had the satisfaction of hearing it crack under her boot.

"Mother, we must use light energy!" yelled Hamel.

"I said no. I want no trace of you on her."

"There will be traces of her on each of us, can't you see?" he said, pointing to his bloody face where she'd bitten him.

"Of course. She's mad. She attacked us. Your injuries will be the proof. You didn't even have time to defend yourselves," said Kemara. "My shield energy is all that will be detected. I protected my children naturally."

"You mean your dogs," said Rella, landing a blow that sent Marvn reeling. All her battle training came back to her in flashes of muscle memory. Her feet danced on the boards of the deck, keeping the three brothers bumping into each other. Even without using her magic, Rella was fast. More of a warrior than any of them would ever be.

She could still inflict pain. Rella threw Hamel to the ground, but Lukor and Marvn grabbed her and pulled at the straps of her armor. Marvn was enjoying himself. A satisfied sneer flashed across his face as he ripped off her breastplate, leaving bloody scratches on her shoulders.

Lukor's broken knee didn't seem to hurt him. That must be Kemara's doing—healing magic. Yet it did slow him down. He couldn't put his full weight on it. Ignoring the hands grabbing at her clothes, Rella lashed out her foot, again connecting with Lukor—his face this time. A loud crack sounded across the deck, and everyone knew his jaw was broken.

Rella threw back her head and laughed as he stumbled toward his mother, holding his jaw in place. She twisted and struggled against the other two, but they were bigger and stronger.

If she couldn't win, at least she'd inflict as much damage as she could. With one last effort, she put one fist in her other hand, and using her elbow as a weapon, struck Marvn's nose as hard as she could. No sooner had she felt his nose break than Hamel's fist slammed into her gut, again and again, before smashing into her face. The last thing she heard before giving herself up to the void was Captain Bernst's voice angry and spitting. "Cowards. All of ye, cowards…"

CHAPTER 23

Dagstyrr felt refreshed and better than he had in some time. The waters may have had some rejuvenating magic about them, or perhaps the exercise he'd long been denied on board had relaxed him. Clean and dressed in some of Calstir's fresh linens, he donned his armor while waiting for Calstir to finish with his ministers.

He could see them in the next room sitting around a table and speaking with smiling faces. If there was anything amiss, then he didn't see it, yet it was difficult to tell with light fae who hid their emotions well. A trickle of water from his damp hair pushed its way down the back of his neck under his shirt, and he gave an involuntary shiver.

If Calstir was smart, he was priming those ten ministers to side with him before he brought up the subject of Rella's new state. If his ministers were in agreement, the rest of the court should be easier to convince. For a moment he allowed himself to imagine Rella here, garbed in blue and white silk and conversing with the courtiers. Even among her own kind, she'd stand out like a beacon.

"Pah!" It was useless. She didn't belong here, and he knew it.

A prickle sent another shiver down his spine. His nerves screamed something was wrong, yet everything appeared normal. Well, as normal as possible in these exotic surroundings. Dagstyrr strapped on his sword belt and drew his blade just in case.

His eyes and ears scanned for any clue that something was wrong. Inside Calstir's apartments, everything appeared well.

He saw the courtiers and Calstir stand up. Every one of them had a smile on their face. Dagstyrr wondered for a moment whether the warnings flashing through his body were just his overwrought imagination. Perhaps it was a result of all this marble and luxury. However, he'd learned many years ago to always trust his gut.

Calstir approached with a smile playing on his handsome face. "Dagstyrr, you will be happy to know we've come to an agreement. We will present it to the court immediately, and everything will then be back to normal here in Casta. The coronation will take place tomorrow morning, though I'm afraid you won't be able to stay for that. Light fae only at such ceremonies. I know you understand."

"I do, my Lord," said Dagstyrr, his heart lifting at the prospect of getting out of here, and grateful he wouldn't have to come up with an excuse to leave. Beautiful as it was, this grand palace filled him with unease. The sooner he was away from it, the better.

"Will you escort me one last time, Dagstyrr of Halfenhaw?"

"Of course," said Dagstyrr, putting away his sword and taking his place beside Calstir. The ministers, who had ignored him completely, formed a phalanx that led the way downstairs toward the crystal throne of Casta. The great marble hall was full of courtiers and ministers, and heaven knew whom else. The energy was tight, like the air before a great storm, when clouds cracked with lightning as a warning of the tempest to come.

Calstir made his way to the throne amid polite applause. Dagstyrr couldn't help feeling the tension was partly because these fae were so restrained. Their perfect faces beaming up at the throne belied the gentle clapping. These people were happy to see Calstir. His presence saved them all from a war involving the three cousins who would have fought each other for the throne.

The ministers took up positions around the hall, each whispering to separate groups of courtiers. *They probably represent different noble families,* thought Dagstyrr. He watched as words were passed from person to person. Nods and smiles accompanied the spread of the news—a good sign.

Dagstyrr took up his position just behind the blue crystal throne. Everyone ignored him. A human wasn't a threat here, and they were in the mood to indulge Calstir's eccentricities. Yet his gut instinct screamed that something was wrong.

Then, to confirm his fears, Bernst's voice echoed in his head. *Call Drago, lad.* Shocked, Dagstyrr struggled to keep his expression neutral. For a second, he wondered whether the captain had over imbibed and was drunk, but Bernst would not have him call Drago lightly. The frustrating thing was he couldn't converse with Captain Bernst as he could with Drago. With Bernst it was a one-way communication only.

Dagstyrr couldn't help grinning. He imagined for a moment the look on these light fae faces if his eyes suddenly started glowing with dragon fire eyes as he spoke to Drago. Perhaps that's what Bernst wanted to happen?

They've taken her.

Now his senses were on high alert. Rella was in danger, and for some reason, Bernst couldn't help her. Where? Where had they taken her, and who were "they"? Irritation over the one-way communication with Bernst really kicked in.

He put his hand to his sword and bent to speak directly to the prince, but a commotion from the far end of the hall caused Calstir to raise a hand to ward him off. As the prince stood, Dagstyrr came to Calstir's side determined to talk to him. He saw a path being made for Lady Kemara and three men, who were dragging something behind them.

Dagstyrr knew immediately the bloodied body being dragged along by the cousins was Rella. Fury erupted in his head as he pulled his sword from its scabbard, the sound reverberating around the stunned court. Calstir's hand went out. "Let me deal with this."

Dagstyrr didn't hesitate. "You deal with them. I'll look after her!" he shouted, leaping down from the dais and running toward the Kemara brothers. One of them clutched his face while the other two dragged a bloodied Rella cursing and spitting along the marble floor, with blue light chains restraining her hands.

The Kemara family was unfazed by his approach even smiling up at Calstir as they made their way towards the throne. "You need to learn some manners, human," sneered Lady Kemara. Then lifted her hand and sent a jolt of energy flashing toward Dagstyrr as he ran past.

For a split second, he enjoyed the look of consternation on her face when it slowed and fizzled harmlessly around him, dissipated by his mother's magic. He ran on with sword drawn until he reached Rella. They'd dropped her half-naked on the floor like a bag of bloodied rags and carried on toward the throne.

He wanted to kill them. Instead, he sheathed his sword and bent down gently, turning Rella over and lifting her onto his bent knee. He pushed her golden hair away from her face. Her one eye was swollen shut, her face badly bruised. She had scratches moving from her neck down under her white shift, which was all she wore.

Dagstyrr's heart turned to stone at the sight of her. The Kemara family deserved all they were about to get. They were powerful, but Calstir's magic was stronger by far.

He used his mother's protective energy to wipe away the remnants of light fae ropes that bound her magical hands and gagged her, thankful for his mother's foresight in giving him this gift.

"Let me up."

Dagstyrr lifted her gently to her feet, his fury growing as he realized how badly she was hurt.

∾

Rella stood on trembling feet. She was filthy and dripped blood on the pristine floor. Fury grew in her to match the pain of her humiliation. After a quick assessment, she knew there was no one injury severe enough to kill her. Her right hand was severely broken in several places, and she suspected she had a few broken ribs. But thankfully, there were no major bones broken. It was nothing compared to what she was about to unleash on the Kemara family, as she pulled her magic to battle readiness.

The courtiers stepped away giving them a wide berth, which suited her purpose just fine. Dagstyrr stayed close.

She felt his mother's gift of protection from magic extend to her, but it wasn't designed to protect from so many. Astrid hadn't reckoned on a how much force light fae could produce en masse, and these were the most potent light fae anywhere.

"Rella, I'll kill them for you, slowly," he whispered.

Mocking laughter sounded to his right. "We can all hear you, you know?" said Marvn, dabbing a cloth to his bloodied nose.

Rella was surprised to see the man still standing. Was her brother not going to defend her? She looked to Calstir, who stood smiling in front of the blue crystal throne. "Thank you, Lord Marvn. I will deal with this now."

The stark truth finally dawned on her. "You," she gasped, all strength deserting her. She stood with Dagstyrr's protective hand touching her elbow. Rella stared into the cold blue eyes of her brother. "You did this?"

"Who else?" said Calstir, taking a few steps toward her. "No one here would dare lay a hand on my sister without my express orders. I've told you all along: the court of Casta is united and will do my bidding. My ministers and I discussed your punishment this very afternoon, and we are agreed."

"Her punishment!" roared Dagstyrr. "After what she sacrificed for you?"

"In my court, we do not have one rule for my sister and a different rule for everyone else. You're human, so I'm indulging you, but do not push me too far," warned Calstir.

Rella felt she was at last awakening from an uncomfortable dream into a nightmare reality. She was light fae turned dark. She was an anathema to all light fae, a creature to be hunted and destroyed before she descended into madness and created havoc by dragging others with her. That was what they believed.

"She swam through *shit* for you. So did I. No one else here would deign to rescue their prince!" shouted Dagstyrr, his eyes raking the amused faces of the court. They had pulled back now, leaving a wide circle around the hapless pair, no one wanting to risk any association or sympathy with them, lest their loyalty be questioned.

"I told Rella to leave Calstir where he was," said Lady Kemara addressing the whole assembly. "She received fair warning."

"Princess Rella risked everything to rescue her brother and save Casta from civil war!" shouted Dagstyrr. "Three brothers all wanting the one throne!"

Lady Kemara's face turned to stone. "That would never have happened. What do you know, human?" She turned to Calstir. "Let's finish this now."

Rella knew now, at last. There was no point in arguing with them. There was only one way forward as far as the court were concerned—Rella's death. Nothing would move them from that path now.

"You do not order the king," Dagstyrr shouted, playing for time. A murmur went around the gathering. "Is the love of family worth nothing in Casta? Is loyalty to the crown worth nothing? How about compassion, or bravery beyond the call of duty? All this and more has Rella of the Royal House of Casta demonstrated."

Her heart soared to hear him defend her with such passion.

In contrast, her brother's silence cut her far deeper than any humiliation the cousins could inflict. His sky-blue eyes —emotionless, as expected of a king of Casta—cut to her very soul even as his gaze captured hers.

Dagstyrr's fury was unsettling the courtiers. "You should be on your knees to her!" he roared. "All of you, on your knees to the only one brave enough to snatch your prince from that prison of hell."

"Enough, Dagstyrr," said Calstir softly. "No one is questioning her bravery or yours. Her loyalty and love for me and Casta are not in question. However, she chose to turn dark knowing full well what the consequences would be," said Calstir with a finality that froze his face into a mask.

"Is that so unforgivable?"

Rella understood what Dagstyrr could not. There was no forgiveness here. Her brother's betrayal was absolute. He hadn't even tried to persuade them to let her live.

It had been hundreds of years since anyone in Casta had turned dark, and they were going to exact the age-old punishment—testing by the Crystal Mountain healers to confirm she was mad, then death. Those tests always ended in death.

"Yes, Dagstyrr, it is unforgivable in their eyes," said Rella, softly.

"You don't understand and never will. You're human," said Calstir, against a backdrop of mounting conversations growing ever more antagonistic. "I have indulged you enough. It is time you left us. Leave the prisoner and go, or I'll not be responsible for your safety."

The Mermaid's *almost ready, lad. Had to get rid of those blasted light fae ropes.*

"You hypocrite," said Rella, putting as much contempt into her voice as was possible. "It was a dark fae ship that carried you home, crewed by dark fae. It was that same dark fae crew that worked day and night to cure your addiction..."

At the mention of addiction, Calstir turned his face, and

everyone else looked away. "That's right, deny it. It was dark fae medicine that saved you. Yet, you and I know you'll never be cured, will you brother?" Rella's voice rang crystal clear across the hall.

With every word Calstir's temper rose showing only as a tapping of his fingers against his royal robes. Yet every member of the court must have been aware of it.

"You will always be an addict," said Rella, pushing home her point.

Calstir rounded at her. "I am not without pity, sister. Nor am I ungrateful." His voice thundered across the gathering as only a high light fae's could. "You made a promise to the Dark Emperor. My ministers and I have decided to let you keep that promise. I would not see my sister die."

A chill ran up Rella's spine. She'd rather die.

"I have already sent envoys to greet him at the border. He will be here soon. Until then, you will be in the custody of…" She saw him falter. Was he about to give her back into the hands of the Kemara cousins? "In my custody."

"Like hell, I will." She adopted battle stance and summoned all the magic in her body. Dark green clouds seeped out of her ready fingers and crawled along the floor.

Reacting as one, the court turned away, their hands in front of their faces as if she'd invoked a poison. She saw Calstir shudder as she sent muddy green magic crawling across the floor toward him before dissipating into the atmosphere. Even after all he'd done, she still loved him.

∼

Dagstyrr. Talk to your dragon, lad. Bernst's voice sounded in his head once more, and this time Dagstyrr understood.

Calstir raised his hand as if to strike Rella but instead

just held it there pointing at her. "It is true. I am not cured yet, but as soon as our healers from the Crystal Mountain arrive, my true healing will start. I will be whole again."

The tapping had stopped, and from the look of the courtiers, they appeared to be buying every word of it.

"Don't delude yourself, brother. You will always be an addict," said Rella, with a finality that shut down any argument.

Drago, hear me now. I'm in a bit of a pickle, and your eyes would help. The heat started in Dagstyrr's feet and mounted to engulf his whole body, his breath hot and dry as it left his mouth. A gasp went up, and people scrambled to widen the distance between them.

I think you're going to need more than my eyes, said Drago.

It was Lady Kemara who first regained her composure. "A dragon-talker. Oh, Calstir, no wonder you allowed this human into the court. We must keep him."

That was not exactly the reaction Dagstyrr had expected. He kept his eyes on Calstir. *The addict can sense me. He wants my blood,* said Drago.

You can see? said Dagstyrr.

Your eyes are mine. I suggest you back slowly out of the marble hall, hurling as many insults at them as you can. Just don't get too angry, I don't want you breathing fire. You must stay alive to fulfill your promise, Drago's slow voice rumbled in his head.

Breathing fire!

With a quick glance at Rella, Dagstyrr reached for her hand and started to back toward the open doors. One look to the guards, and when they saw his flaming eyes, they disappeared into the shadows. The whole court stood stock still, except for Calstir who followed slowly like a man in a trance.

"Why didn't you tell me?" he pleaded.

"Stay back, Calstir!" roared Dagstyrr, his voice deep and hoarse from the heat Drago's presence caused in his body.

"I will do you no harm," said Calstir. "The ministers and I have made arrangements for Rella. You didn't think I'd have her killed, did you? No, no it's time for her to pay the price, the price *she* negotiated. She is no longer my responsibility."

Rella's hand tightened in his, her face white with suppressed emotion. Dagstyrr continued to back toward the doors.

"You would say anything to get what you want, wouldn't you, Calstir? Your soft words and rich trappings do not fool me. Remember, I was there for every moment of your recovery. I know you, Calstir."

A collective gasp rippled through the crowd.

"Why didn't you let me know you were a dragon-talker?" Calstir was almost drooling at the word "dragon."

"It's none of your business."

"But I would have prepared a place for you at court. You would live the life of a high light fae lord. Even now, I am prepared to offer you a place. What do you say?"

"I'm no high fae anything. I'm human. Remember?" They were almost at the door. The rest of the court was amassing behind Calstir.

"I'm leaving now, with Rella. Keep everyone away from us, and I'll do no harm to your precious palace," said Dagstyrr, with absolutely no idea what harm he might do a marble palace. But they didn't know that.

"Go, if you must," said Lady Kemara, "but leave Rella. The Dark Emperor will be here for her soon."

Despite the heat of Drago's intrusion into his mind and

body, Dagstyrr felt another shiver run over him. "The Dark Emperor?"

"She is promised to him. That is the price she agreed to, and that is what she must pay," said Calstir.

"Why don't you take her place, Calstir? After all, it was done to rescue you, wasn't it?" Dagstyrr stepped outside. They'd have to turn and run soon. Backing down such a long flight of stairs was impossible.

Calstir laughed. "I'm hardly his type."

"It is true," said Rella. "I am to be queen of the dark fae, and rule the Dark Forest." Despite her cold delivery of the facts, she gave an involuntary shudder. "They think it's kinder than death."

"You must leave her here for the Dark Emperor," said Lady Kemara. "Otherwise it will mean war between Casta and the Dark Kingdom."

If the Dark Emperor is on his way you'd better get out of there, now, said Drago, and a flare of heat coursed through Dagstyrr. *If there are any puddles of water along the way, step in them. It will help hide you both.*

What?

Just do as I say.

Dagstyrr and Rella turned as one and ran down the steps. A scream worthy of sea harpies escaped the palace when the courtiers saw Rella fleeing. The sound of hundreds of feet thundering toward them echoed around the marble columns. There were no puddles, but there was a series of descending fountains covering the gardens between the palace and the docks.

"Here goes nothing," said Dagstyrr, leaping up and wading through the knee-high water. Steam rose in billows around him. *Thank you, Drago.*

"Keep hold of my hand," said Dagstyrr, afraid he might

lose Rella in the rising vapor billowing behind them. Leaping from pool to pool, Dagstyrr and Rella left a wide trail of burning-hot steam behind. He made sure Rella was just ahead of him otherwise she'd be scalded.

Steam rose like a thick fog over everything. It would be impossible for their pursuers to pinpoint their exact position. But Dagstyrr knew it wouldn't take long to work out that they were heading for the *Mermaid*. Then they'd be overtaken. They had to move fast.

Rella moaned. The sound almost broke his heart. She was hurt, but he had to get her away from here, or they'd hand her over to the Dark Emperor.

She must have sensed his hesitation. "I'm all right. Hurry, or they'll catch us!" she shouted. Dagstyrr remembered the look of horror on Rella's face as she'd described the Dark Emperor. That memory spurred him on.

As each jump took them to a lower pool, the fountains began exploding as the boiling water gushed through the pipes. Dagstyrr took a moment and looked back; the whole front of the palace was engulfed in steam. No one could find a quick way through that—he hoped. Dagstyrr heard Drago laugh gently at the sight.

At last, they were within reach of the *Mermaid*. Captain Bernst was casting off, but the gangway was still down, and crewmen held the ship in place with billhooks. Rella stumbled. Dagstyrr picked her up and ran along the gangplank, feeling it move just before he jumped and landed on deck. "Thanks for waiting," he said, "but you might not be too happy when you hear what I've done."

"Never mind that now, lad. Say goodbye to Drago and get Rella into her cabin. I'll be there as fast as I can," said Captain Bernst.

I heard him. Farewell, for now, Dagstyrr of Halfenhaw. I will hear from you soon, and I hope you are on your way here when that happens. Give my love to your lady.

Farewell, Drago, said Dagstyrr without taking the time to correct him about Rella being his lady. Dragons probably had other ideas about what constituted a mate. There was a smoky singed smell coming from his feet, and Dagstyrr realized he was about to set the deck on fire. In a flash, Bernst saw the problem and poured a bucket of water over his ruined boots.

"Now, get her into the cabin. I've work to do here," said Bernst. "Calstir will send his ships after us. We must be swift."

"I can walk," said Rella, sliding from him and marching toward her cabin with one hand cupping her damaged elbow.

Dagstyrr bent his head and eased into the cabin. He grasped her arms to help her down onto the cushions. He choked at the sight of her battered body. Unable to trust himself to speak, he stepped outside and waved to summon Billy.

"I'll have hot water and fresh linens for you in a trice, sir," said Billy, anticipating his orders.

The boy knew more about preparing Rella's bathwater than he did, so he left him to it. Dagstyrr lifted her broken hand, and he saw the lacerations and bruises. "It looks like you landed a good one." With a kiss, he replaced her hand. It would take Captain Bernst to heal bones. Her lower legs were pink from the hot steam.

"Does it hurt?"

"Don't be kind to me, Dagstyrr. I don't think I can bear it," she said. "I should have known better than to return to Casta. You tried to tell me, and I didn't listen. I put you in grave danger. Now, Captain Bernst and the *Mermaid* are in danger too."

"Come, Rella, your wounds will heal," he said, though he wasn't sure she'd ever recover from Calstir's betrayal.

"I should have listened to you. Even after your mother's reaction, I chose to believe my brother could sway the court in my favor. He didn't even try." A tear slipped down her face, and she swiped it away with her good hand. "I must be very foolish to have put my faith in an addict."

Seeing her swollen face, her delicate features all battered and bruised, stirred a desire in him to protect her, and more. "You had faith in a brother whose life you'd saved. It is understandable."

She closed her eyes and leaned back against the bright silk. Even in this battered state, she was the most beautiful woman he'd ever seen, and he wanted to gather her in his arms and wipe away all the hurt and treachery assaulting her.

"It is unforgivable," she said. "I should have known better. We are brought up to fear and despise those who turn dark for it is believed they always go mad. A madness so deep and dark, they spread evil wherever they go. We are taught to destroy them as soon as we encounter them. It is ingrained in us. That's why your mother attacked me," she said, sadly. "I should have known my brother wasn't strong enough to go against our indoctrination."

The scent of roses and peppermint filled the small space and brought back a reminder of the look he'd glimpsed on Calstir's face when Dagstyrr had innocently claimed this as his favorite scent. He took her gently into his arms and stroked her hair. Having Calstir as an enemy was no joke.

"You are not mad, Rella. Don't say that. You trusted your

brother, that's all. After what you did for him, you had a right to expect his loyalty."

"Bernst warned us both to never trust an addict. I should have listened," said Rella.

"Do you think the Crystal Mountain healers will be able to help him?"

"You saw him. He sensed Drago's presence in you, and he became enthralled. I think my brother will be fighting his addiction for the rest of his life."

"Which makes him very unpredictable," said Dagstyrr. "Not a good candidate for king."

"I hope he gets the help he needs. The idea of him losing the throne, and Casta being thrown into civil war is what drove me to rescue him in the first place. I didn't do it lightly, you know."

"I know."

"If you had known him before, you'd understand. He was a man of honor, who championed those not as fortunate as himself. He has a great aptitude for the law, and he's a renowned speaker. He was the perfect choice to succeed my father," said Rella, remembering her father pacing the floor as he hashed out new legislation with his ministers, and Calstir sitting patiently taking it all in—learning kingship from the master.

"You thought he'd be incapable of betraying you. I understand that. Now, he is a different man. You must come to terms with that, Rella. You can never trust him," said Dagstyrr, looking away. He knew that even now she didn't want to hear that her brother was changed forever. But the truth was, Calstir had his own agenda, and it didn't include a dark fae sister.

He was shocked to hear her laugh. It was a joyless, empty sound he'd never thought to hear from her. "Don't you think I know that? I may have been blind where Calstir was concerned, but his betrayal has opened my eyes. To hand me over to the Dark Emperor...?" She froze. "That was a double betrayal. First, Calstir doesn't even try to reconcile the court to my changed appearance, and then he wants to hand me over to that monster," she said. "I am alone now. I will just have to get used to the idea. I'd sign on the *Mermaid* as a hand if Captain Bernst would have me."

"Which he won't, because he's dark fae and doesn't want the wrath of the Dark Emperor to follow him," said Dagstyrr.

"Exactly."

Dagstyrr gazed at her, willing her to turn to him. She would never be alone while he was alive, but he needed to know she wanted him by her side. "You need never be alone," he said, quietly, but he could see she hadn't heard him. She gazed into the middle distance, her thoughts miles away from here.

"I hope I don't go mad," she whispered.

"Remember, it is thousands of years since those warnings were given. Since then, there must have been others who turned dark. I've never heard of anyone going mad and creating evil, have you?"

"No. No, you are right. It is probably foolish talk to frighten us into staying light."

"Tales for naughty children," he said.

"Aye."

"You will never be alone, you know," he said, softly.

She turned to him and smiled, her dark eyes brimming with unshed tears. "I know." Rella reached for him with her one good hand just as Billy appeared.

"The water's good and hot, and I've left fresh towels by the side with some ointments," said Billy. "I'm so sorry, sir."

"What have you to be sorry about, Billy?"

"I shouldn't have told her about her piggin' brother," said Billy, with a vehemence that surprised Dagstyrr. "Shoulda left him to rot in that place."

"This is not your fault, Billy. You did the right thing. I feel at fault too, but this is down to Calstir. Let's lay blame where it's due."

"Aye, sir," said Billy, wiping tears and a little snot from his face onto the one sleeve of his shirt. Dagstyrr could still hardly believe that someone in the court of Casta had so callously taken the boy's other arm when all he'd done was tell the court about Calstir's imprisonment in the citadel. Rella had deflected the blow meant to kill. Bernst had healed him—that said it all.

"I'll get the galley cooking as soon as we're away from here."

"Thanks, Billy."

CHAPTER 24

Rella dozed in the warm, soothing water. She wanted to stay here forever and let Dagstyrr's strong hands gently cleanse her cuts. The healing scents of herbs and flowers filled her body, working their special everyday magic. If she did not move, everything would be perfect. Unfortunately, thirst reared its ugly head, and she licked her cracked lips, tasting blood. It stung.

Slowly but surely, all the abuse she'd suffered made itself known in stings, and aches. She put her good hand to a rib and found it broken. Her swollen elbow hurt terribly. It was then she remembered why and smiled, remembering the crack of Marvn's nose.

"You're awake?" asked Dagstyrr, his voice deep with emotion.

"No, I don't want to wake. I want to stay here in this bath until I don't hurt anymore," she mumbled, her eyes still closed. "But it's too late. I am awake, and everything hurts."

"Here, try this," said Dagstyrr, supporting the back of her head and putting a cup to her lips.

"What is it?" she said, drinking it down thirstily without waiting for an answer.

"One of the captain's remedies. I trust his knowledge," said Dagstyrr a smile playing on his mouth.

She lifted a hand to her swollen eye, grimacing as she felt a bloody crust over the swelling. "One day I'll teach those boys a lesson," she said, meaning her Kemara cousins.

"Not if I find them first," said Dagstyrr, his jaw set in grim determination.

Rella lifted her hand and cupped his jaw. Immediately, his tension relaxed a bit. "Dagstyrr, they are light fae. For all your bravery and skill, you are only human." She saw her words momentarily wound his pride, but sooner or later he was going to have to come to terms with the fact he couldn't fight fae on equal terms.

Then he smiled. "Ah, but I am not alone," he said, gently cleansing her eye.

"What do you mean?" she said. Surely he didn't mean her?

"I have Drago."

"Yes, you most certainly do," she said, remembering the fountains exploding.

It was then Rella noticed the strange campfire smell emanating from him. The front of his hair, and his shirt were scorched. She put up a hand and touched the ends of his hair. It crumbled in her hand like dust. "Drago."

"Let's get ourselves cleaned and fed. Then we'll talk. I think Captain Bernst needs to be part of the conversation. I don't think he's going to like what we have to say," said Dagstyrr, lifting her from the water and onto a warm towel.

Rella laughed. "I'm not a baby. Get into the water, and I will see to myself."

"Are you sure?"

"Yes," she said. It was very tempting to allow him to dry and dress her, but that would be selfish. She understood how he felt about her, and she wasn't immune to his charms either.

He stripped off his badly singed shirt. Then Rella turned her back, gently patting herself dry. Once she heard him immerse himself in the water, she turned to him. "Promise me you'll never lie to me."

His dark blue eyes smoldered with emotion. "I promise, Rella. We are in this thing together now, whether we like it or not. You need never doubt me."

She believed him. "Good, because I don't think I could stand it." She wanted to linger beside him. Wash his back perhaps? Catching a glimpse of her image in her mirror divested her of any such thoughts. No man, human or fae, would welcome her touch. She looked like a monster. No wonder he could look upon her nakedness and not be aroused by it. Throwing on a white silk robe, she retired to the cushioned area they used for eating and talking.

∼

Dagstyrr tried not to focus on Rella's injuries. He knew she was self-conscious about them. Growing up with three light fae brothers, he'd learned to keep quiet at such moments. Now was not the time to tell her that seeing her bravery only endeared her to him. She was the most beautiful creature he'd ever held in his arms. It had been hard to put her down and step away. So, he busied himself pouring drinks and serving the meal.

It was a simple one of bread and soup. Dagstyrr was hungrier than he'd realized, and his thirst was raging—no doubt the after-effects of Drago's presence. As he spooned the delicious soup into his mouth, he thought of Drago and wondered what else they could achieve together. He vaguely remembered him saying something about breathing fire. Surely that was impossible?

One thing was for sure. If he was to stand any chance of rescuing one hundred and sixty-eight dragons, not counting hatchlings or eggs, he must fully understand how his connection to Drago worked.

Captain Bernst entered the cabin interrupting his reverie. "Please join us, Captain," said Dagstyrr. "I'll not want to tell this tale more than once. But first, tell me how you let them get to Rella when she was still onboard the *Mermaid*. I thought she had some protection here?"

Rella's hand on his shirtsleeve stopped him short. "They tricked us," she said.

"Aye. Came down here disguised as an escort. We all thought they'd come to take Rella up to the palace in fine style. A hero's welcome," said Bernst with disgust. "They had me and the crew roped against the bulwark in the blink of an eye. Then the cousins attacked."

Listening to the captain's account of the attack on Rella, Dagstyrr lost his appetite for food. When Bernst described those thugs stripping an unconscious Rella of the rest of her uniform, Dagstyrr could barely contain his fury. Only Rella's hand on his arm stilled his trembling muscles.

"Once they left, it didn't take long for us to break the light ropes that bound us. I knew where they were taking her and had to trust that you'd get her out. So, I concentrated on getting the *Mermaid* ready to depart."

"Thank you for your warning and your advice," said Dagstyrr.

"So, what happened up there?" said Bernst.

Rella reached forward and filled their cups with Samish

wine, keeping her broken hand protected against her cracked ribs. Dagstyrr nodded his thanks. He needed something stronger than water if he was expected to tell such a sorry tale. He'd much rather gloss over the crueler parts, but Captain Bernst deserved to know the truth.

With a deep sigh, he took Rella's good hand in his and started with how Calstir had cleverly lulled him into a sense of ease by appearing to take him into his confidence. Then how Calstir had met with his ministers in full sight, but not hearing. "I should have known their camaraderie wasn't right. That his ministers were not going to be happy unless he had a scapegoat to offer them."

"You couldn't have known," said Rella.

"I honestly believed we were gathered in the great hall to welcome you home a hero. Then Lady Kemara came in..."

Dagstyrr told Captain Bernst the rest of the tale in all its gory detail, leaving nothing out. When it came to Calstir having summoned the Dark Emperor, Rella's hand started to pull from his, but he hung on to it and finished the story.

"That is what I wish I didn't have to tell you, Captain. Not only are we running from the light fae of Casta, we are also running from the Dark Emperor himself. If what I understand is right, you owe him allegiance. He is your master."

Bernst's face was black with rage by this time. "I have no master," he said, bringing his fist down on the table. "Least of all him."

Dagstyrr could tell something was very wrong. He'd never seen the captain look so worried, not even when Drago was hunting them.

"Mind you, he's not to be trifled with, that's for sure," said Bernst, rubbing his hand over his stubbly chin. "From what you tell me, Casta has no choice now. The Dark

Emperor will challenge Casta to battle unless they can produce Rella," said Bernst. "They'll have to be quick too. He's not known for his patience."

"No, no Calstir will look for a diplomatic solution," said Rella. "He'll invite him to the palace. Well, he has already sent an escort to bring him to the palace. Calstir will wine and dine him. He'll lavish him with flattery and entertain him until he finds a resolution. My brother can be very charming and charismatic when he chooses."

"That's as may be, but if I know the Dark Emperor, only one thing will satisfy him—you."

"Well, he isn't going to get her," stated Dagstyrr, his gaze never leaving the captain's one bloodshot eye. If treachery were building on board, Dagstyrr would be ready for it.

"No, lad, he isn't. I promise you that," said Bernst, and Dagstyrr believed he meant it. "I'm going to have to make some arrangements. A change of plan," he said, wiping his mouth with a napkin.

As Bernst ducked out the door, Dagstyrr turned to Rella. "I'm sorry."

"For what?"

"I'm sorry your brother has betrayed you. You of all people deserve his loyalty."

"I should have known. Calstir's always had a ruthless streak in him, and he always obeys the rules," said Rella. She remembered Viktar, her father's first warrior and legendary strategist, could never get it through Calstir's head that sometimes the rules needed to be broken. A true leader, like Viktar, knew when to break them, especially when honor demanded it. "He was my loving brother, and family always meant so much to him—before he was an addict. I was a fool to trust him."

"No, you are never that, Rella. If anyone is a fool, it is Calstir."

"He believes that if he obeys the rules, everything will work out—and the rules say I must die. He must think he's doing me a great favor turning me over to the Dark Emperor instead. Calstir at his most indulgent."

"You told him about the Dark Emperor when he was still imprisoned in the citadel?'

"I had to explain this," she said, indicating her brown eyes and mark. "But he couldn't have sent a message to the Dark Emperor until he set foot on Casta. Even the mountain elves he uses as messengers can't travel that far in a day. By the time the Dark Emperor receives his invitation and then travels here with his entourage, we'll be far away," said Rella, still as a statue.

Dagstyrr wished she'd rant and rave. She was hurting physically, but far more so emotionally, from her brother's betrayal. Why couldn't she just let it out in a rage against injustice? He thought again of how he'd found her in Hedabar, a high light fae princess living on the streets, stinking of the sewer, and so disguised she passed for a boy—all for Calstir. She was much stronger than anyone imagined.

"I think it's time you rested. Who knows what tomorrow will bring?"

Captain Bernst knocked and entered without waiting for an invitation. "Those broken bones in your hand, and your rib. Heal them before you sleep, Rella. Otherwise, you might find they set wrong. However, and this is important, don't heal anything else." Then he left as quickly as he'd appeared, leaving Rella looking puzzled.

"Dagstyrr, I don't know how. I've never tried to heal anyone with my new magic. I only ever used dark-magic to summon more Samish wine, or warm my bathwater," she said, lifting her broken hand and staring at it.

Dagstyrr laughed. "I thought that bottle was lasting a long time. But didn't you use it to impress my mother with a budding rose, and more recently to threaten the court?"

"Don't laugh. Those were desperate circumstances. I have no idea how to heal."

"Yes, I think you do. Otherwise, our good Captain Bernst wouldn't expect you to do it," he said. "You must use that green forest energy you have at your fingertips. That stuff you hate so much. You just said you've been experimenting with it. Let it show you the way."

"What would you know?" she said, surprise in her voice.

"It's worth a try." He shrugged.

"I know how to summon it, but I think using it to heal will require more skill than I have," said Rella. "My blue light fae energy is all about speed, will, and fighting, I know how to use that very well, but we didn't waste our time with healing. We had specialists for that."

"The Crystal Mountain light fae, yes, I know. Still, try it. Gently though," urged Dagstyrr. "I'm sure the captain can help with any mistakes..."

"You mean any damage?"

He shrugged. "That too."

~

Rella drove everything else from her mind and brought forth the dark green energy she so despised. Despite Dagstyrr's confidence, this was a daunting task. She could end up making things far worse if she didn't get it right.

Slowly, the robust green energy started to coalesce at her fingertips. She closed her eyes and directed it carefully over her ribs, sensing its probing energy looking for an injury and retreating when it found none.

Eventually, it found the broken rib. Rella saw in her mind's eye the broken bone slowly knitting together under the direction of the dark fae energy. It was not instantaneous, as she'd imagined, but a slow growing of bone, one piece perfectly matching the other until they were one, and yes, it was leaving a scar on her rib that no one would ever see.

Instinctively, she stopped short of completing the healing. Rella felt the bone should finish the job without her help. She'd accelerated the natural process, but she wasn't confident enough to take it any further.

Pleased with her first attempt at healing, she opened her eyes to see Dagstyrr's worried face gazing down on her. "I'm all right. The rib is healed," she said, watching "I told you so" wash over his handsome face. *No one else cares for me as he does,* she thought. *He is a good man. A pity he's human. Then again, if he were light fae, he'd not be helping me. He'd be out there, hunting me down with the rest of Casta.*

"What are you thinking, Rella?"

"What do you mean?"

He smiled, disarming her.

"I think I've healed my rib," she said self-consciously.

"That's good, but I was talking about the scowl on your face when you opened your eyes and saw me. If I'm not wanted..."

"No. Stay, please. I was thinking of my family," she said, ruefully, "or should I say, lack of family."

"I understand," he whispered.

"No you don't, Dagstyrr of Halfenhaw!" she said, frustrated at his ignorance. "You have a real family, a wonderful family, with a great earl for a father who's not above cooking in a kitchen, and a light fae princess for a mother who breastfed you herself so that you'd be protected from magic all your life. You have three brothers who love you and would do for you as you have done for them.

"Erik is virtually full light fae," she continued, "and when he comes to your defense, all will quake at his prowess. Sigmund and Thorsten will always welcome you to their hearths and defend you against any who dare threaten you."

"I had no idea you felt this way."

Rella was breathing hard; her anger and pain poured out of her like an exploding geyser. She couldn't stop it. Until this moment, Rella hadn't realized how much she envied Dagstyrr. He might be human, but he was more blessed than she would ever be. "Get out!"

CHAPTER 25

She threw you out?

"Yep." Dagstyrr leaned against the prow, one hand on the figurehead.

She'll come around, said the *Mermaid*.

"I hope so," said Dagstyrr, sincerely. "She's obstinate, frustrating, wonderful..."

You mean, you love her?

"Very well. Yes. She's so vulnerable and angry. All at the same time."

She'd not thank you for saying that.

"Don't I know it," said Dagstyrr with a grin. "Rella's also strong, brave, resourceful... I could go on, but I'd hate to bore you."

She's also beautiful.

"Ah, yes, don't think I hadn't noticed. In truth, she's the most beautiful woman I've ever seen, but she's so much more than that," said Dagstyrr. "I didn't know she had a temper, did you?"

Most people do. Don't tell me you thought her so pretty she'd be without such harsh emotions, said the *Mermaid*, laughing.

Dagstyrr noticed the captain hovering close by. "What is it, Captain? I have no secrets from the *Mermaid*," he said.

"We want to cloak the ship in a fogbank for the night. It can be dangerous. I suggest you stay inside until the morning," said Captain Bernst.

"You mean I might fall overboard? Have you forgotten I've been sailing since I was a child?"

"Don't laugh, I've seen it happen, and to more experienced sailors than you, lad," said Captain Bernst, turning his back and heading for the stern, where he preferred to sit and watch his crew.

"Very well. Goodnight, *Mermaid*," Dagstyrr said with a small bow, then made his way to Rella's cabin. He hoped she'd receive him. He didn't fancy spending the night hard against the bulwark, scared to move.

He needn't have worried. Rella was already in her sleeping chamber and didn't make a sound when he bedded down on the cushions beside the curtain. He hoped she'd managed to heal the broken bones in her hand. If they healed badly, it would affect her use of sword and knife, and she'd be furious with herself.

He wanted to reach out beyond the curtain and pull her into his arms, to hold and protect her forevermore. With a sigh, he pulled off his shirt and boots and lying down, turned his back on temptation.

He could hear her steady breathing on the other side of the silk partition. After a few moments, just as sleep was claiming him, he felt a hand creep over his waist and around him. With a smile, he raised it and tested every finger. Assured, he kissed each finger, then replaced her hand on his body, placing his callused hand on top. He'd sleep well now.

The morning came with a storm. Rella had slept well, better than she deserved with all her cuts and bruises. Why had Captain Bernst told her not to heal them? She must find out, and soon.

The rolling of the ship forced Rella and Dagstyrr to rise before dawn. Throwing on a silk overdress, she settled against the cushions, content to stay in her cabin until the storm passed. Thoughts of the Dark Emperor descending on Casta with his entourage of strange creatures made this storm seem a mere trifle. That was the disaster she feared—Casta at war. There would be so many deaths, and all because she hadn't kept her promise and pay the agreed price.

Dagstyrr washed on deck, as was his habit, leaving her some privacy to attend to her toilette. Today he returned quickly, with fresh bread and cheese wrapped in a large napkin and tucked inside his tunic, thus saving it from the worst of the seawater surging over the sides of the small ship.

"Here," he said, putting their breakfast on the table. "It's the best the galley can do under these circumstances." Water dripped from his dark hair and down the front of his shirt.

The cheese was good and sharp and the bread soft and sweet. Rella was hungry and ate in silence. It would be so easy to stay on board the *Mermaid*, return to Halfenhaw, pick up the other two ships, then sail away with Dagstyrr to whatever fate and dragons awaited them. However, Rella had never been one for passive acceptance of whatever vagaries life had in store for her.

She might be dark fae now, but she was also a high

princess, and not one to hide. She was a warrior, a maker of destiny. What she needed was a plan. As she reached across the table for the jug of water, the bruises and crusty cuts on her body made their presence felt. "If I don't have a good reason from Bernst for keeping these cuts and bruises, I will heal them myself this afternoon," she said, irritated. "I'm tired of seeing out of one eye only."

"He's busy with this storm," said Dagstyrr, who seemed lost in thought.

She refused to complain about the way her injuries made her look, which was frightful. Dagstyrr's opinion of her was absurdly important to her at this moment, and she didn't want him to think her vain. No doubt, as a human he'd sustained similar injuries, so he should think nothing of it.

The ship lurched hard to port sending their food sliding off the table onto the floor, where the water gushed in under the door. Rella slid hard against Dagstyrr, who had no time to react. It was upon this mess that Captain Bernst landed after bursting through the door of the cabin. "I know it's rough, but you're both leaving the ship as soon this storm abates. I reckon we've seen the worst of it," he said, pushing up from the soft landing the cushions had given him.

"Do you think the Dark Emperor will follow the *Mermaid*?" said Dagstyrr.

"I know he will. It's important neither of you are here when he catches up with us. I told you I had to change plans, this is it."

He braced one hand on the doorframe, the other wiping seawater from his face. "I'll send Billy in to help you."

"Where are we?" said Dagstyrr.

"Somewhere the Dark Emperor won't think to look for you, I hope"

"You're abandoning us?" said Rella, stunned at the abrupt change. She would have continued, had Dagstyrr's hand on her arm not stayed her for a moment.

"Captain Bernst is correct, Rella. We cannot bring harm to the *Mermaid*. He can go on to Halfenhaw and claim his prize. Let my family know what has happened. Right Captain?"

"Aye, but meanwhile, you two will need to live as ordinary humans, quietly, and making sure to arouse no suspicion. If I'm not mistaken, the Dark Emperor will put out rewards as soon as he knows you've escaped him. You must live completely as human, Rella. Remember, a spider or a flower can talk to him as well as you or I. There must be no indication that you are anything other than what you appear to be."

"Is that why you told me not to heal my cuts and bruises?"

"Aye. I'll send Billy with you. He'll help you adjust to living an ordinary life."

"That won't be necessary, Captain. You forget, I am fully human," said Dagstyrr.

"Aye, a lordling of Halfenhaw. Tell me, how often have you been paid a wage?"

"Never," admitted Dagstyrr, starting to understand it wasn't just the human part that they must obey but also the "ordinary."

"Billy can help you with that. You'll arrive as husband, wife, and son. You're a surly brute, Dagstyrr. Rella, you're a mouthy wife who deserves all she gets. Billy is your son, kind and eager to lend a hand. That way the villagers will give you two a wide berth but allow Billy into their gatherings. He'll be your eyes and ears."

"You've got this all figured out," said Dagstyrr, his jaw set hard to match his frown.

"Someone had to. Now, get a move on," said Bernst, leaving the cabin.

Rella stared at the closed door. "Why is he so surly with us?"

"He has big responsibilities, and we've put them in danger," said Dagstyrr.

"It wasn't your fault, or Billy's."

"Well, the Dark Emperor knows I'm with you now, thanks to our spectacular exit from court, and Billy would be in too much danger if we left him behind. From what I've heard the Dark Emperor hates humans. Believe me, Bernst's kinder than most captains. There's some I know would throw us overboard and claim ignorance of us. Or worse, take us straight to the Dark Emperor for a fat reward."

Rella thought about it before turning to Dagstyrr. "You're right. I've been showing the same arrogance as Calstir. Assuming what's good for me is good for everyone, and that is not true."

Dagstyrr stood and pulled her up into his arms, and she went gratefully. At least she'd have his strength and protection to succor her through the days to come. "We'd better start packing," said Dagstyrr, planting a light kiss on her head.

Billy came in shyly. "I've clothes for you, mistress. Captain says to leave all those silks and fineries here."

"Thank you, son," said Dagstyrr, taking the bundle from him with a wink.

Billy lowered his head, but not before Rella saw a small smile appear. Unfortunately, she was frustrated at the idea of hiding out for an indeterminate length of time. She was used to planning ahead.

Once Billy left the cabin, Dagstyrr said, "I don't suppose it will be for too long. Besides, it will give us some time to plan our next move."

He knew her too well.

∾

They were put ashore on a rowboat upon a sandy beach in the middle of nowhere. A man waiting on shore, jumped into the boat as soon as they were out. "The house is empty. Look after the horses!" he yelled over the noise of waves crashing ashore.

He must be one of Captain Bernst's many cousins, thought Rella. The storm was dying, but the squalls this close to shore made it hard to stand. Rella lifted her bundle of clothes and followed Dagstyrr up the sandy dunes.

With one eye swollen shut and sand in the other, it was almost impossible for her to see. Billy, shouldering his bundle, took her hand and led her steadily along. Dagstyrr strode on ahead never even looking back.

Eventually, Dagstyrr stopped. He raised his arm, pointed, and then continued. Rella was becoming more furious every moment. The poor leather shoes on her feet were letting in stones, and she kept having to stop and empty them. The brown cloth wrap Bernst had given her was coming undone, and wet ropes of hair plastered her face. As a warrior she'd faced many hardships, but this was intolerable. She couldn't even use her magic to make things more comfortable.

Billy took no notice of the wind or rain. Was this truly what it was like being human in these northern waters? Hedabar was bad enough, but this was so much worse. It was so cold.

Rella knew she would end up using her magic in this place. She was a fae warrior, not some victim cowering from those who were after her.

She saw a modest house at the end of the meandering road. Four horses huddled under a shelter in a corner of the field, and Rella knew exactly how they felt. Their dejected heads hung low, and, even though they couldn't hear, she whispered to them, "It won't last much longer."

Dagstyrr was already at the house. She saw him knock on the wooden door, and go in.

"We're nearly there, mistress," called Billy over the wind.

Why didn't Dagstyrr come and carry her? Then she laughed. Hadn't she objected strongly every time he did?

"What's funny, mistress?" asked Billy.

"Life, Billy, never works out the way you expect."

"That's very true, mistress."

The wind shifted to drive the rain directly in their faces as they slogged up the long, muddy path leading to the house. Rella pushed open the door, and Billy slipped past just as the wind slammed the door shut behind them, startling her.

The house consisted of one room with an inglenook fireplace, a table and chairs, and an alcove in which a large feather bed awaited. There was a stone sink at the far end under a window overlooking a patch of sorry-looking vegetables. To the right, she saw what looked like a door to a small pantry.

Dagstyrr stood looking out the window with his back to them. He turned as Rella placed her bundle of sodden clothes on the table.

"Billy," said Dagstyrr, "get the fire going and put water on to boil. Rella, you can hang up our wet clothes here," he said, lowering a contraption on a pulley system that hung in front of the fireplace. "Then I suggest you find dusters and polish and get to work. Find out if there's any food in that larder."

Rella opened her mouth to speak, but Dagstyrr beat her to it.

"I'm going to make sure the horses have dry feed," he said, pulling on a broad felt hat that must have come with the house. "I'll see if the barn looks in good shape. You'll bed down there, Billy."

"I'll enjoy that. It's a long time since I had a billet that didn't rock," said the boy, busily brushing out the cinders still in the grate from the last occupants.

Rella stood with her hands on her hips, at a loss as she watched his back disappear into the storm. What was driving Dagstyrr? Well, she'd make sure they were comfortable. Perhaps then he'd open up to her.

She walked into the dusty larder, full of spiderwebs and dead moths. Taking the time to feel her energy build, she summoned forth her dark magic and slowly healed every cut, scratch, and bruise until she felt normal again. Captain Bernst was too cautious, and Dagstyrr had to learn that hiding from her enemies was not in her nature.

"Now for some food." First, she gently persuaded all the living creatures hiding in the larder to vacate. Then she sought out crumbs of food left behind. Using their energy signature to guide her, she filled the larder with simple things to eat: bread, cheese, herbed sausage, and a few vegetables. "There, that's not too much," she said, starting to enjoy her new dark fae magic. It was so practical.

She re-entered the one room just as Billy finished laying the fire. Without thinking, she walked over and lit it for him.

"Mistress!" He recoiled in horror. "Remember what the captain said about not using magic."

"I'm sure he only meant outside, where others can see us," said Rella wiping away months of dust and dirt with a wave of her hand.

"What about the spiders? The captain said they could talk to..."

"I asked them nicely to leave. I didn't damage anything they weren't already finished with. Besides, you-know-who won't be looking for us yet. He won't even know I'm gone from Casta."

"How do you know?"

"Even the Dark Emperor can't defy time and space. He must have a way to go before he reaches Casta."

"Well, I guess there's no harm just this once," said Billy with a grin. "How about you drying out our clothes and I'll get some supper in the pot?"

"Good idea, Billy. Perhaps some food in his stomach will cheer Dagstyrr up. Something is troubling him, and I swear I don't know what," said Rella, laying out their clothes before drying them, folding them, and placing them in the chest by the door.

"You should call Dagstyrr and me Father and Mother for the time being."

"Nope. Won't do it. Don't ask me why, cause I won't tell you nothing neither."

Rella's concern for Billy's past grew, but she didn't push him. "Very well, but if there are others around, try and manage a 'Ma' or 'Pa.'"

"Hmm."

As Rella sorted through their garments, she thought of her uniform and regretted its loss. She valued her white-kilted leather uniform above all else. She itched to heft a weapon and feel the weight of a war helmet. She wanted to be a warrior again.

Perhaps that was what troubled Dagstyrr. Exchanging his armor for a felt hat and his sword for a plow must be hard.

∽

Dagstyrr approached the horses shivering in the lean-to shelter. He carried a large bucket of oats. Lifting the tin lid he'd used to keep the rain off, he held out a handful to the big stallion that was keeping the mare and fillies behind him. Not yet trusting Dagstyrr, the stallion came forward slowly and lifted his huge black head. His eyes rolled this way and that, looking for deception where there was none.

After a second and third handful of oats, Dagstyrr poured some into the feed bin so that all the horses could enjoy it. He gently stroked the stallion's face, sliding his hand farther and farther down his neck to his withers.

It felt good to deal with ordinary chores. It gave him a few moments to consider the future. Rella was not going to allow Bernst, or anyone else, to prevent her from following the path she thought was hers. If a war started, she'd want to drop everything and join the fight—but how? She'd no longer be welcome as a commander of Casta troops. They'd hand her over to the Dark Emperor in an instant. So what could she do? Surely, she wouldn't sacrifice herself by going to him voluntarily?

Dagstyrr would rather die than see that happen.

He knew Calstir well enough to know he'd happily go to war with the Dark Emperor to defend Casta. Calstir saw himself as a great king, and that's what mighty kings did.

Somehow he must convince her that it was others who caused it. If anyone was to blame, it was Calstir and the

Dark Emperor. Whatever happened, she must not go anywhere near the Dark Emperor.

"When this weather clears, we'll go for a ride, boy." As if he understood, the big horse nodded, his head his wet mane splashing Dagstyrr's face.

Dagstyrr suspected this farm belonged to the captain. He'd seen a small village below them in a hollow, less than a mile away. They were far enough away not to bother strangers, and knowing Bernst, they were probably used to strangers here. The rain stopped suddenly, and the wind started to lose ferocity, but dark clouds scudded across the skies, promising more bad weather to come.

The farm was an excellent place to hide, but Dagstyrr couldn't afford to hide out. He too had a quest. He needed to raise what forces he could to rescue Drago and his kin.

One of the young fillies sidestepped her sire and nuzzled his hand, looking for treats, her nose impossibly soft. "What's your name, girl? Moon. I think I'll call you Dark Moon," said Dagstyrr, though he couldn't think why.

The horses followed him to the barn. He would get them into a routine of spending their days in the paddock and nights in the barn. It would mean Billy mucking out, but the horses would be company for him in the night. Dagstyrr thought it a good compromise.

After rubbing them down, he made sure the horses had plenty of fresh hay and water; then he inspected the rest of the barn, which was dry and secure. Billy would be comfortable in the hayloft.

Somehow, he must convince Rella to own her new position in life. To see the truth of how amazing she truly was. That was the key. Only then would she have the strength to defy the Dark Emperor. She could learn from Captain Bernst.

With a lighter step, he made his way to the dripping house. That storm had proved too much for the wooden gutters and water still poured off the roof and beams. He opened the door to find Rella bathing in a tin tub in front of the fire, the familiar scent of roses and peppermint filling the air. A red-faced Billy stood with his back to her, stirring a pot over the open fire. The place was sparkling clean, a vision of domestic bliss.

Dagstyrr saw red.

CHAPTER 26

Rella smiled up at Dagstyrr but saw the dark shadow that had taken root in his handsome face had not relented. "Are you not pleased?" she asked, her soapy arms indicating the warm welcoming home she'd made for them.

He ignored her, which stung more than she wanted to admit.

"Billy, is that food ready?" he said.

"Aye, it is," answered the boy never taking his eyes from the pot.

"Take yours out to the barn. There's plenty of blankets, and you'll have the horses for company."

Billy dished out a bowl of stew and sidled away from Rella and out the door as quickly as he could. She didn't blame him. Dagstyrr was insufferable. Well, it was time to get to the bottom of it. She stood, letting the water drip off her, not caring that he could see her naked, her mark exposed for him to see in all its horror.

"Why are you so cruel? Billy has done nothing wrong."

"Get dressed. We'll eat, then talk," said Dagstyrr, heading for the stewpot and ladle.

Rella saw the exhaustion on his face. It etched small lines at the edges of his eyes and deepened the hollow of his cheeks. With a wave of her smallest finger, she could wipe it out. As a fae, she could fill him with vigor and energy, but she knew it would only increase the anger building in him if she did.

Dutifully, she donned her mud-brown dress and wrapped her hair in a fresh linen cloth. She brought bread to the table and served the stew in silence. The food was exceptionally good, but Rella took no pleasure in it. She watched Dagstyrr spoon it into his mouth as if it were the poorest tavern fare fit only to sustain, not pleasure, the body.

With a sigh, he sat back and pushed his empty plate away. "That was good."

"So, not all manners have deserted you then?"

"I have things on my mind."

"Drago?"

"Yes."

"Well don't take it out on me or Billy. Talk to me about it," she said.

"Don't you think you could have discussed it with me before defying Bernst's orders, Rella? What kind of example is that for Billy?"

"I was tired, hungry, and miserable," she stated. "Every inch of me hurt. I put an end to it."

"Did you not listen to Captain Bernst?"

"Aye, I listened, I heard, and I understood him. However, I'm a light fae princess, and I don't take orders from him any more than he takes orders from the Dark Emperor."

"Dark. You're dark fae and not one of their princesses."

His words cut her like a knife. Forcing her to face what she wanted to deny. Wounded far more than she would ever have him know, she fought the tears welling up in her eyes and swallowed the salty taste in the back of her throat. Rella turned her head and blinked rapidly until she felt able to answer. "Something has happened to you, Dagstyrr. You have become cruel."

"If I sound cruel, it is because you refuse to accept reality, Rella. Calstir betrayed you in the worst possible way, and the Dark Emperor is coming for you." He stood and rounded the table and, taking her elbow, he raised her to her feet and drew her toward the only mirror in the place. "Look. Take a long hard look at yourself, Rella. You are dark fae. Just as powerful and strong a warrior as you ever were, but dark all the same."

She flinched under his scrutiny, not wanting to face her brown-eyed image in the mirror.

"We have made a sorry mess of things, you and I, and unless we face the truth head on, we are defeated," he added.

Rella turned her head so the mark on her face was not visible in the mirror and leaned her head back against his chest. He took her chin and moved her head to the side so that the mark was once again visible in the mirror. A tear slipped down her face. "Why are you so cruel, Dagstyrr of Halfenhaw?"

"I don't want to be cruel," his said, his voice roughened by emotion. "Why are you so blind, Rella of the dark fae?"

"I am not of the dark fae, nor am I blind," she said. "I see only too well. I have been betrayed by the one person supposed to protect me. I gave Calstir all he has. I gave him his freedom; his crown, his position, and it cost me everything—who I am, who I was yet to become, my home, my sword, my very face!" she shouted to the mirror.

"Then do something about it."

"I cannot be consort to the Dark Emperor," she said with a shudder that reverberated down her whole body. She remembered the earthy smell that permeated his palace at Thingstyrbol, the way he looked at her like she was a tasty morsel for him to savor.

"Of course not," he said, and she felt his hands tense on her shoulders. "Don't even say such a thing."

"Casta will be thrown into a war with the Dark Emperor. People will die because of me. Can I be that selfish?"

"So, you no longer believe that Calstir will try and avoid going to war."

"I have tried to deny it, but it's time for me to face the truth about my brother. There will be a war for sure. Calstir will enjoy leading Casta's troops."

"Yes. I fear he will. Do you think the Dark Emperor is strong enough to defeat him?"

"I have been thinking about the Dark Emperor. I am beginning to believe he was once light fae. If so, he may be mad. An army led by such a creature will be formidable."

"You will not go to him?" said Dagstyrr his voice rough with emotion.

"Never."

"I believe he hates Casta. If Calstir had succeeded in handing me over to be his consort, he would thumb his nose, and then he'd go to war anyway. I fear it is a war he wants, whether I go to him or not."

"He was light fae? So, he is like you. Why didn't you tell me this before? I thought no light fae had turned dark in hundreds of years," said Dagstyrr.

"No one seems to know about him, but the more I think about it, the more I'm convinced he was once light fae."

"What makes you think so?"

"When he touched me, I sensed something in him that I didn't expect."

"The knowing."

"The what?"

"Erik calls it 'the knowing.'"

"That's a good name for it. We have no particular name for it. It's a sensing of magic that happens when one fae touches another," said Rella, remembering the Dark Emperor's touch. Was it madness she'd felt?

"Who do you think will win if it comes to a full-scale battle?"

"Casta," she said automatically. "I know their troops. They are well trained and organized. If the fight is on Casta land, they will win the first battle for sure."

"Then if Calstir wants to stop a war, that is when he'll start negotiations. He'll find terms acceptable to the Dark Emperor. It is no longer your problem, Rella. If what you say about him wanting war is true, it never *was* your problem."

"It is my problem. These are my people about to die. I started it all when I went to the Dark Emperor."

"No, you didn't, the Dark Emperor did. Please, don't think like that."

She let herself go limp. What was the use of fighting him? He was relentless, and may the gods help her, he was right. "Tell me then," she said. "How am I to think?"

"Like Rella. Like the clever, resourceful, noble fae you are."

"I don't know who I am anymore, Dagstyrr."

She saw a slow smile spread across his face, and his eyes light up. "Yes you do. Your defiance of the captain's orders says it all. You're still the powerful, warrior fae you always were. A uniform doesn't make you a warrior. It's what's inside you, here, that matters." He pointed to her chest.

He was right. On the ship, she'd allowed self-pity to blind her. She was as strong as she'd always been. If she could get Calstir out of the citadel, she could defeat the Dark Emperor and put an end to him and his war with Casta. "You are so right, Dagstyrr. Just don't expect me to live cold, hungry, and bruised, for that is not who I am. I am Rella, a warrior fae, and I take orders from no one," she said, lifting her head a little higher.

His eyes in the mirror sought hers, and she felt the impact of their dark blue depths. He was a very special human, indeed. "Very well, just keep your magic indoors for now," he said.

He made it all sound so simple.

"Agreed. I have some wine. If you are interested?" she said, changing the subject.

"The wine sounds good," he conceded. "I am hoping, that as long as your magic is behind closed doors, it will go undetected by the villagers. For that is what I believe Captain Bernst feared. Remember, the dark fae in these parts live unnoticed among humans. It is how they stay safe," he said, with a smile.

"What do you mean?"

"You must do whatever you think is right, Rella. I have every faith in you."

"Of course," she said, grinning up at him. They still hadn't discussed Drago, she realized.

Dagstyrr smiled down at her, making her feel very self-conscious. She'd never questioned what kind of person she was before. But being an outcast was like being stripped naked. You had to question everything about yourself.

"I hadn't meant to endanger anyone," said Rella pouring wine into rough wooden cups. "I will make sure to keep all magic indoors. Though I had intended to help those vegetables in the garden."

As Rella spoke, she knew this was dark fae magic talking. She'd never felt the desire to grow anything before she'd acquired this green magic, never mind vegetables.

"Don't worry. Set Billy to hoe and weed them, and as soon as the sun comes out, they will thrive quite naturally all by themselves," said Dagstyrr. "Hopefully, Bernst will be back before too long."

The high feather bed in the alcove called to her, but she was determined not to suggest they retire. She wanted him so badly, but was it fair to Dagstyrr to saddle him with a mate who hadn't even come to terms with what she was? A mate who might yet go mad?

Dagstyrr deserved more.

Yet this growing attraction between them could not be ignored much longer. Every time he stood close her pulse quickened like a lovesick girl's.

"I think it's time for bed," he said, looking everywhere but at her. "If you want, I can sleep on the floor."

"No. I mean...I put a bolster down the middle earlier. It will be just like it was on the ship. No need for the floor," she said, busy clearing the table.

CHAPTER 27

Dagstyrr awoke to the sound of Billy stoking the fire. Pulling back the curtain, he saw the boy struggle to lift a heavy pot onto the hook one handed. He got up and grabbed the handle before Billy sent the water splashing over the coals that were just starting to catch.

"Thank you, sir," said Billy. "I've soaked the porridge overnight. My ma always had a pot stirring early, and as we're to live like humans, I thought it a good idea."

"An excellent idea, Billy. How did you sleep?"

"Well, thank you, sir. I made a good bed of hay and plenty of blankets. The horses make me feel safe. They'd kick up a ruckus if there was anything amiss."

Rella emerged from behind the curtain fully dressed. "Did I hear mention of porridge?"

They ate some time later, enjoying the sun streaming through the window. "We need some rules around here," said Rella, as Billy set about washing up the bowls. "I'm not to use magic outdoors, only indoors from now on. That will lighten the chores for all of us. Meantime, I must find out more about this dark magic, and how it works. Who I am."

Billy's laugh bounced off the window. "You're Rella, Princess Rella."

Dagstyrr laughed too. "That she is, Billy, but dark fae magic is new to her. She needs to take the time to understand it. I'll work with the horses. I need to know I can trust them on a journey if Bernst is delayed too long, and we have to leave. At some point, I'll need to find a good smith. My hand feels empty without a sword in it, and I'm sure Rella's does too," he said, winking at her. She scowled as if he'd just read her mind and revealed a secret.

"What about me?" said Billy, looking down at his empty sleeve. "I'll never be able to hold a sword and fight like a man."

"I've known two one-armed swordsmen in my time. If it's what you really want, Billy, it can be done," said Dagstyrr. "Or perhaps you'll prefer the ax? Meantime, we still need you to tend the vegetable garden and muck out the stables."

"No trouble, them's light chores," said Billy, with a smile. "I think sword is better, like Rella and Cap'n Bernst."

The sun shining in the front window suddenly dimmed, and Dagstyrr's senses went on high alert. "What is that?" he said, striding across the room to look out the front window. He moved quickly, throwing open the door. Rella and Billy joined him. In the far distance, a dark green cloud had risen above the forest blotting out the sun. He saw Rella's hand go to her throat and heard her gasp.

"So, that is dark fae battle magic?" whispered Billy.

"I think so," answered Rella.

As they watched, more green mist billowed up from the earth, and then the sky was riven with bright blue flashes of light fae strikes.

"I don't understand," said Rella. "How could this be happening so soon?"

Dagstyrr frowned at the panic sounding in her voice. "Calstir must have taken the Casta army to meet the Dark Emperor. It is what I would have done," he said casually, trying to calm her.

"But how could the Dark Emperor's army be on the road so quickly?" said Rella.

"Calstir sent a messenger to the Dark Emperor the moment he arrived in Casta. A second messenger telling him you'd run away would only have been a few hours behind. Once out of Casta, they could probably use the Dark Emperor's own relay system to send messages. Who knows? He may already have been on his way." Dagstyrr put his arm around her shoulders and she leaned into him.

"Aye, and the Dark Emperor can run like a deer at the head of his army, all day and all night if necessary," said a deep voice that sent chills down Dagstyrr's spine.

All three froze.

An extraordinary man was seated on a tree stump not six feet away from the door. He looked ancient. His face was lined like crumpled leather, and his white hair and beard wafted in the breeze beneath his woolen hat. Though he appeared no taller than Billy, his shoes indicated his feet were large, and his hands were adorned with fingers twice the length of his palms. "Who are you?" said Dagstyrr, pushing Rella and Billy behind him.

"What are you?" said Billy, unabashed.

"He's a mountain elf," said Rella, sounding wary.

"Is he like the Dark Emperor?" said Billy, now wary.

"The one calling himself the Dark Emperor is an abomination who usurped the throne of the Dark Queen."

"This is true," said Rella. "This gentleman is a mountain

elf, quite different." Rella knew the mountain elves rarely showed themselves to others, and never to humans. His people were dark fae who lived in the mountains with their own culture, king, and court. They rarely mixed with other dark fae, but from what he'd just said, they were not allies of the Dark Emperor.

"You've seen my kind before, mistress?"

"Aye. In the citadel," she said sadly.

The little man's face turned almost black with temper. "What do you know of the citadel, mistress?"

"I have been there. I rescued my brother from the vizier," said Rella.

"Impossible!"

"Not impossible. She helped me rescue my three brothers," said Dagstyrr, not sure how much they should tell the curious fellow.

"You must be Dagstyrr of Halfenhaw."

"How do you know who I am?"

"There is only one person rescued kin from the citadel. Dagstyrr of Halfenhaw."

"Who are you? Why are you here?" said Dagstyrr. If this mountain elf could find them, so could Calstir or the Dark Emperor.

"I am Englesten, a friend. It's all over the high mountains, the tale of the human who rescued three light fae brothers and a prince from the vizier."

Rella and Dagstyrr looked at each other, frowning. Their story had been corrupted in its retelling and Rella's part had been written out of it.

Just then, a flash of blue fire lit the sky, splitting the green cloud. "They're at it in earnest now," said Englesten.

"I wish I could see what's going on," said Dagstyrr.

"Me too," said Rella.

"Do you trust me?" said Englesten.

"Your kind have never hurt mine," said Rella.

"We prefer to keep to ourselves."

Englesten closed his eyes and reached out with his long fingers to grab, first Dagstyrr's hand, then Rella's. Immediately, Dagstyrr was in the thick of battle, not only seeing the carnage but smelling the death and fear all around him. Blue bolts tore through groups of dark fae, followed by a screaming charge of light fae warriors with their swords in hand.

The dark fae magic crept along the forest floor like a thick carpet, then rose up and engulfed large groups of light fae leaving them slow and lethargic, unable to swing a sword fast enough to beat back their foe. Each side was losing warriors at an incredible rate.

Dagstyrr pulled his hand from Englesten's. "Enough, thank you," said Dagstyrr. It was unlike any other battle he'd seen, but some things were always the same: the fear, the blood, the noise, and the panic—a deathly nightmare.

Dagstyrr looked at Rella. Her face mirrored the turmoil in his head. "Enough, Rella," he said, taking her hand from Englesten's. "There is no need to punish yourself."

"I caused this."

"No, you didn't," said Dagstyrr drawing her aside where the mountain elf wouldn't overhear.

"I'm glad I saw it. It has helped me make a decision," said Rella, strangely calm.

The determination in her voice worried Dagstyrr. "Should we let him stay? I'm worried about how he found us so easily."

"He knows I could kill him in a instant. I don't think he's a threat," she said.

"Still, I want him gone," said Dagstyrr. Then again, the

odd fellow did seem to be more interested in Dagstyrr than Rella, so perhaps he was harmless.

They let the strange little man stay and rest. For a few hours, the four of them watched the battle energies light the sky in all the shades of blue and green they could imagine. Sometimes one side appeared to be winning, sometimes the other. With every flash of battle energy, Dagstyrr could see Rella's guilt etch itself on her beautiful face. He knew she imagined her warriors there without her and guilt for the carnage grew.

What they were watching in the sky was only an indication of the devastation and death that littered the battlefield. Dagstyrr could almost taste the battle in his mouth.

Billy, who was oblivious to the horror of the slaughter, brought out bread rolls for them to eat. Dagstyrr could see down to the village, where people stood outside their houses, watching the unnatural display. They had no idea what was happening.

Dagstyrr kept the horses in the barn in case it spooked them. Even so, as a particularly bright spark of blue cracked across the sky, he could hear them whinny. Rella called Billy into the house, whispering to him.

When next they emerged, Billy ran off toward the village. "Where have you sent him?"

"Just for some supplies."

"We don't need supplies," said Dagstyrr.

"I do," said Rella, her chin set determinedly.

"Women always need their supplies, Dagstyrr of Halfenhaw. Our lives are generally better for letting them have their way," said the mountain elf.

"Perhaps, but I don't want anything to happen to Billy. I'm going after him."

"People might question who you are," said Rella anxiously. "That's why I sent Billy. He's human."

"So am I," said Dagstyrr. "I'll go with him. Make sure he's all right.

Englesten stood. "Then I'll be off. I just wanted to let you know that when the time comes, the mountain elves are with you, Dagstyrr. Some of our people are in the citadel, and we want to help you get them out."

"I think there's been some confusion. I'm going to rescue the dragons, not the prisoners."

"The rumor is, you're planning on rescuing all the prisoners," said Englesten, obviously distressed.

"No, that was never my plan. I would not bring your people false hope, Englesten. Even if it were possible to rescue everyone, I doubt they'd survive long without powerful magical healing, or the dragon's blood they're addicted to," said Dagstyrr. "Once I rescue the dragons, there will be no more dragon's blood."

"Still, we aim to be with you. When the time comes, I'll bring an army of mountain elves. We are short of stature but big in fighting skills," boasted the little man. "And stealth. We're very good with stealth. Remember that, Dagstyrr of Halfenhaw."

Dagstyrr couldn't believe what he was hearing. Did the whole world know of Drago and Dagstyrr's promise to rescue him? He watched Englesten wave and then take off, running toward the forest, which he reached remarkably quickly.

"I wonder who Englesten's loved one in the citadel is," said Dagstyrr before turning and following Billy.

Another strike of bright blue energy flashed across the sky piercing a large cloud of green before charging to the ground. It made little inroad into the huge turgid mass boiling over the battle.

∽

Rella watched the battle signs. With every blast of blue or billowing cloud of green, her fingers twitched to be in the thick of it. "I am a warrior first," she whispered to herself. Looking down at her hands, she remembered the bright blue energy that used to spark from them.

"I am light fae. I am dark fae. I am a warrior. I am noble fae." She looked up, and there in the sky above the land, the turbulence mirrored the turmoil inside her. She reached out to a flower growing by the door, a rose. Holding her hand above it, she pulled its energy into her fingers. It was sweet and surprisingly strong. Sitting down on a smooth rock, she allowed the earth's energy to enter her. It filled her up. So strong, so very strong and vital, it was like nothing she'd imagined. It was time to stop fighting it and learn how to use it.

Rella sat and pondered her situation. One thing was for sure, she couldn't stay here too long. If Englesten had found them, so could others.

Dagstyrr was very insightful. Rella couldn't help wishing she had some of his ability to see the truth of a matter and act accordingly. She, it seemed was easily deceived, especially by those she loved. That put them all in danger.

At the thought of Calstir, a shiver ran down her spine. Her pain at his betrayal was morphing into rage. She looked again at the turbulent skies, the green shot through with shards of bright fae blue. "He doesn't deserve to have me for a sister!" she screamed into the wind, and with that scream came a torrent of tears.

Angry for showing such weakness, she stood, held up her hands, and discharged the magical energy there in a small show of strength. Dark green burst from her hands, powerful and strong. Then an extraordinary thing happened: blue energy followed it. Bright and light it came in spurts at first, then as a brilliant blue stream winding itself into the green—not destroying it. Then it was gone.

How could this be?

She dismissed it as some remnants of light fae energy left deep within her. Then a feeling of awe filled her. Could it be?

Careful to hide behind the house, away from prying eyes, she stretched out her hand and let her magic flow gently to the ground. There it was again, both green and blue. She had both at her fingertips.

Rella smiled. At last, she was ready to take charge of her life. Once a sword was in her hand, she'd feel her magic burgeoning for release in battle. All she needed now was a new cohort to command. Then the Dark Emperor's days would be numbered.

∞

The battle between Casta and the Dark Emperor raged on long after Dagstyrr and Billy returned. It took all of Rella's determination to conjure a simple meal. She knew Billy would be hungry, even if she and Dagstyrr couldn't stomach food. Soon the battle would be over, and no matter who won or lost, the dead and dying would litter the field. From what they could see, it looked like the two armies were evenly matched. Rella suspected both would claim victory.

Frustrated at having to watch the battle from afar when she could do nothing about it, she went inside. Billy followed her. "I have what you asked for, mistress," he said, pulling his hand from deep within his trouser pocket.

She smiled as, with great ceremony, he laid his treasures out on the table. First, shards of metal, steel, and iron from the smithy; then a short lace of leather from the tannery; a pretty stone from the path; a shard of oak; and a scraping of multi-layered paint from the garden gate. "Is it all right?"

"Yes, Billy, it looks fine," said Rella, rubbing the steel between two fingers and sensing its crazy blended life force. Everything had a life force, but when two natural elements were bonded together, the result was a dizzying mix of energies. "You've done well," she said with a smile. "Now, off with you," she said, ruffling his hair. "You look tired. It's been a difficult day."

"You can say that again. I've heard of mountain elves, but never thought to meet one. Do you think they can be dangerous?"

"All creatures can be dangerous, Billy. If there are enough of them, even a harmless insect can devastate a crop or make people desert their homes," she said. "But don't you worry. I think Englesten's concern is for a loved one imprisoned in the citadel. He doesn't want to harm us."

"I trust you're right, mistress," he said with a barely stifled yawn.

"Finish your supper, Billy, then off you go. There will be plenty of work to do tomorrow," she said patting his head, and was rewarded with a loving smile. Rella hadn't the heart to tell the boy that the mountain elves were among the fiercest and most dangerous of all fae. They were unpredictable and owed allegiance to none but themselves.

Rella locked the door behind him, not wanting to be disturbed in her work. She'd rarely had the need to use this kind of magic before, but she was grateful her tutors insisted on her learning it. First, she took the steel shard and fashioned it into two swords, using some leather to cover the wooden grips and polished granite for the pommels. Though one was larger, they were identical, extremely sharp, and strong.

Then she fashioned a half dozen lesser blades. They were smaller but just as deadly. There were plenty of wood scraps and bones to use as handles. Two were long and very thin bladed, two were short swords, and two were eating knives but with serrated edges.

Her uniform was next. Calstir may have confiscated her Casta uniform, but she was going to make her own. She fashioned the brown leather into a broad breastplate studded with steel bosses. Then, using more steel and leather, she fashioned greaves, gauntlets, and a helmet. Finally she made a brown leather kilt. Its pleats hung perfectly and fitted as well as her white Casta kilt ever had.

She looked at her reflection in the dark window. All she needed was some horsehair to decorate her helmet, but that could wait for another day. She'd made a sword and knives for Dagstyrr. Now she made him a mail hauberk, a helmet with gorget, and greaves. A leather gambeson followed. She could find no silk, but with a piece of best white lawn, she fashioned an elegant cape, similar in style to the one he wore at Hedabar. A pair of studded gauntlets and a shield completed his gift.

Her shield she made last, for she couldn't think what device to embellish it with. Eventually, she settled for a bright blue field representing light fae, overlaid with dark green stripes that represented dark fae. In the middle was a bright white star, to represent who she was becoming—her very best self. The device would mean nothing to anyone else, but that was all right.

CHAPTER 28

Dagstyrr saw the battle lights dim and grow smaller. Either they'd stopped for the night, or the battle was over. He had no way to know. Despite his anger against Calstir smoldering in his heart, he wanted the light fae to win. For if the Dark Emperor won, Dagstyrr couldn't imagine what terrors would rampage through the world. If he were mad, as Rella suspected, then his madness would infect all his troops. Eventually, it would spread to all the reaches of his kingdom, and that was a vast territory. Nothing good would come of the Dark Emperor's victory, of that he was sure.

Dagstyrr checked on the horses. The smell of fresh hay and horseflesh greeted him as he opened the barn door. They were calm, and only the stallion paid him any attention, with a nod of his great black head and a roll of his eyes. Dagstyrr went to him and ran his hands over his face and neck, allowing the horse to nuzzle him. "There, big boy," he whispered. "Tomorrow we'll go for a good gallop up on the hills."

He checked on Billy snug in his hay bed, sleeping the

sleep of the innocent. Life had been cruel to the boy, but it never dampened his spirit. Bending down, he touched the boy's forehead. "I'll see you learn to fight, Billy. Don't you worry," he whispered. Even if he had to send Billy to his father's sword master, he'd find a way to honor that promise. "There's plenty of time for that," said Dagstyrr to himself.

The boy snuffled in his sleep, suddenly appearing even younger.

He made sure the animals had everything they needed then shut the door and made his way to the cottage. He'd known Rella was up to something when he'd heard the snick of the door locking. As long as she kept it indoors, it shouldn't be a problem. The last rays of the dying sun were sending red streaks across the darkening sky. He felt hope for tomorrow, perhaps hope for no more fae lying dead or dying on a battlefield.

He knew she longed to be in the thick of it. Selfishly, he was very glad she wasn't. Dagstyrr was torn between going to rescue Drago without her and taking her with him. He only wanted to keep her safe, but he suspected the choice wouldn't be his.

Pushing at the door to the cottage to see whether it was still locked, he was pleased to find it opened easily. He immediately smelled leather and steel. Rella stood proudly by the table, displaying weapons and armor. "What do you think?" she said.

What can't she do? thought Dagstyrr, amazed. This was incredible magic, even for full-blooded fae.

Dagstyrr lifted the larger sword and hefted it, checking its balance, then running his thumb along the blade. He couldn't hide the broad smile stealing across his face. "Ah, you know the way to a man's heart right enough, Princess." The blade was magnificent. Plain, without fancy embellishment, but splendid in structure and perfectly weighted, and it fit his hand like it was made for him—which, of course, it was.

Rella bounced excitedly on her toes. "Look here. I've fashioned knives as well. I wasn't sure whether to make one for Billy or not. I think he is too young."

The knives glistened on the table, sharp and lethal. "I think a small knife won't do any harm," said Dagstyrr, admiring her handiwork.

"Come, try this on," she said, indicating a magnificent chainmail shirt. "I want to know how it fits."

Dagstyrr laughed. "If you insist."

With her help, he donned the armor and found it fit better than any he'd ever owned. "I didn't know you were so aware of my exact size," he said with a twinkle in his eye, trying to bring about one of her rare, but oh-so-pretty, blushes.

He succeeded.

"Monster! I make you a gift, and you tease me."

"I would like to see you in yours," he said, waving a hand at the brown kilt decorating the chair by the fireside.

"Then you must go outside and wait until I have it on."

"When did you become so modest?"

"Out," she said, pointing to the door, hands on hips in imitation of an angry housewife.

Dagstyrr laughed. "Very well," he said, turning and ducking outside, where the air was clear and fresh, like after a storm. But this particular storm was not over yet.

The pleasure his new sword and armor brought could not be denied. This meant one thing: she knew as well as he did that they could not stay here.

∼

Rella put on her new uniform. It was hers and hers alone. One day she'd lead a whole army of fae wearing this uniform. This was the day her new cohort was born—an army of one.

The kilt fit perfectly, as she knew it would. The breastplate, gauntlets, and greaves molded to her, and she moved in it like a warrior should. Like a fae warrior should. Light as air and fast as a blink, as her sword master used to say.

With her sword buckled at her side and her knives secreted about her person, she lifted her helmet and pulled her long braid through the top hole designed to accommodate it. Then, as she admired her reflection in the darkened window, she lifted the round shield—Rella's shield, the first of many.

The white splash in the middle glowed in the dim light of the cottage, a star of hope. The blue field and green stripes complemented each other as if their origin was the same, and Rella thought perhaps it was. For all fae energy, light and dark, came from the same source. Though she supposed such radical thinking would never be fashionable.

Everyone knew that they both started off the same thousands of years ago, but now they appeared as divergent as a fish and a cat. There was no putting them back together again.

The window reflected a strong warrior, ready for a fight. For the first time in a long time, she felt right. Her image reflected who she was inside. Proudly, she opened the door to show Dagstyrr the real Rella, hoping he'd feel about her the same way she felt about him. For this new Rella would no longer hide her truth.

CHAPTER 29

Dagstyrr watched her emerge from the cottage fully battle ready, her head high and a sparkle in her eye. He knew at once that this warrior before him was the true Rella. At last, she was working it out for herself. Rella, the warrior fae princess. She entranced him as she drew her sword and spun slowly for him to admire her work before crouching in a defensive stance, her shield up and her weapon threatening.

Slowly drawing his weapon but unable to keep the broad smile from his face, he circled her. His experience with his light fae brothers had taught him always to feint unless you could double-feint, which was even better. Fae were so much faster. They saw your move before you'd committed to it.

Sometimes, it was best to let them win the first move, and then surprise them when their guard was down. He'd try it with Rella. He suspected she'd only ever fought other fae, so would think him easy prey.

Dagstyrr continued to circle. They were both grinning at each other, two warriors, happy to be back in armor with swords in hand. She jumped, turning in midair, her sword meeting his in one fluid movement. Her smile belied the strength it took.

He continued to circle. His awareness focused on Rella's feet. He knew that when one foot was about to leave the ground to reposition, that's when she'd strike. He watched the rhythm of her feet turning in place, following his movement. The tips of their swords were inches apart, and he had the longer reach, but she had the speed, and speed always won.

The sun had long since set, and the moon had yet to rise beyond the forest. She was a shadow, and he knew he must also look like a shadow to her—two dangerous shades circling each other in the gloom of evening. Then she struck. In a flash, the tip of her blade was at his throat. As soon as he felt her move, he'd swept his blade down and across her path causing her to jump, twist, and fall back just as her blade touched him.

"If this were a real fight, you'd be dead," she said, annoyance bristling from every fiber of her new uniform.

He laughed. "I'd still have surprised you."

She smiled, "True. Perhaps we should spar some more. I've never fought a human."

"I can tell. I, on the other hand, have sparred with fae all of my life."

"Then you have something to teach me."

"I am honored," he said, bowing over his sword. Then Dagstyrr started to teach Rella everything he knew of combat between fae and humans. She was faster, but she needed to learn a few dirty tricks.

He was just the human to teach her.

They worked for hours, feinting, fighting, charging, and retreating. Dagstyrr thoroughly enjoyed instructing her, and he was patient. But she learned quickly. He never had to repeat a lesson. There were a few moves she showed him that he'd never seen before. Perhaps his brothers weren't such good swordsmen as they thought they were.

They continued until the moon rose eerily against a black, star-studded blanket of sky. Without a word, they sheathed their weapons. Rella raised her hands and face to the moon and stars, drawing their energies into herself.

Dagstyrr watched her, reminded of Calstir's bed in the palace, placed directly under the influence of the night sky. She was dark fae now, and he knew she pulled her magical energy from the earth, so why was she so intent on sky energy?

Her slender neck exposed to the caress of the moonshine tempted him, and he envied the moon. He wanted to press his mouth to her soft skin. Her limbs were long and elegant despite their strength, her face in profile an image of perfection. Dagstyrr wanted her more than he had ever wanted anything in his life. He felt tension flood his body—the tension that came whenever his thoughts dwelt on her. Every inch of him yearned for her touch, her smile, just the scent of her.

But he had nothing to offer her but an impossible quest, and she deserved so much more.

∼

Rella felt the night sky's energy beam down upon her, and she absorbed it. At the same time, the earth's energy was sucked up through her feet. She didn't understand what had happened to her, but she had both light fae and dark fae magic at her fingertips. What did it mean?

"Reminiscing?" said Dagstyrr.

His voice, close to her, ear jolted her out of her reverie. "Not quite," she said.

It was then she noticed he was sweating and must be tired, to say nothing of the dust and dirt coating his new armor. She too wore a fine sheen of sweat and dust, but the energy zipping through her left no thought of fatigue.

She led him into the little house, and they helped each other off with their armor. She warmed the water in the bath and insisted he go first while she set the table with a selection of tempting food.

"So, Rella, when do we leave?"

"You really are the most annoying man," she said, banging down a plate of roast vegetables. She turned to him. "Are you sure you can't read my mind?"

"The moment the battle started, you and I both knew we couldn't stay here. As tempting as it is to pretend we're a normal family, the danger is too great." His dark blue eyes sought hers, and she saw the pain of unpalatable truth there. "We are being hunted, and so, like good little prey we must run," he said.

"Aye, if Englesten found us, so will others. Too many have died today because of me. Those villagers and Billy are innocents. I will not have them harmed," she said, hanging her head with the weight of it. "So, yes, we must go."

"When are you planning to leave?'

"Tomorrow."

"Very well. If we are leaving Billy behind, I will make sure he has some coin, and if you fill the larder he should be safe until Captain Bernst comes for him," said Dagstyrr, holding out his soapy hand for her.

∼

To his delight, she came. Pulling off the short shift she'd worn under her uniform and laughing, she stepped into the bathtub, sending water cascading over the sides. "What are you doing woman?"

"I'm dirty."

"I can see that," he said, unable to stop smiling in wonder. Rella's skin was soft as rainwater against his. He pulled her to his chest and ran the rose-scented soap up her arm and across her collarbone. Such exquisite torture. His breath quickened.

Unable to resist any longer, he ran his hands up the length of her perfect body. Rella bent her head back until it nestled against his neck. He saw her close her eyes with pleasure, a smile teasing the corners of her mouth. "Are you sure this is what you want, Rella?" His voice was deep and throaty from the effort of not ravishing her right there.

"It is time," she said, opening her eyes and gazing up at him. "Don't you think?"

"I do. This is not something I will do lightly, Rella. You must understand that. I want you for my woman for as long as I live," he said, aware her lifetime was going to be so much longer than his.

"We are hunted warriors, you and me. I fear we may not have so long to live, and so I intend to live the rest of my life on my terms," she said.

"Does that mean no?"

"That means I am yours, Dagstyrr of Halfenhaw, for as long as one of us is still alive. More than that, I cannot promise, and neither can you."

Dagstyrr's heart soared. "I think it's time," he said, standing and lifting her out of the bathwater that miraculously had not cooled, and taking her to the bed in the alcove, where he laid her down. Unashamedly, she raised her arms to welcome him, but this was not anything he intended to hurry.

∽

Rella thought the ecstasy of lovemaking with a human was a dark fae fable—she was wrong.

The cloak of protective safety he brought with him enveloped her. He gave himself so utterly, adoring every inch of her far-from-perfect body, and she reveled in the big human warrior whose love and worship she drank like an elixir. His roughened hands scraped deliciously across her skin and traced the mark, but she didn't care.

His dark hair fell over her face, and she opened her mouth to his kiss. Warm and demanding he claimed her as no other had done before. She gave herself up to the sensation of him, sweeping her hands over his muscled back, tracing every contour and committing it to memory. If she were to have him for only a short while, she'd need a lot of memories to last the rest of her life.

"I love you, Dagstyrr," she whispered and felt his reaction like a ripple of laughter in every muscle of his body.

"I love you too, Rella." Her body celebrated, and joy rose in her heart. "I think you know who you are now."

"I do." She smiled.

It took time to explore his body, and she reveled in it. Every mark and scar depicted a wound he'd suffered. Far from revulsion, she found her love grow with every one of them. The story of his life was written on his body. He exposed his past to her without fear of rejection or shame.

The hours passed, and still they had no fill of each other. When the time came to seal their love, he took her gently at first. Lost in a river of sensation, she thrust hard against him, demanding and voracious in her appetite, wanting to drown in the marvel that was Dagstyrr.

He responded to her demands in kind, taking her harder and faster until with a roar of pleasure and sparking blue and green energies, they fell into each other's arms sated.

Dagstyrr lay beside her. They looked up at the light show she'd produced without meaning to. Once her breath returned to normal, she raised her hand to it. He did the same. "This is what I wanted to show you, my love," she said.

He stared hard at it for some time, watching the display slow and dissipate. "I had no idea. Is it normal?"

Cautiously, she asked, "Is what normal?"

"This beautiful light display. It is magic energy, is it not?'

"Yes, it is magic energy. I shouldn't have let it out, but I was distracted."

"You can control it?"

"To a point, yes. That is not what I meant, though. Do you not see?"

She watched it dawn on him. He turned to her in amazement. "Blue *and* green."

"Yes."

"Since when has this been happening?"

"It just started, but I think it's been building for a while. I know who I am, but I don't know what I am, and I don't care."

"I've never cared what you are, Rella. I only care about who you are. You are the most beautiful, skilled warrior princess it has ever been my privilege to know, and now you're my woman," he said, lacing his fingers with hers.

Rella knew she should object to his owning her, but part of her liked being called his woman, so she let it go. After all, she owned him too, now that he was her mate. Later, they rose and ate, only to return to their bed and make love all over again. Eventually, lost in the wonder of each other, they slept.

At some point in the night, Dagstyrr propped himself up on one arm and tracing her profile with his finger, said, "I'm beginning to regret leaving tomorrow before Billy wakes. He won't like being left behind, even if it is for his protection."

"It will be kinder in the long run." Rella turned her face away, sad at the deceit. "He'll get over it. He'll know it is for his protection, and he'll forgive me."

Dagstyrr pulled her into the circle of his arms and sighed. "I hope so. I do worry about him." They lay wrapped together as Rella thought of all the changes the day had brought and wondered at what tomorrow would bring.

Eventually, she felt Dagstyrr fall asleep at her side, his arm around her secure and protective. She wanted this night to last forever. She was happier than she'd ever been, and her heart soared, despite the shadow of the Dark Emperor hanging over them like poison.

She'd caused a terrible war. Men and women were dying tonight because of her. The weeping and wailing of grieving families echoed in her imagination and would not let her sleep.

Images of her comrades fallen and wounded churned through her mind. She saw the faces of her friends lying on the battlefield and the Dark Emperor laughing at her.

Her nightmares only confirmed her decision. Only she could put a stop to it.

CHAPTER 30

Dagstyrr stretched and opened his eyes to bright sunlight streaming into the cottage, and Billy hammering on the door. "Wake up, wake up and open the door!" he shouted, then kicked at the stout timbers.

Dagstyrr stretched out his arm for Rella. She wasn't there. "Ok, ok, Billy, I'm coming." Where was she? Had something happened to her?

Naked, he reached the door and yanked it open. "What's ..."

"Gone, she's gone!" cried Billy, tears pouring down his face. "She left me, she left me here, and she went," he said, pointing toward the forest.

A chill stilled Dagstyrr. "What do you mean, she's gone?" He turned, grabbed his clothes, and pulled them on. It was then he noticed the large amount of fresh food and a magnificent pair of leather boots that stood on a chair. Propped against the boots was a note.

"See, I told you," said Billy, wiping his snot and tears from his face.

With great trepidation, Dagstyrr reached for the letter addressed to him. His heart thundered so hard his hand shook. Even before he read it, he knew, and his anger grew like a lump of steel in his breast.

Ignoring Billy, who took one look at him and then made himself busy with the fire, Dagstyrr sat down at the table and read:

My love, I have made many enemies, and now they will hunt me down. Strange, is it not, that when you set out to do what is right and good, you end up doing more harm than you can imagine?

I am going to put right what I allowed to go wrong. I am a warrior. It is what I know.

Calstir is no longer the strong king he might once have been. Perhaps Lady Kemara was correct. Maybe I should have left him to rot in the vizier's citadel. Unfortunately, it is not in my nature to do so. If I had to do it all again, I would change nothing.

I am not sorry I embroiled you in my escape plan, and I'm glad your brothers are safe.

Most of all, I have no regrets about loving you.

It is because I love you so much that I must go. You have a dangerous quest ahead of you. If I thought for a moment I could aid you in that quest, I would stay, but I fear my enemies would find us first. Your family would suffer for ten generations. They don't deserve that. No one does.

The mountain elves are strong allies, but they are always self-serving. Remember that. Captain Bernst will be back soon. I have put a spell on the farm. Neither you nor Billy can leave until either a month has passed or Captain Bernst returns. His magical signature will break the spell.

With me gone, you will not be in any danger.

I will think of you each day and miss you every moment we are apart. I love you more than my life.

Farewell, beloved, until I see the sky darken with one hundred and sixty-eight dragons, not counting hatchlings or eggs. When that day comes, I will come to you with joy and love, ready to live the life we have left together.

Make it soon, my love.
Yours in fae, dark and light,
Forever your loving woman, Rella.

Stunned, Dagstyrr let the letter fall to the floor. What was it she'd said last night when they talked about leaving Billy behind? *He'll know it is for his protection, and he'll forgive me.*

Dagstyrr felt no forgiveness, only hurt, anger, and betrayal. He watched Billy serve porridge into two bowls and cautiously push one toward him. Fury poured from every inch of Dagstyrr. It made the boy wary of him.

Rella, without even asking him, or discussing it, had sacrificed herself for him.

Oh, Rella. He closed his eyes and saw her smile up at him. Her scent filled his head with the essence of her. How was he to go on without her? He saw again her pride in her new uniform and heard her laugh. Felt once more the impossibly soft skin of her thigh under his rough palm. With great clarity, he suddenly understood where she'd gone—to kill the Dark Emperor.

"So," said Billy, interrupting Dagstyrr's reverie between mouthfuls of porridge, "when do we go and get her?"

The End

ACKNOWLEDGMENTS

Although writing is a solitary occupation, no book exists without the help and guidance of those who have gone before. I have been exceptionally gifted with the wisdom of so many—too many to mention here. I owe a special thanks to my critique group, Naomi, Shereen, and Solveig whose unending patience keeps me on the straight and narrow. Kathleen and Nancy who are so very generous with their knowledge and advice. To Jacqui, and Taryn and last, but by no mean least, Lynsey G. for her editing skills.

Any mistakes in this book are mine alone. I hate typos, but sometimes they slip through. Please send any errors to **jane@janearmor.com**. I am very grateful to any eagle-eyed readers who take the time to contact me.

FROM THE AUTHOR

Hi,

Thank you for taking the time to read my book. I hope you have enjoyed reading Rella and Dagstyrr's story as much as I enjoyed writing it. I am always happy to hear from my readers and you can reach me easily at JaneArmor.com. If you have the time, I would love to read your review of *Dark Fae* on Amazon, Goodreads, or just tell your friends. It would mean a lot to me.

I am working hard on launching the second book in this series, *Wild Fae,* and have just started my first draft of the third book in the series, *Dragon Fae*.

You can find an excerpt of *Wild Fae* on the next few pages. I hope you enjoy it.

Yours truly,
 Jane

Review *Dark Fae* on
Amazon, Goodreads, and BookBub

WILD FAE – EXCERPT
Copyright © Jane Wallace #1170881 June 2020

CHAPTER 1

Rella led her group of wild fae misfits through the groaning battlefield with a heavy heart. Now that the fighting was over, their work began. They'd save those they could and bring a swift end to those who asked for it.

Skirmishes between Casta and the Dark Emperor had grown fiercer and bloodier in recent weeks. The acrid stench of battle magic lay heavy in the air as they worked their way through the dead and the dying.

Moans of pain reached Rella's acute hearing. Leaving her companions to administer to the dying, she sought out the injured fae. The iron scent of blood and the fizzling blue battle magic of a dying light fae urged her forward. The warrior hid in the undergrowth, his handsome, chiseled features given up his agony. Glittering prettily in the mud, his silver and blue armor declared him a young lord. He wore three medals, all given for bravery in battle. One such as this would be deeply mourned. The wound to his abdomen gaped open, causing his innards to fall into the dirt. There was little help for him. "Have pity, mistress. I must live!" he cried.

Cases like this were always the most difficult—beyond help, but refusing to acknowledge they were dying.

"He knows you're going to kill him," said Beatty, an ancient mountain elf, short of stature, but with elongated hands and feet. His brown wizened features challenged her to refute his wisdom. "It would be for the best, I'm thinking."

Rella looked into the dying fae's bright blue eyes. She

sensed his magic was strong, but he was dying. Soon his magic would desert him in painful spurts until, with a final flash of light, it would leave him and he'd be gone. The fae warrior was young and full of determination. If they had the skills to heal him, such willpower could see him live a long and useful life. Every life saved eased Rella's guilt.

"What is your name?" she asked, kneeling by his side and taking his hand.

"Fedric, mistress, and I want to live. Help me," he said.

Her heart sank. Fedric's wound was beyond her considerable skills. "Do you know who I am?"

"You are the Dark Queen," he said.

This was not the first time she'd heard that name applied to her. Rella glanced at Beatty, who shrugged and turned his face from her. He'd already given his opinion on Fedric's chances, and it wasn't good.

"Ask Gimrir to come."

"He won't like it. Are you sure?" said Beatty, sheathing his sword with a clang.

She whipped around to face Beatty, her speed a warning of danger to the mountain elf. "Just do it," she snarled. Beatty left, muttering to himself. It was a difficult enough decision without him questioning her, but she understood why he did. Gimrir's magic was ancient and only used sparingly. He was a spirit of the sacred oaks, torn from his home by the war she'd started between her brother's kingdom of Casta and that abomination, the Dark Emperor.

Rella put her hand to the young light fae's forehead and felt his will to live. "Do you understand what it means if we heal you?"

His eyes sought hers, and she saw a glimmer of fear wiped away by firm resolve. "Aye, I must go dark. I must join your army."

"Nonsense. Whether you go dark or not will depend on how much dark magic we use to heal you," said Rella, inspecting his wound. "I don't have an army, and if I did, light fae would not be welcome. I don't know where these ideas spring from."

He grimaced. Rella moved her hand over his head, letting her dark green healing magic flow around him, giving him some relief from the pain. She dared not try to heal such a complicated wound on her own.

"I don't care about the price. I want to live."

Just then, Gimrir appeared out of the gathering gloom. Although he was almost seven feet tall, his beard reached to his knees, and he was dressed in homespun linen from head to toe. One glance proclaimed him a spirit-fae, for both he and his clothing were almost transparent. He was a dark fae so rare, few had ever seen his kind, and those who did saw no more than a momentary glimmer of light. Rella left her charge and went to where Gimrir stood under a clutch of rowan trees.

"Why do you want to save the boy, Rella?" Gimrir's deep voice was soft with compassion.

"He wants to live."

"Most creatures want to live, especially the young. That is not enough."

Rella sighed. "He has an attitude, and maybe not a good one, but his will is strong."

Gimrir lifted a questioning eyebrow as Rella struggled with a more satisfactory answer. "I don't know, Gimrir," she said, frustration raising her voice.

The spirit-fae leaned forward and patted her shoulder. "You're tired. It's been a long day for all of us. Very well, let me see him."

"Thank you." The spirit-fae had a reassuring way of making her feel that he always had her back.

Gimrir knelt by the young fae's side. "I don't know what I can do," he said, focusing on the young man's wound.

Rella saw Fedric's hand try to grasp the old man's sleeve. "I need to live," he said. "I will pay the price."

Gimrir looked into his eyes for what seemed like an age before turning to Rella. "We will try. I promise nothing."

Rella nodded and left him to his work while she continued with hers. All wounded fae gradually lost control of their magic energy unless healing took place. It spurted uncontrollably from their hands until they died. To see so many lifeless bodies, their magic lost forever, was a tragedy.

Here and there across the fields and forest floor, shows of magic energy separated the dead from the dying. They managed to save four others that day and send them home. The price was always the same, whether they were dark fae or light fae. They each swore never to fight against Rella or her companions, known to all as the wild fae and made up of dark fae refugees and outlaws. No fae would break that promise for fear of rejection in the afterlife.

Unfortunately, Rella and her crew had to dispatch far more than they saved. It was always thus.

As they worked, Rella kept her guard up. She was sure the Dark Emperor's army had retreated beyond this forest to the untamed lands at the foot of the mountains, but she was ever alert. If one of his scouting parties were to capture her, it would be a great victory for them, and all her plans would come to naught.

Recently, the light fae had not been so diligent at tracking her movements. She suspected they knew where she was, but weren't eager to capture her and hand her over to the Dark Emperor. That would bring an end to the war.

Which meant someone at the court of Casta wanted this war to continue. She refused to believe it was her brother, King Calstir, despite his betrayal.

Rella still blamed herself for starting this war. She would end it on her terms. To do so, she must kill the Dark Emperor, and so free the dark fae from his oppressive rule.

Rella and her companions made sure they left the battlefield before relatives of the dead arrived to claim their bodies. Sometimes the wild fae were late leaving. When that happened, they would have to hide and watch the recovery of the dead. That was hard on them. The keening cries of relatives when they discovered a loved one shredded their nerves. Especially if it was someone they had mercifully dispatched to the afterlife. Tonight, however, was a good night. They had saved those they could, brought mercy to those who asked for it, and taken Fedric with them. The healing he required would be too complicated for the battlefield. Perhaps she should have listened to Beatty after all.

∾

Back at their encampment, Rella entered the dim interior of her tent and warmed her bathwater with a wave of her fingers. It had taken some time, but she was no longer reluctant to use her dark magic to its fullest potential. When she stepped into the warm water scented with rose and mint, she thought of Dagstyrr, and the bath they had shared before mating for the first time.

A mating that had bound them together, forever.

Where was he? Had he forgiven her yet for leaving him? She laid her head back, letting the warm water soothe her aching limbs. She imagined him at the prow of the *Knucker*, sailing fast and free with the wind in his hair toward

Hedabar with Captain Bernst commanding the *Mermaid* and the *Viper* bringing up the rear. How many more, she wondered, had he managed to recruit in his mission to save the dragon Drago and his family?

"One hundred and sixty-eight dragons, not counting hatchlings or eggs." She quoted the number of dragons in Hedabar's dungeons. To free them all seemed an impossible task for any human, but Dagstyrr of Halfenhaw was no ordinary human. One day she would see the sky darken with the flight of dragons. When that day came, she'd stop whatever she was doing and go to him. For then, his promise to free Drago would be fulfilled, and they could be together. First, however, she must do her part and put an end to this war by putting an end to the Dark Emperor.

Emerging from the water and dressing in a simple tunic of unembellished forest green, she left her tent to walk the camp. In her imagination, Dagstyrr walked with her, and in her mind, she pointed out things of interest to him. She missed him far more than she would have thought possible. His absence was like a void deep within her psyche.

The wild fae camp was growing every day. She no longer had to recruit. Dark fae refugees flocked to her banner. Some were full of impossible hopes, but many were merely sick of living under the cruelty of their self-styled emperor.

Once the Dark Emperor was gone, the dark fae would return to the benevolent reign of their chosen queen, whoever she might be. With a Dark Queen on the throne of Thingstyrbol once more, peace would descend upon the world. Both light and dark fae would return to their homes and live in tenuous harmony.

The camp Rella walked through was a myriad of fae beings. She had not seen so many different fae since the prison cells in the citadel in Hedabar.

A woman approached. From the look of her, she was a dark fae halfling and worked hard for her living. Her hands were red and callused, her step heavy. "Mistress Rella, might I do your laundry? I do a good job. See here?" The woman lifted her basket to show off the snowy white linen inside.

Rella didn't need a laundress. However, she did want to get to know the dark fae and halflings in her charge. "What is your name?"

"Polly, mistress," she said with a curtsey.

"Very well. What can I give you for your services?"

"My daughter's just birthed her first babe. I'd happily exchange a year of cleaning linen for a good knife. It is for his dedication ceremony."

Rella smiled. She slipped a black knife from her belt. Chased in silver filigree, it was sharp as well as decorative. Perfect for a young dark fae's dedication ceremony. "Will this do?"

Polly's eyes widened. "I should think it will, mistress."

"Very well. It's a fair price. Where is the new babe's father?"

At that, Polly's eyes clouded. "Hedabar, mistress."

"Take the knife, and save me a piece of cake from the dedication," said Rella, walking away and wishing she could do more.

She and Dagstyrr were the only ones to ever successfully rescue family members from the prison cells of the citadel on the island of Hedabar. Because of that, people looked to her to free their relatives from the vizier, but she had a more urgent task. Besides, once Dagstyrr freed the dragons, the vizier's reign would end, and the citadel would collapse.

Rella, born a light fae princess, had started this war when she broke the only law held sacred by the dark fae: she'd refused to pay the price she'd agreed upon with the

Dark Emperor in exchange for her ability to walk unknown among humans. They should shun her. Yet they came in droves and swore allegiance to her. The dark fae were hard to understand, even if she was now one of them.

Startled out of her reverie by the tall figure of Gimrir stalking toward her, Rella watched as he passed silently between the tents and wooden shacks of her followers. He stopped and waved for her to accompany him. Rella caught him up in a trice. "Is it Fedric?"

"There is a decision to be made. Only you can make it," said Gimrir, so solemnly her heart sank.

She followed him back to the base of an enormous tree where dryads occupied the upper branches, and Gimrir made his home at its gnarled base. "What is wrong, Gimrir?"

"The boy has only one wound. Which is strange after such a fierce battle. Nevertheless, that wound is very severe. The boy is strong, just as you predicted. I think his determination will indeed win through as long as I can piece his poor guts back together."

"And can you?"

"Only with your help," he said. "Your ...very special help."

A cold shiver ran down Rella's spine. Gimrir was one of the few beings who knew of her strange magic. Born light fae and having chosen to turn dark, her bright blue flashes of light fae magic had given way to the billowing green magic of the dark fae. Then, an extraordinary thing had happened. The blue returned, and now it worked in concert with the green, a strange phenomenon that Rella wanted to keep quiet. There were enough ridiculous rumors spread about her. "Is there no other way?"

"I've already tried many times and failed. Guts are slippery and confusing to the likes of me. Your clever blue energy can show the way, while your green does the healing. I will keep him sedated. It is the only way."

"I've never attempted this kind of healing. I have no experience."

"I will help you. If we are quick, no one need know."

Loath to risk anyone seeing her using both green and blue magic together, Rella glanced at the young light fae lying within Gimrir's healing circle. His innards still lay exposed to the night air. "You know that with this much dark magic in him, his eyes will change color. He won't be able to return to Casta. We'll probably have to keep him here." Rella struggled with the choice in front of her. If she helped, his life as he knew it was over. If she didn't, he would be dead by morning. "Damn! I should have put him out of his misery on the field."

"But you did not, and this is the consequence."

A breeze whispered through the long grasses where Fedric lay. He was very young and handsome, a prime example of a light fae warrior. Rella sighed. It seemed to her that whenever she attempted a kindness, it went horribly wrong. "Very well, Gimrir."

∽

Check JaneArmor.com for release dates.

ALSO BY JANE ARMOR

The Fae Series

Dark Fae - Book 1

Wild Fae - Book 2

Dragon Fae - Book 3

Contact Jane at her website: JaneArmor.com

Printed in Great Britain
by Amazon